Straightening Ali

Amjeed Kabil

Herndon, VA

Straightening Ali

Amjeed Kabil

Herndon, VA

Published in the United States

STARbooks Press
PO Box 711612
Herndon VA 20171

Printed in the United States

Many thanks to graphic artist John Nail for the cover design.
Mr. Nail may be reached at: tojonail@bellsouth.net.

Book and text design by Milton Stern. Mr. Stern can be reached
at: miltonstern@miltonstern.com.

Contents

Chapter One

"We've been waiting so long for you to get married, but as you don't seem to want to make an effort, we've gone ahead and arranged your wedding for you," Ali's mother said, kissing him excitedly on both of his cheeks, while gripping him tightly in a bear hug. Meanwhile, Ali's older brother and sister, Yunus and Yasmin, looked at him intently with the same self-satisfied smug expressions plastered on their faces.

"What?" Shock was the only way to describe Ali's reaction. His voice seemed to fail him, and his breathing was uncomfortable. "You've arranged my wedding?" he said, struggling to speak. "How? Why? Who?" he spluttered. His mother's embrace suddenly felt claustrophobic, as if she were trying to take away his freedom, and he pushed her clinging arms away. Maybe it was all a joke. They liked sick jokes in the Mirza family.

"Yes, aren't you delighted that you're finally going to get married?" his sister Yasmin exclaimed. "You're always far too busy to even think about seeing any of the eligible girls that we want to introduce you to, so we thought we'd sift through the catalogue and pick out the good ones."

"Just imagine if we didn't do this for you. All of the best girls would be gone, and you'd have ended up left on the shelf, alone without any children, or even worse, have to marry a divorcee! If it wasn't for us sorting things out, you might have died without giving Ammi any grandchildren," Yasmin beamed, showing her pearly white teeth and feeling proud that she had gone beyond her sisterly duty and done him such a huge favor. Somehow she managed to ignore or misunderstand the stricken look on Ali's face.

"We've even set the date for your wedding," Yunus added, delighting in the look of disbelief on Ali's face.

"You've set a date for my wedding without even asking me? You're all joking aren't you?" Ali asked, trying not to sound too distressed. The thing he'd dreaded most was happening so suddenly, and he was living his worst nightmare.

Amjeed Kabil

"You're getting married in two weeks time, on November seventeenth," Yunus said. He seemed to enjoy the anguish he was causing Ali. It was as if he still resented the fact that Ali had been born and taken away his position as the only cherished boy in the family.

"Two weeks?" Ali said, his mind reeling. "It's too soon," he thought. He could feel a shadow over his head and a suffocating feeling envelope him.

"We've very little time to arrange everything, but we'll manage it. Ammi has lots of contacts," Yasmin said grinning at Ali's horrified expression, somehow still mistaking it for something else. "I have a photograph of your fiancée here somewhere. You must want to see what she looks like."

She rummaged in the large multicolored wool handbag from Islamabad that she always carried with her and carefully pulled out a small silver picture frame, which she placed gently in Ali's lap. "Here, don't say we don't do anything for you. Her name is Sajda. Isn't she beautiful? Ammi thinks she is beautiful," she said, referring to their mother, who was now sitting happily next to Ali.

Ali still couldn't believe that his family was doing this to him. How could they find a girl, fix a date, and not even mention it to him? Why hadn't he suspected that this plan was being hatched? They had been so nice to him lately, and even Yunus had made some attempts to be pleasant. In hindsight, Ali realized that he should have made some plans for this very moment, but he had never foreseen that he would be confronted by a marriage proposal in this way.

"Ahhh Sajda. She is so light skinned, like a goree. She's twenty years old, only four years younger than you," his mother said.

"Twenty is hardly an age to get married," Ali thought, unable to find his voice. He still felt dumbstruck and unsure of how to respond. He couldn't bring himself to look at the photograph, knowing that in doing so, it would make the absurdity of his situation all too real.

"A husband should always be older than his wife. Your father was fourteen years older, so this is nothing," Ali's mother murmured wistfully. "Ah, your father and I were so happy. I was only fifteen when we married. It was the happiest day of

2

my life. We had never met before the wedding day, but the moment I met him, I knew I was in love."

There was no more avoiding it. It was really happening. Maybe he'd feel differently if he saw her face. Ali looked at the photo frame lying in his lap and tried to ignore his mother reminiscing about his father. She had a habit of doing this sometimes, usually as a ploy to distract from what was really going on.

The photo frame held a color studio portrait of a young girl dressed in traditional Pakistani clothes, a green salwar and kameez suit. It was embroidered at the collar with small swirling patterns, and her head was covered in matching sequined dupatta in true Pakistani style. The girl was smiling almost shyly into the camera. She had the most striking and beautiful brown eyes that were accentuated by a line of dark kohl running along her eyelids. She wore some red lipstick, and at the side of her mouth, she had created a fake beauty spot. The attempt to look traditional failed if you looked closely enough. Ali noticed that on her feet she was wearing the tallest high-heeled shoes he'd ever seen.

Ali clutched the frame tightly in his hands, his knuckles showing white with the strain. He was unable to believe what he'd just been told. He wondered why the girl in the photograph had agreed to marry him. It was clear from looking at her that she was determined to impress whoever looked at the photograph, but it did not have the desired effect on Ali. All he felt was indifference.

"I'm from a different generation, Ammi. My generation makes its own choices. I won't be another statistic who has a failed arranged marriage. I am not getting married." The words that Ali had been trying to say were finally out.

"On my wedding day, I wore the most beautiful red sharara with a wonderful hand stitched dupatta to go with it. When your father saw me, he said he knew that he would love me forever," his mother continued, oblivious to Ali's statement.

"She's a virgin. Her dad said he guaranteed it. He just came out with it. Even Ammi was embarrassed," Yasmin said smirking. "She was going to ask Sajda's mother the question a little more discretely. I'm sure he would have given us a certificate from the doctor if we'd asked for it."

"I'd give her one," Yunus said under his breath, making sure that only Ali heard. He glanced appreciatively at the picture frame. "She wouldn't have been a virgin for long if she'd met me first."

"Stop! All of you stop!" Ali's words just came out. He didn't know where he had managed to find the strength to verbalize his thoughts. "How can you arrange my wedding without even asking me? We've never discussed it. None of you have even mentioned it to me before," he screamed, slamming the photo frame angrily onto the floor. The frame managed to bounce across the laminate floor without shattering, the face on it unmarred by the attack. "We're not living in Pakistan, we're living in England. You can't do this to me. You've not asked me what I want."

"Ali, we don't need to ask you anything. Your wedding has been arranged because it's part of our custom and religion. It's the parents' Islamic duty to find their child a partner to marry so that they can procreate," Yasmin said, as if explaining it to a disobedient child.

"I'm a free man, and in case you've forgotten, I'm over eighteen, and I don't have to put up with this crap. I'm not this family's property, which means you can't go around setting up a wedding for me," yelled Ali. "I'm not getting married. Not now! Not ever!"

"Who the hell do you think you are?" Yasmin asked, her face darkening. "You're not any different from Yunus and me. You forget that even though you wear your English clothes, live in Birmingham, and have had an English education, you still have Pakistani blood flowing through your veins. You might be living in England, but you are a Pakistani and a Muslim, too, so don't you dare forget that. You're a part of this family, and you will bloody well do as you're told. It was our mother who gave birth to you. That woman sitting there," yelled Yasmin pointing her finger dramatically at Ammi. "She deserves the right to see her youngest son married, settled and happy."

Ammi sat on the brown leather couch looking sadly at her disobedient son. Since her husband had died, she had stopped dying her hair black. It was now gray but streaked with the occasional black strand. Her eyes were surrounded by wrinkles, but the rest of her face looked soft with a youthful zeal. She never wore make up and swore on the cream that she had imported from Pakistan for keeping her skin soft and wrinkle free. As a widow, she no longer wore brightly colored clothes and instead wore shades of white and cream.

She thumbed a necklace of wooden prayer beads in her hand while reciting a prayer as her daughter Yasmin explained Ali's obligations to the family.

"It was Ammi who carried you for nine months in her womb and raised you all these years. You wouldn't be here if it wasn't for her. Don't you think you owe her something? Or are you the ungrateful, selfish bastard that everyone thinks you are?"

"I'm not ungrateful and I'll contribute to this family in my own way, but I'm not contributing by getting married," Ali said.

"We're your family, and you'll bloody well listen to what we ask you to do!" Yasmin yelled back, her face showing a red flush.

"It's not something I want. If I'd wanted to get married, I would have told you. I can make decisions about my life, myself, without anyone interfering. I don't need decisions about something as important as this made for me!" Ali said trying to remain calm.

"We know what's right for you. We're the ones who know you best, sometimes better than you know yourself. We know what you want deep down, and we've done this for your benefit. Do you really want to grow old without any children to look after you? Who do you think is going to care for you in your old age?" asked Yasmin, her voice wavering, as if close to tears.

"No one," murmured Ali's mother sadly. She counted through her prayer beads as she recited a prayer that she hoped would deliver Ali onto the right path.

"No one else is going to care for you when you are old and feeble. Do you really want to go into an old people's home, alone and helpless, or do you think your kafir friends are going to look after you?" Yasmin shouted as she worked herself back into an angry state.

"I've told you all before that I don't want to get married, and you know why I don't," Ali cried despairingly, not wanting to go back over old ground with them again.

"Yes, we've all heard it from you before. Get the violins out! You think you're gay. You're confused. You're unsure. So what? It does not stop you from getting married," Yasmin insisted.

"You're not gay. You were studying. You became stressed out with your university work and found yourself thinking you're attracted to men. You're not attracted to men. How could you be? God made Adam and Eve, not Adam and Steve," Yunus laughed, thinking he'd said something clever. "Adam and Steve," he repeated, laughing again.

"Shut up," Ali yelled at him angrily. Ali's relationship with Yunus had never been good. They had nothing in common. Yunus was into macho pursuits like his car and the gym, and he had always found Ali to be a bit effeminate, even before Ali told the family he was gay. Since then, the relationship between them had deteriorated with Yunus behaving in an antagonistic and aggressive way towards him.

"We are not going to shut up. We are your family. It's us you need to be listening to. You listen too much to your white university friends. All of you trying so hard to be different. How can you expect them to understand your culture and your religion?" Yasmin asked angrily. "Just stop listening to your friends and listen to your family. Think for yourself, be your own man. Being gay is sinful in our religion. Forget about it. Get married and leave this life you've been leading in the past. Islam will forgive you."

"Think for myself? Be my own man? How can you say that when you've just arranged my wedding without asking me? You know I'm gay, so how can you expect me to get married?" Ali said, bewildered by her conflicting attitude.

Yasmin was the only person in the family who practiced a fundamentalist form of Islam. She had done so since she came back from Coventry University, having joined the Islamic Society while studying there. She never left the house without wearing her hijab, and every so often came out with a ruling decreed by the Islamic Society. Most recently, she had banned everyone, including Ammi, from watching *Eastenders*, simply because the Islamic Society believed it to be anti-Islamic.

"You're not gay. Stop believing what this kafir culture wants you to believe. You have always wanted children. Remember when you were little and you used to say you wanted six children. What's changed now? Gays can't have children. Do you really think two men can make babies? Your bum is for going to the toilet, not for making babies. It's not natural. It's perverted, and you're not a pervert. In Islam, you would be stoned for being gay," shrieked Yasmin.

"Stop screaming at me, Yasmin. I don't want any children. You're all enough to put anyone off from having children for life. I don't want to get married, so call it off if you want to see me again. If you don't, I will move out and never come back," Ali said. He felt sick at the thought of resorting to this threat, as he knew how it would make his mother feel, but he had no option other than to trade emotional blackmail with emotional blackmail.

There was shocked silence in the room. Both Ali's mother and sister looked stunned, and even Yunus had wiped the inane smirk from his face.

"Call it off? How could you ask that? We went and arranged it today! We can't cancel it! Yunus, Mum and I went all the way to Nottingham to ask for Sajda's hand in marriage, and she accepted. How do you think she will feel if we suddenly turn round and say that you don't want to marry her?" asked Yasmin, her voice dropping to a whisper.

"I don't care how she feels. I don't know her! Do any of you care about how I feel? Knowing that you've all gone behind my back and set up a wedding for me when I've told you so many times that I'm gay? You've had years to deal with it, but you still decide to marry me off," Ali retorted angrily. "Don't you think she needs to know that I'm gay before you go any further with this ridiculous plan?"

"Ali, you have to marry her. It's too late to back out now. Do you really want to be responsible for making so many people unhappy? You will destroy that young girl's life and reputation if you don't marry her. Do you think anyone else will want to marry her if you cancel the wedding? You will bring shame on both of our families," Yasmin said, angry tears running from her eyes.

"I don't care! I don't give a damn," Ali replied crossly.

"How could you say that Ali? How can you be so heartless and cruel? Ammi did not bring you up to be cruel. How could you hurt Sajda when she loves you so much?" asked

7

Yasmin. She picked up the picture frame from the floor and shoved it in Ali's face. "Look at her. She deserves better than this."

"Sajda loves me so much?" exclaimed Ali sounding bewildered. "How can you say that she loves me when she doesn't even know me? What are you all on?"

"She loves you," Ali's mother replied. She had been crying silently. Her prayer beads had slipped from her hands and were lying on the floor. It was as if she had not expected this response from Ali. "She knew she was going to marry you for a long time. Her family has been waiting for us to ask for her hand in marriage. All of us knew you would both end up together, but we were waiting for the right moment."

"Ammi, why are we still talking to him and trying to get him to listen to reason? Let me break his legs," said Yunus aggressively. "He never listens. A good beating will straighten him out and stop him playing with those white, batty boys."

"No, don't touch my precious son. He has always been a good boy," Ali's mother said protectively, crying out in distress. "He will listen to me. Ali is a good boy, and good sons always listen to their mothers. He will make me proud."

"Look, everyone gets married Ali," Yasmin said. "You're behaving like a spoilt little child. You've obviously been speaking to your white friends, but they don't know anything. They don't understand our values, our beliefs, or our culture. So how can you listen to them and ignore what we have to say?"

"My friends understand everything, and they even manage to accept me for who I am. Why can't you do the same?" asked Ali.

"Are any of these friends from Pakistani families? I don't think so. I suppose there's your best friend, Haseena, but that bitch knows nothing about her own culture. You're Pakistani, a Muslim. We've always taught you to know better. You were brought up to respect your elders and to listen to them. What do you think dad would say if he was alive today? Dad would never have allowed you to behave like this," Yasmin said, sounding exasperated. "He would have shipped you off to Pakistan, taken your passport, and married you off to some village idiot."

"I don't care! You can't run my life for me. This is not Pakistan," Ali screamed back at her hysterically.

"What are you trying to do Ali? Destroy our father's memory? Dad would be so disappointed in you if he knew you were behaving like this. Don't let dad down. Get married. He would have wanted this for you. He would have been so proud," Yasmin said in earnest.

"I'm not getting married," Ali shouted again. "Why aren't you listening to me? How many times do I have to repeat myself?"

"Hush, hush," Ali's mother said gently. She muttered a prayer in Arabic and blew in Ali's direction, as if to blow the goodness of the prayer over him. "Be a good boy, listen to your Ammi. Get married. You have always been my favorite son. You have always made me proud of everything you've done. Please don't let me down now. If you don't get married, it will kill me. I won't be able to carry on anymore. The only thought that has kept me going since your father died is that you would get married and give me some grandchildren." She burst into tears, sobbing loudly.

"I'm diabetic and getting old. I don't have many years ahead of me. I want to see some grandchildren from you. I want to see them before I die. Please, Ali, get married for my sake if no one else's. I'm begging you. I'll touch your feet, if that's what you want me to do." Ali's mother fell onto her knees, dramatically prostrating herself in front of him. "Please get married," she begged, grabbing onto his feet, tears streaming from her eyes.

"Ammi, please don't do this. You know I can't get married, and I've told you why," Ali said.

"When you were little, you always said that you would get married when you grew up," she whimpered, her breathing loud and hoarse between her words.

"That was when I was little, Ammi. I'm grown up now, and I want different things. Please get up." His mother ignored him, continuing to whimper and gasp for breath pathetically.

"Look, I'm going. I can't deal with all of you when you're like this. I'll stay over with one of my friends for a couple of days until you've all calmed down. Please cancel the wedding while I'm gone." Ali headed for the door, pulling his feet out of his mothers grasp and trying to make a quick exit.

Yunus got to the door first and held it shut. "Where do you think you're going? No one said you could leave, yet," he said threateningly. He pushed Ali away from the door. "Listen to what we have to say. Stop being selfish, or I'll break your legs you queer bastard! I've had an arranged marriage, and so will Yasmin, so why don't you just agree and everything will be fine. You'll be sorted for life or would you rather be a queer batty boy."

"Look what happened to your marriage, Yunus. She left you after two years. How can you want the same for me when you know that arranged marriages don't work? Why are you interfering in my life? You're no longer married, so why don't you marry her yourself instead?" Ali suggested.

"Don't talk to me about my marriage you queer fucker," Yunus yelled. He lunged at Ali and grabbed him by his crotch, squeezing Ali's testicles hard. Ali winced in pain. "If you don't listen to Ammi, I'll rip these off for you! Then we'll see how you like playing with your white bum boys." He let go and punched Ali square in the face. "Sit down and listen like a good little boy."

The punch hit Ali's nose making a crunching sound. He felt blood dripping from his nostrils and sat down on the floor crying in pain and shock. None of this was fair. He could not believe what was happening. It was as if the freedom that he'd had while at university was slowly slipping away from his grasp.

He had fought with Yunus since they were young. In some ways it was for the best as it had taught him how to stand up to the bullies in the classroom. Yunus was always physically stronger than he, so there was no way that Ali would be able to beat him in a fight, but that did not matter as Ali always fought back. However, right now, he felt defeated as he looked round at his family standing around him with their minds set firmly against giving him his freedom. It felt as if all his strength had been sucked out, and he was unable to fight any more.

Ali's mother watched sadly. She clasped her hands together in prayer and asked for forgiveness from God for any sin that she may have committed that had made her son turn against her.

She then turned her face to the little glass replica of Mecca Medina that had been brought back by Yasmin from her Hajj and hoped for divine intervention. When none came, she turned back to her son. Seeing him on the ground crying made her heart clench in pain, and she sought to comfort him. "Ali, I will buy you a new house with a lovely garden, wherever you want. You don't need to live anywhere near us if you hate us so much. All you have to do is say that you will get married."

"Ammi, I don't hate anyone! I love you all very much. I just don't want to get married. I don't want to live a lie," said Ali tearfully through the blood that was dripping down his face. He tried to wipe it away, but instead his hand came back covered in blood. He looked at the red liquid on his hand and whimpered wretchedly. "If I say yes, I will be their victim forever," he thought.

"What about a new car to go with your new house," Ali's mother said ignoring his plea. "You would like that, wouldn't you? A lovely new car? What do you say, Ali? I will buy that for you tomorrow if only you agree to the wedding."

"No, Mum, I am not getting married. You can't bribe me. I don't want anything from you. I'm happy with the car I've got," Ali said. "Please, I'm begging you. Don't ask me to do this."

"What have I done, God? What have I done to deserve this heartless son?" his mother cried dramatically. "You're my favorite son. I've always looked after you and given you what you wanted. Why don't you do as I ask? Why do you want to hurt me so much? Do you mean to destroy your father's memory? He would have been so happy about your wedding. All you want to do is hurt and shame me." Ali's mother started counting through the prayer beads manically, repeating the same word over and over again in Arabic.

"Ammi, please don't ask me to marry. I don't want to," Ali begged. "Ask me anything else, and I will do it, just not that."

"Stop being so heartless to Ammi, Ali. Why are you trying to hurt her? I'm going to hate you for the rest of your life if you don't listen to her and get married. We'll all hate you," Yasmin shouted angrily. "Your name will be mud in this family. We will never speak to you again, ever! She does not have long to live, so why can't you make her final years happy?"

As if on cue, Ali's mother suddenly fell to the floor screaming in apparent agony. "The pain, the pain. I'm going to die," she screeched, clutching her chest.

Yasmin rushed to her aid. "Ammi, what's happened?" she asked her mother, who only moaned in response. Yasmin turned round to Ali and immediately found someone to blame. "Look what you've done, you bastard. You've given her a heart attack. Yunus, call the ambulance, quickly."

Yunus grabbed Ali by the throat. "I'll kill you if Mum dies," he said angrily, spittle flying rabidly from his mouth. He let go and grabbed the phone from the oak dining table.

"Don't call the ambulance yet, Yunus," Ali's mother whimpered pathetically from the floor. "Ali, come to me. I want to speak to you."

"I'll help you," Yunus said grabbing Ali by his hair. Ali screamed in pain as he was dragged across the floor to where Ammi lay. Yunus lifted Ali by his hair until his face was level with his mother's.

"Son, please say you'll get married. I don't want to die leaving you without a wife, knowing that you'll never marry. Please let me die happy," Ali's mother whispered. "Let my last moments be happy ones. Promise me you will marry."

"Ammi, I will get married. I don't want you to die. I'm so sorry. I will get married," Ali said in anguish. He was willing to do anything to make sure that his mother might live, even if it meant giving up his freedom and any future happiness. He did not want to be blamed by his family for his mother's death for the rest of his life.

"Ali, you have made me so happy." She leaned over to Ali's bloodied face and gave him a kiss, wiping the blood with her dupatta, which was ruined as the cream cloth absorbed the crimson liquid. "I won't need the ambulance after all, Yunus. The thought of seeing my youngest son's wedding has made me happy, and I feel so much better. Ali, you're a good son and a good Muslim boy. I will put some money in your bank account for you to buy yourself a car. I am so proud of you. Your father would be so happy if he was alive today."

"I don't want any money, Ammi. I'm marrying so that you are happy," Ali said with the dawning suspicion that his mother may have faked the sudden heart attack. He discreetly wiped the blood from his hand onto the beige rug beneath the coffee table in petty revenge. "Just remember that I will be dying inside on my wedding day," he added melodramatically "You will be happy, you will see," his mother said contentedly. She looked up at one of the paintings of Mecca hanging on the wall, recited a prayer under her breath and exhaled. "Sajda will make you a lovely bride, and you will both give me beautiful grandchildren. Carry me to my bedroom Yunus. I feel very tired. This day has drained me, and I need to rest."

Chapter Two

"Bonjour," said Ali, trying to make his accent sound as French as possible. If he hadn't had a Birmingham accent, he may have succeeded, but somehow he still managed to retain his Brummie tones while speaking the limited French that he knew.

"Bonjour monsieur," said the person at the other end of the phone. "Est-ce que je peux vous aider?"

"Steve Smith, chambre quatre vingts-six, s'il vous plait," replied Ali, hurriedly hoping that the receptionist was not going to try to enter into a conversation. The receptionist muttered something incomprehensible in French before putting Ali through.

Ali had successfully completed the first stage of getting through to Steve, who was studying in Strasbourg as part of his French degree. He lived in a hall of residence, which had its own receptionist to put all telephone calls through to the individual rooms.

Ali dreaded having to communicate in French with the receptionist when he phoned. Steve had given Ali fully written instructions as to how he should ask in French to be connected. The instructions were brief, so Ali did not get too confused, and Ali had telephoned enough times by now to be able to recite the French he had been taught from memory, but he still found it stressful making the call and always ended up referring to the written instructions.

The line went dead for several seconds, and then there was a ringing sound. The phone was answered after two rings. "Bonjour," said a male voice on the other end of the phone.

"Steve, how are you?" Ali asked, delighted to hear Steve's voice. His concern about making the call dissipated into the cold night's air. Ali was standing inside a public phone box in a quiet side street away from the family home in order to avoid being seen using the phone by family or community members.

"I'm fine thanks. What's up? How come you're ringing me so late?" asked Steve more sharply than Ali had expected.

"I'm really sorry. Did I wake you? If I did, I didn't mean to," Ali said crestfallen, the euphoria of getting through to Steve quickly drying up. He shivered as a gust of cold wind blew through the missing glass panels of the phone box. Ali checked the time on his watch. It showed ten o'clock, meaning that it was eleven o'clock in France. He'd forgotten about the time difference.

"I'm sorry for sounding so grumpy. I was just in the middle of translating some complicated text. How are you?" Steve asked, switching quickly from seeming annoyed to sounding pleased to hear from Ali.

"That's okay, Steve. I have something to tell you," Ali said, his voice suddenly strained and shaking with emotion with what he was about to say. Ali loved Steve very much and did not know how to break the news about the wedding. How do you tell the one you love that you are marrying someone else because you were told to?

"Okay," Steve said slowly after a long pause. "What is it?"

Ali struggled to find the words to explain what had happened. "Well you know when you asked me if I would ever have an arranged marriage?" asked Ali.

The phone went deathly silent for a moment. "Yes, I do. You promised me that it would never happen." Steve's voice sounded worried as he ran over all of the things that Ali might be about to tell him in his mind.

"Things have changed," Ali said sadly, trying hard not to cry and let his emotions get in the way.

"What are you saying Ali? Are you telling me that you're getting married?" Steve asked almost shouting down the phone.

"I'm sorry." Ali said, glad that Steve had made the situation a little easier to explain by guessing what he wanted to say. "We all had a massive discussion today, and I've agreed to get married," he said unhappily.

"What do you mean you've agreed to get married?" Steve asked angrily. "What about me? You're dating me! Where do I come into the equation?"

"They told me today that they'd arranged my wedding, and there was no way that they were going to let me get out of it. They didn't even ask me. They just went ahead and arranged everything," the shocked disbelief in Ali's voice was still obvious. "Then, they forced me to agree."

"Why? Why did you say yes, Ali? You're gay for God's sake. How the hell can you get married? You've been going out with me for more than two years. Do I mean nothing to you? Don't you love me?" Steve shouted down the phone angrily.

"I do love you. You mean everything to me, but my mother nearly had a heart attack today, and she says she doesn't have long to live." Ali cried. "You should have seen the state she was in. I had to agree as it's the only thing that's keeping her alive. You don't have a clue what it's like to be in a Pakistani family. We have obligations and responsibilities. I just knew you wouldn't understand."

"I do understand! Don't you dare throw that in my face. I've stood by you for all this time. You could have said no. You're gay, so how do you expect to live a lie?" Steve asked, unsure what battle he was trying to win. He knew that once Ali had agreed to do something he always went ahead with it, no matter what the consequences.

"I'm going to have to. I'll change. I'm going to be straight," Ali said determinedly, wondering whether this was something that he could hope to achieve.

"So when is the wedding?" Steve asked.

"It's very soon," Ali said, trying to sound vague. "I'm not too sure." He looked out of the missing glass panel of the phone box and shivered again. It was dark outside, and the sky looked pink as if there was going to be snow. Ali hated the snow and shivered again.

"Ali, you know when it is, so tell me," said Steve, reading Ali like a book.

"It's in two weeks time if you really want to know," Ali said. He had been reluctant to part with this information, worried what Steve might do. What if Steve turned up to the wedding and told all of the guests that he was gay, shaming him and his family in front of the community? It could ruin everything and devastate his family.

"Two weeks!" Steve exclaimed. "And you say they only told you today? You're lying! You must have known for longer than that," he said accusingly.

"Honestly, I didn't know until today. It's in two weeks, and I'm not joking," Ali said. "If it helps, I'm not exactly over the moon about it either."

"Two weeks! Why so quick? What is your family so worried about?" asked Steve.

"I don't know. I've finished my studies, and I guess they think it's the right time," Ali said. "They want the best for me. They just want to see me happy in their own way."

"They're probably worried that you're going to elope with some white boy," said Steve sarcastically. "I wouldn't be surprised if your family know everything about you already. They have a knack of finding things out."

"Steve, you know that if you asked me to leave and run away with you I would leave right now," Ali said interrupting Steve. Ali's head was suddenly filled with the romanticism of it all. The idea of packing his suitcase and following his heart seemed to be a second away from reality. "I can do it," he affirmed silently to himself.

"I can't ask you to leave, Ali," said Steve sounding surprised but sad. "I wish I could though," he muttered longingly down the phone.

"Why can't you ask me to leave?" Ali asked. Deep down, Ali had known what the response was going to be, but he'd found the courage to speak his heart's desire, and that moment seemed to have gone now. Steve had rejected the rosy future that Ali had glimpsed for them both.

"You know you have to make that choice yourself. I can't make your decisions for you. I don't want to be the one you blame for leaving your family if it all went wrong. You have to decide whether you can leave or not. I can't ask you," Steve said, sounding worried and concerned for Ali. "You have to leave for yourself, not for me."

"I just want you to ask me to leave. The decision will be mine. All I want you to do is ask. If you say the words, I will leave today," said Ali meaning every word.

"I can't ask you. It's going to have to be your choice," Steve said. "So do you know who you're marrying?" he asked, moving on from the subject.

"It's a girl from Nottingham. I've not met her yet. I don't think I'm allowed to until the wedding day," said Ali worrying about the change of subject. "If Steve really loved me, he would

18

ask me to leave, even if I couldn't," he thought. "Maybe getting married will be for the best."

"She knows you're gay though?" asked Steve, although he clearly knew the answer to the question already.

"I don't know," Ali replied.

"Well, I'm assuming that your family has told her that you're gay," Steve said. "Or are they going to deceive her family?"

"Like I said, I don't know," Ali muttered crossly.

"Well, knowing your family, I'm sure it's not something they're going to advertise," Steve said

"If you knew the answer, why did you ask me? Why are you being so mean? I thought you might just be a little supportive," Ali said, feeling upset at Steve's attitude.

"I am being supportive. I'm still talking to you aren't I? It's not every day that you get a call from your boyfriend telling you he's getting married and then wants you to be supportive!" Steve said, sounding incredulous. "You're forgetting that it's a shock for me, too."

"I know, I'm sorry," Ali said feeling guilty. He'd dropped a large bombshell and was still expecting a lot from Steve.

"You know it's not going to last, don't you?" said Steve after a brief silence.

"Isn't it? Why not?" Ali asked, not really interested in hearing Steve's reply. "I think it will last as long as I work at it." A large part of Ali felt that he was creating an illusion for himself in which he was married and living happily with his wife. The other part of him agreed with Steve and imagined that the marriage couldn't possibly last. How could it?

"You might work at it as hard as you want, but it still won't work you know. I mean, how are you planning on doing it?" Steve asked suggestively.

"Doing it? Doing what?" asked Ali, pretending not to understand Steve's question, and feeling annoyed. It was as if Steve did not want him to leave, which as far as Ali was concerned meant that he did not want commitment, yet he still seemed desperate for Ali's marriage to fail.

"You know what I mean. Doing it! Having sex! You can't take gay porn into the bedroom with you on your wedding night. So how are you going to do it? Does a woman turn you on? Can you make love to her on the wedding night?" Steve asked, throwing the questions at Ali in a brutal attempt to drum home the reality of what Ali was getting himself into.

"I'm not going to answer that. Stop being so coarse. It will work. I'll make sure it does," Ali said. "I will try and get to know her first, and eventually, I'm sure I'll fall in love with her." The rose-tinted picture that Ali had built up in his mind was still there although somewhat dented by Steve's artillery of questions.

"I give it a year. I can guarantee that it won't work," Steve said, sounding very sure of himself. "I know you, and I know you can't do it."

"Steve, I'm not getting into an argument about whether I can make my marriage work or not. I can't see you anymore, and it's best if I don't call you again. I have to move on with my life now," Ali said angrily. "It's not as if I will be able to see you when I get married anyway." That was it. Ali had ended his relationship, but as soon as the words were out, he wanted to take them back. He couldn't though, as this was the right thing to do.

"I love you, Ali, and I know you have to do this, but I will wait for you," said Steve making his decision. "I will wait for one whole year."

"No, I don't want you to wait for me. You need to get on with your own life. You'll probably meet someone with far less baggage who you'll be much happier with," Ali said trying to be brave but really wanting to tell him the opposite. What Steve was offering was tempting. It was designed to make his marriage fail though, and he wanted to ensure that he gave his marriage a one hundred percent chance of survival.

"I won't meet anyone else. You're the only one for me," replied Steve. "I love you so much. You are worth waiting for. If you're happily married in a year's time, I will move on with my life, but until then, I can wait."

"I don't want you to wait. I think it's sweet and romantic that you want to, but you shouldn't waste your time waiting for something to happen. It's better that we finish it and both move on with our lives," Ali said. It was so hard to say, but Ali didn't want to be trapped by both the marriage and Steve.

"I don't want to move on. I love you, plain and simple. I've not met anyone else like you," Steve said. "I'm sorry for being so horrible to you earlier, but you are dumping me, and really, I should be angry and bitter towards you, but I'm not. I love you."

"It's so hard. I never wanted to get married. Why does shit like this always happen to me?" Ali said starting to cry, his resolve slipping completely.

"Stop crying. It's okay," Steve murmured lovingly over the phone.

"I'm sorry. I'm fine. You know I sometimes wake up hoping to discover that this has all been some horrible dream," Ali said through the tears. The tears felt cold on his face, and he wiped them with the sleeve of his jacket and shivered.

"So will you wait for me or are you just saying that?" Ali asked hesitantly, giving in and seeking the reassurance that Steve might still be there for him.

"Yes, for a year from the day of your wedding, I promise," Steve replied.

"A whole year, that's like twelve months. It's a long time to wait when there are no guarantees," Ali said, unsure whether Steve would really want to wait for him.

"Yes, but there is one condition. You can't have any children with her. If you do, then it's over. I won't be waiting for you. It's too messy if there are children involved," Steve said.

"What if my wife wants children?" Ali asked worriedly. "I will have to have children if she wants children."

"Do you want to have children?" Steve asked.

"No, definitely not," Ali replied adamantly. "I've always been told how many children I should have, but I've never wanted children."

"Well, that's all that really matters, isn't it? You should at least do one thing for yourself," Steve said.

"I guess so, but what if I'm happily settled down with my wife a year from now. What will you do then?" Ali asked.

"I'll be very sad, but I'll move on and try to get on with my life," said Steve.

"I bet you'll meet someone as soon as you put the phone down. That's how quickly you'll get on with your life," Ali said trying to make a joke of it, but actually voicing his insecurities.

"No, that won't happen," Steve declared. "I will wait for you. I really will. I promise. I love you, and if you happen to

21

decide that you want to leave a little sooner then that's okay with me, too."

"I have to give it a try for at least a year, whatever happens," Ali said sadly. Suddenly, the automated voice of the telephone operator cut into the call. "You have one minute of credit remaining."

"I've got to go. I don't have any more coins left," cried Ali. He had been topping up the coins in the payphone continually throughout the conversation, but now he'd run out. He checked his wallet again, but all he found were a few coppers.

"I love you lots," said Steve blowing a kiss down the phone. "Don't you dare forget me once you're married."

"I'll never forget you, whatever happens," Ali cried back. "I love you, too. I'm sorry I've hurt you."

"I know, I really do understand what you're going through," Steve replied. "It's okay, don't worry. Whatever happens, you will be alright."

"It's not okay. I'm sorry. I really am. I'll try and call you again when I can get away," yelled Ali as the phone cut off with a click. Ali put the receiver down, and his coins washed down the phone noisily. Since Steve had moved to France, Ali had spent hundreds of pounds feeding the payphone.

Ali opened the door to the phone-box and stepped out into the cold. Although it was early in the year, it was snowing, but the snowflakes melted as soon as they hit the ground. Ali no longer felt the cold for some reason. He hurried back home wondering if anyone had seen him in the phone-box. He shrugged his shoulders. It did not matter anymore, as he was doing what they wanted him to now. Despite the hurt and the pain, Ali smiled to himself. Steve had not let him down.

Chapter Three

Ali was rudely interrupted from his sleep by the voice of his youngest sister, Aneesa, booming loudly at him. "Wake up, Ali, Ammi's arranged for you to see your in-laws."

Ali tried to bury his head deeper into the duvet. He had hoped that somehow the previous day had just been a nightmare. He whimpered self-pityingly to himself before yelling, "Go away," from under the duvet, his voice muffled by the covers.

"If you don't get up, I'm going to pull the duvet off you." Aneesa threatened, her hands reaching for the duvet in readiness. Ali twisted some of the duvet under his feet, just in case she tried to carry out her threat. "Listen, Ammi says that she's arranged for you to meet Sajda, so you've got to get up."

"I'm not going. I'm not getting up!" Ali yelled. He had come home to find his bedroom in disarray. His posters of Madonna that had been on the walls for years had been ripped off, while the old wallpaper underneath, which he had painstakingly painted green had been stripped away to reveal the bare plaster of the walls. Someone had even loaded his collection of vinyl records into several boxes for storage. It was as if all traces of his identity had been clinically removed from the room, so that his family could create a new one for him.

"You have to get up. It's a chance for you to meet your fiancée and not everyone gets the opportunity to do that. Ammi's trying to be modern about your wedding because you've got a degree. You're so lucky," she said, joyfully delighting in her mother's forward thinking attitude.

Aneesa was the youngest member of the household. She was eighteen years old, full of boundless energy and never showed any sign of distress or unhappiness. She always seemed positive, probably because she never got drawn into the arguments between the other siblings.

She maintained her own strong moral code and a self-righteous attitude, which embraced the cultural values of

Pakistan. She had been to Pakistan several times and had even lived there for a year at one time.

She always insisted that she would only marry through an arranged marriage and was known to break friendships or stop talking to other Pakistani girls if she found out that they were dating boys or even talking to them. She would distance herself from these girls, labeling them as "slags," along with general disparaging comments such as "What would their parents think if they knew, have they no shame?" Despite this, she kept her views about family matters to herself, especially where Ali was concerned.

"Go away, Aneesa," Ali shouted, sitting up in the bed. "You know what I think of this wedding, and I am not going to see her. I don't have to, and I don't want to."

"You have to go. You need to check her out," Aneesa continued ignoring Ali's words. She was wearing a trendy pair of blue jeans and a black baggy sweater with a white t-shirt underneath. Her face looked traditionally Pakistani, quite darkly tanned with attractive sharp features that still carried some puppy fat. "You can't trust photographs these days, not with all that digital imaging and camera lighting. You remember what happened to cousin Imran. You don't want that happening to you."

"I don't care what happened to Imran. Stop talking rubbish and go away. I'm your older brother, so show me a little respect!" Ali yelled. He took a few deep breaths to calm himself, remembering that it was not Aneesa that he was angry at but the rest of the family.

"You must remember what happened to cousin Imran? They took him to Pakistan last year and look who he ended up marrying. They told him that she was beautiful. I saw her photographs, and she looked fantastic. Don't tell me you weren't shocked when you met her? She was so ugly!" It seemed Aneesa didn't trust the verdict of the rest of the family about Sajda and was concerned about what Ali might end up with.

"Aneesa, just go and tell Ammi that I am not going to visit Sajda's bloody family," Ali said, shouting in frustration.

"You have to. If you don't go, her family will be upset with you," she said tugging the duvet again, not that it mattered whether she pulled it off now, as Ali was wide awake and sitting up in bed. "It's tradition as well. You have to take some clothes for her."

"I don't care about tradition. Just leave me alone," Ali told Aneesa crossly. He loved her the most of all the family members, and she rarely did anything to annoy him, but today she had somehow managed to become the messenger for everyone, which he found infuriating.

"Ammi says that she met Sajda about a year ago and that she's beautiful, but then Mum thinks that Imran's wife is beautiful, so it's best to see for yourself," Aneesa continued worriedly, ignoring Ali's rant.

"Aren't you listening to me? I am not going. I've agreed to this ridiculous wedding, and I'll turn up on the wedding day, but you can tell everyone from me to go to hell," Ali said crossly, lying back on the duvet covers, his body tense and angry.

"Why should I? You can tell Yasmin and Yunus yourself. That's if you really want to upset them. Don't go if you think you can handle them," Aneesa said sounding annoyed. She secretly agreed with Ali that Yasmin and Yunus behaved like tyrants, but was too scared to say anything in case she got caught in the firing line.

"I thought you couldn't see any of the bride's family before the wedding," Ali said questioningly. He wasn't familiar with any of the wedding customs, but he was positive that there was something weird about the two families not meeting until the wedding day once the wedding date was confirmed.

"Are you thick or something? You can see the family anytime you want; it's your fiancée that you can't. Ammi's sorted that out though. She was on the phone last night. She's told Sajda's family that as you're a modern man who was born in England; they have to do things differently. So they've decided to bend some of the rules for you," Aneesa said with relish at the power that her mother wielded.

"Great. That's all I need," muttered Ali. He knew that he would have to go if his mother had already made the arrangements, but he wasn't going to make things easy for anyone.

"You have to go," Aneesa said sharply, knowing that she had nearly won the battle.

"So, are you saying that I can refuse to go ahead with the wedding if I don't like her?" Ali asked.

"Well, not really. It's too late for that," she said after a pause. "Look, Ali, if you're going to argue, you can argue with Mum. I can't be bothered. I'm going to call her," she said, giving Ali an evil look and leaving his bedroom, loudly banging the door shut behind her, a trait she'd picked up from Ali when she was angry. Ali groaned as he heard her shout for their mother, and seconds later his mother materialized at his door with a sad dejected look on her face.

"You have plans more important than visiting your in-laws? Why must you always behave like this?" she asked sadly. "You would not have behaved in this way if your father was alive."

"I'm not going, Ammi. I've agreed to the marriage, so why do I have to visit them now?" Ali asked, knowing that he was going to lose the impending argument with his mother.

"You are worried, that's all. I know you are nervous, but don't be. Your big brother will go with you. I know you're not happy driving on motorways, so he'll drive you there and look after you," his mother said, her voice changing from disappointment to concern.

"I am not going! I have things to do," Ali said belligerently.

"You must go. I have arranged it. It is part of our custom for you to take clothes for your fiancée and to meet your in-laws. They need to speak to you, and make sure that you are happy with the match. You must behave when you go to see them, be respectful and don't talk back at them. They are a very good family, very big in our community. Please don't do anything to bring shame on us when you visit them," Ali's mother instructed, ignoring his protest.

"Well, I'm not going with Yunus. I can make my own way there. He hates me," Ali said finally getting up from the bed. He was wearing a grey kurta salwar suit that his grandmother had sent him from Pakistan, but which he used instead of pajamas. His mother looked at the suit and shook her head, silently wondering why her son was ruining such a perfectly good outfit by sleeping in it.

"Yunus is the head of the family, so he must go with you. We have to be respectful, son. I cannot send you to their house on your own or they will feel insulted. What would people say?" Ali's mother said kissing him on his forehead. "Get ready, or you will be late, and it will not create a good first impression."

Ali flung the duvet onto the floor defiantly and stormed out of the bedroom. Copying Aneesa, he banged the door shut behind him for effect. "Great, another thing you're making me do. When are you all going to stop," he yelled as he headed for the shower in defeat.

Ali hurriedly shaved, then showered quickly in the hope of avoiding Yunus. He rushed out of the bathroom to his bedroom to find a black suit neatly laid out for him on the bed. He felt slightly irritated that his mother had been through his wardrobe and picked out an outfit for him to wear. "Fantastic," he muttered, noticing that she'd even put out his underwear, socks and tie. It was as if he wasn't even allowed to make the smallest decision for himself anymore.

Ali quickly got dressed, choosing a different tie as a small act of rebellion, then rushed down the stairs, seeing if he could get away without anyone noticing.

There was no chance. Yunus was already dressed and waiting for him in the lounge. It seemed that Ali's mother had made sure she had roused him before Ali, knowing that he might try to make a quick exit. There was no way that Ali was getting away.

The suit that Yunus wore was identical to Ali's except for the ties, making Ali groan. Despite the age difference of four years between the two brothers, his mother had still attempted to dress them the same, just as she had done when they were young.

"Shall I make you breakfast before you go?" his mother asked. "I can cook you some aloo paratha."

"It's okay, Ammi, I'm not hungry," Ali said. All of a sudden, he felt very anxious about meeting his in-laws and unsure whether he would be able to keep his food down if he ate.

Ali felt rather strange. He knew that he didn't want to marry, but at the same time, he didn't want to let his family down. His mind seemed to be in conflict, but instead of attempting to evaluate his feelings about the subject, he

27

Amjeed Kabil

decided then it was best to try to block them out for now and consider them later.

"I have made some samosas for you in case you get hungry on the way," his mother said handing him a plastic food container containing the triangle shaped pastries filled with spicy mixed vegetables and potato.

"Thanks, Ammi, but I'm not hungry," Ali said, taking the food container anyway knowing that his mother would force it on him.

"This is for your Sajda," she said handing him a large square box hand painted with floral designs in red and gold. "It's the engagement present for you to give to her." She took the lid off the box, and let Ali peer inside. He gasped when he saw what it contained. It was the most exquisite dress he'd ever seen, folded neatly. It was a burgundy shade of brown, with sequined jewels sewn around the neckline that glittered gently in the light.

"You can get the general idea without taking it out of the box," said Ali's mother. She saw the look on Ali's face and knew that her son approved. "It was hand made in Pakistan and cost a lot of money. It's only the best for my son's fiancée." She carefully put the lid down on the box and handed it to Ali.

"Thank you, Ammi," he said trying to sound grateful as he took the box. Despite his reluctance to get married, his mother was trying her best. "What an ungrateful son I am. I should be happy today," he thought, giving a smile to try to hide the pain that he really felt for his mother's sake.

Ali's mother kissed him on his cheeks before bundling him out of the house with Yunus.

"Oi, faggot, you're coming with me in my car," Yunus said grabbing Ali and pushing him towards the bright red Toyota with blacked out windows that was parked in the driveway. "You can leave your disgusting rust bucket behind." He kicked Ali's car to demonstrate his feelings as he walked past it.

Ali sighed and followed Yunus obediently. This was going to be a long journey, and there was no point in antagonizing him. Ali got in the car as his mother waved goodbye. Aneesa and Yasmin hadn't come out to say goodbye. It seemed that Ammi wanted to keep things quiet for the time being in case the neighbors were watching.

28

The car had a luxury interior that gave off a strong, leathery smell. This mixed with the stale smell of cigarettes and Yunus's strong aftershave to create an oppressive stench in the car. Ali pressed the button to open the car's automatic windows, but Yunus pressed the button straight away to close them again. Ali sat back unhappily in his seat aware that Yunus was deliberately trying to provoke him.

Within minutes, Yunus hit the M6 motorway, driving extremely fast and well over the speed limit. He knew that Ali wasn't comfortable with motorway driving and rarely managed to drive up to the motorway speed limit. Taking one hand off the steering wheel, Yunus removed a pack of cigarettes from his jacket pocket and opened it pulling out a cigarette at the same time. He paused to light it with the car's cigarette lighter and then took one long puff from the cigarette.

At twenty eight years old, Yunus still behaved immaturely when it came to his relationship with Ali, always competing and attempting to outdo him. If Ali's mother cooked something special for Ali, then Yunus wanted the same. If she brought him new clothes or gave him money, then Yunus got the same by throwing a tantrum.

In appearance, Yunus was very handsome, and he knew it. He was obsessed with going to the gym and drank protein concoctions that he made up from huge plastic cartons of powder. He had almond colored eyes, which were rather striking, and his ability to charm the girls meant that he had most of them falling at his feet.

However, Yunus's own marriage had ended after just two years, and no one in the family ever mentioned why. Ali had been living away at the University Halls of Residence when it had happened. One day, his sister-in-law was living in the extension that had been added to the house for her, and the next she had disappeared. She was referred to as the "tart" by his sisters, but Yunus had never mentioned her. Ali imagined that she'd had an affair and run away.

"So how many white boys have given it to you up the arse?" Yunus asked suddenly after a lengthy silence.

Caught by the vulgarity of the question, Ali thought about ignoring it, but his annoyance got the better of him. "Lots and lots," he replied. "You know, to be honest, I've lost count. I really can't get enough. It's like the best feeling ever, pleasure and pain all rolled into one."

"You dirty fucking bastard! How could you like it up your arse? It's sick," Yunus said turning to look at Ali, utterly disgusted.

"You just haven't tried it, yet. You should. All men should. When you do you'll love it, or have you tried it already and can't say?" Ali asked, doing his best to shock Yunus, but also knowing what the reaction would be. It was dangerous to wind Yunus up, but he couldn't stop himself.

"You dirty little wanker. I like women. Pussy! I only fuck pussy!" he said, punching Ali savagely on the arm.

Ali winced in pain and rubbed his arm. "I think you're scared that you'll like it too much," he said seething with silent rage, his earlier plan of not antagonizing Yunus slowly falling apart. Yunus made him so angry that he shook with rage. Ali took some deep breaths to calm himself. It didn't help his asthma when he got angry.

"Have you fucked a woman yet? You must have fucked that slag you hang around with?" Yunus asked, trying to aggravate Ali further. Yunus was desperate to "straighten" Ali out. He loved Ali, but found him effeminate and worried what would happen if he didn't help him to toughen up. Ali's gay lifestyle shamed him in front of his friends, and he was sick of lying to them about Ali's numerous "girlfriends." "Why can't Ali be a real man?" he thought despairingly.

"No, not really," Ali replied sharply wanting to say more to defend his friend.

"You're lying! You mean you've never fucked that slut? What's her name?" Yunus said pretending to have forgotten her name. "Oh yes, Haseena. A good-looking guy like you should be able to fuck an old slag like that. What the fuck's wrong with you?" He looked at Ali and shook his head in disappointment.

"There's nothing wrong with me. It's you who has the problem," Ali retorted. He knew this would happen. He always suffered a barrage of abuse whenever he was alone with Yunus. "It's my own fault," Ali thought, "I should have kept quiet and not answered back."

"She's a fat, old slag, but even I'd give her one. So what the fuck's wrong with you?" He asked again in disgust. "I'll hire you a prostitute. In fact, why don't I pay that slut Haseena. You need to have sex with a woman before you get married. What will your wife think knowing you're a fucking virgin? You need to know what you're doing on your wedding night."

"It's ok. I'm sure I'll manage," Ali said, repulsed by the suggestion. Ali had never slept with a woman, and since agreeing to the wedding was worried what might happen on the wedding night. He blocked the thought from his mind and decided to think about it some other time. Ali had become an expert at blocking upsetting thoughts like this lately.

"You're a virgin right? Being buggered by a man doesn't count. You're a virgin until you fuck a woman. That's when you become a real man," Yunus said using his twisted logic on Ali. "Don't you feel the slightest bit ashamed of yourself? Doesn't picking up men for sex in toilets make you feel dirty?"

"What are you on about?" exclaimed Ali.

"You gays meet in toilets, don't you?" said Yunus more as a statement than a question.

"Oh, you should see me on a Friday night. I'm always dressed up and ready to go round to the toilets in the city center," Ali said sarcastically.

"You dirty fucker," said Yunus, failing to pick up the sarcasm in Ali's voice. "Have you been skiing?"

"Skiing? No," said Ali feeling bewildered at the change of subject.

"Skiing," Yunus repeated, taking both hands off the steering wheel and gesturing with his hands as if he was holding two ski sticks. "It's what you poofs always do together."

"Oh you mean threesomes. I've lost count," Ali said inwardly appalled by his own replies, although for some reason he felt compelled to respond to Yunus, no matter how crude his own reply. He knew that he was cementing Yunus's stereotype of gay men, but couldn't find a way to end the conversation.

"You'll have to stop being a poof when you're married. You can't go around getting fucked up the arse by dirty old white men. It's perverted. You should be ashamed of yourself," he said. "When I have kids why should I have to always worry about letting you see them? I should be able to trust you, but I know what you poofs are like, you like to fiddle with children."

"You bastard," Ali shouted angrily. "I'm gay, not a pedophile. I like men not children you idiot, and I certainly am not ashamed of what I am." He couldn't believe how Yunus was relating his sexuality to pedophilia.

"You disgusting bastard! How could you say you like men? If dad was around he would have straightened you out. You're lucky Mum won't let me deal with you my way, otherwise you'd have two broken legs and be sitting at home in a wheelchair," Yunus shouted back.

"Try it, and we will see who'll be going to prison," shouted Ali. "We're not in a village in Pakistan anymore."

"Do you really think you would be able to leave the house with broken legs? You wouldn't get a chance to tell the police. We'd lock you up in a room. That's what they do to people in Pakistan who fuck about like you. You're so lucky Mum doesn't understand that you're a dirty fucker who can't control himself. She thinks you're influenced by the white society. She's too old to understand what gay means."

Ali stopped talking to him, hoping that his silence might encourage the verbal assaults to stop. He stared out of the window pretending to be interested in the scenery while Yunus droned on. They drove past a sign which indicated that they were fifteen miles away from Nottingham, making Ali wince inwardly as he wondered how much longer he would have to spend in the car with Yunus.

"So why do you like being fucked up the arse by old men?" Yunus asked. Ali pretended not to hear him, but Yunus repeated the question, trying to bait Ali. When he failed to get a response he punched Ali and repeated the question again.

Ali finally snapped. "They pay me lots of money, that's why I sleep with old men. Most of them aren't white anyway. You should see the old Muslim guys with the beards. They're my best customers. In fact they're my regulars! I mean fifty pounds for an hour with me is a reasonable price, and the more they pay, the more willing I am."

"What! You're a prostitute, a dirty fucking rent boy?" Yunus asked in shock, seeking confirmation of the revelation. His face was contorted horribly in disbelief.

"Yes," Ali said, knowing that his brother believed him. "I have regular clients, though. I don't need to hang about the street, so don't worry about my safety."

"You're fucking with my head. You can't be a rent boy," Yunus said seeking assurance.

"Why should I fuck with your head? There's quite a market for us Pakistani boys. We're seen as a bit exotic because there are so few of us gay ones about. We can get away with charging a little extra. How do you think I managed to buy my own car? You know I'm not good at saving," Ali said, making his claim more plausible for his brother.

Yunus went quiet for a moment while mulling over Ali's "revelation." "So you're not gay after all. You're just a prostitute. You sleep with men for money, not because they turn you on, but because you want money. I see now. Do you need money that much? Ammi gives you lots of money, so why are you so desperate?"

Ali groaned, realizing his untruth had spawned another theory to explain his sexuality. "Whatever," he muttered, not wanting to enter into another cycle of verbal abuse from Yunus.

This time the silence managed to sustain itself until Yunus stopped to refuel at a service station on the M1, just before the junction for Nottingham. Ali went with him to get himself a chocolate bar. "Walk like a man," Yunus told him as Ali hurried away for a few minutes of respite from Yunus's company.

Ali picked up a Kit Kat from the counter and paid for it. He smiled at the shop assistant when he was given his change, and walked past Yunus, deliberately ignoring him. Ali went outside to wait on the forecourt next to the car for Yunus.

It was nice to be out of the car and away from Yunus. The cool November air hit Ali's face making him gasp, but it was refreshing in comparison to the stench in Yunus's car. "What am I going to do?" he thought despairingly as he remembered where he was going. He didn't have long to sink into his thoughts before Yunus returned.

"Stop giving out gay signals you dirty bastard. You poofs, you can't stop it can you?" Yunus said, getting into the car. Ali got in, unsure what Yunus was talking about. "I have a good mind to beat that poof in the shop up, but the garage has CCTV."

"What are you talking about?" Ali asked, still puzzled by Yunus's comment.

"The queer cashier. I saw you both giving each other gay signals. You should be ashamed of yourself. You're seeing your

33

fiancée today, but you can't leave your gay ways behind," Yunus said.

"What do you mean? I was buying some chocolate and smiled at him when I paid. I was being polite, you stupid bastard," Ali said furiously. "Just leave me alone. I hate you. The only reason I tolerate you is because we have the same mother and father."

"I'll only leave you alone when you tell me you're not going to be a fucking queer boy anymore," Yunus said calmly. He smiled wickedly revealing his recently enameled white teeth.

"Why are you so horrible to me? I'm doing everything that this family wants of me, but you still won't leave me alone," Ali exclaimed. "Why do you carry on like this all the time? What have I done to make you hate me so much?"

"I don't hate you. I love you. You're my brother, and I'm looking out for you. I'm the head of the family, so it's my duty to look after you all. It's a bad world out there, and I don't want you to be a poof all your life. It's not right. I want you to be happy, get married and have children as much as Ammi does," Yunus said, sounding sincere and actually making Ali half believe him.

"You've just talked about what you want," Ali said. "But you've not asked me what I want. I've never wanted to get married. I've never wanted children."

"You don't know what you want, Ali. That's why we've sorted everything out for you. Just leave it to your family. We will look after you," he said caressing Ali's shoulder caringly.

"Leave me alone," Ali said angrily, cringing from Yunus's touch.

"I have to make sure you don't pick up men anymore. If I ever find out you are still getting fucked by men when you're married, I'm going to break your legs. Promise me you won't see any men," he demanded.

Ali ignored him and allowed the rest of his words to disappear into the background with the noise of the car engine. It was pointless having a discussion with Yunus at the best of times, but today, he was at his worst.

Ali's earliest memories of Yunus were of him stealing Ali's milk bottle as a toddler. Years later, this had progressed to violent fights. Ali still carried scars on his hand from when

Yunus had bitten him. Nothing had changed between them since childhood, except perhaps the dislike had become stronger.

"We're nearly there," Yunus said, interrupting Ali's thoughts. When we get there, you are to stay quiet. If you dare say anything out of order, I'll sort you out, you dirty fuck. Go along with whatever your in-laws say. Don't disagree with them. If you mention your dirty habits to anyone, I'll kill you, and I'll sort that bitch Haseena out as well. Do you understand what I'm saying?"

"Yes," said Ali, cowed by his brother's threat.

"If you misbehave, it won't just be your neck on the line. You know what my friends can do," Yunus said threateningly. Ali knew exactly what Yunus's friends were capable of. They were the type who wouldn't hesitate in taking a baseball bat to someone to teach them a lesson, and Yunus had already settled some scores this way.

They turned the corner onto the street where Sajda's parent's lived. It was a quiet suburban street, unlike the busy road where Ali's family lived. Yunus parked his car opposite their driveway. The house was built on an end plot. It was large and detached with a newly finished extension to the side that squeezed the gap between the neighboring property to a tight inch.

"What shitty cars," Yunus hissed noticing the two identical black BMW's parked side by side on the red brick driveway as he got out of the car. The two cars were sparkling as if newly polished in order to exhibit the wealth and prestige of the family inside the house.

As Yunus set the immobilizer alarm on his car, Ali looked up and noticed the bedroom curtains twitch. He looked away quickly, then followed Yunus to the door, holding the gift box that his mother had given him for his fiancée. The front door was plastic and double-glazed. It had "Hussein" boldly written in green and red stained glass in the glass panel above.

"Behave like a fucking man," whispered Yunus and then pressed the doorbell firmly.

Chapter Four

The door was opened by a short overweight woman, who looked to be in her late fifties. She had a round and full face that was wrinkled like old parchment, and her hair was jet black. It was obvious she had recently dyed it.

She ignored Yunus completely and grabbed hold of Ali, kissing him wetly on both of his cheeks, while shoving his face almost hungrily into her pendulous breasts. When she finally pulled away, Ali could feel a slight tenderness on his cheeks where her teeth had left indentations. "Yuck! She has buckteeth," Ali thought, shocked at his own shallowness.

She pulled Ali into the house excitedly. "Welcome. Welcome, my son," she cried in Urdu. Yunus stood at the doorstep looking unhappy at being ignored. Ali wondered if Yunus would react to this or whether he'd been warned to be on his best behavior by their mother. After a few moments, Yunus shrugged his shoulders angrily and followed them inside.

"Buckteeth," Ali thought unable to take his mind off his mother-in-law's teeth. Despite his lack of enthusiasm for his forthcoming wedding, he couldn't help but wonder whether his fiancée looked like the image on the photograph he'd seen or whether she resembled her mother. He found himself praying she hadn't inherited her mother's looks. Strange, but he hoped that his family had made a good match. Maybe it was a fair swap, a gay husband for a rabbit-faced wife.

Ali's mother-in-law seemed to have the most horrendous taste in clothes. She was wearing a hideous, salwar kameez suit that looked almost like wallpaper found in any Pakistani curry house. It was made from a thick burgundy velvet fabric, which was covered with little splashes of bleached green patches, while the dupatta, covering her hair, had large nylon flower petals sewn on it.

She led Ali and Yunus into the house through a long hallway. The smell of freshly cooked curry emanated from the nearby kitchen, making Ali's stomach churn. It had a delicious aroma, but the thought of eating was the last thing on his mind.

His stomach was volatile and his nerves in tatters as he wondered what his in-laws would make of him. It felt as if he were about to walk into an interview.

The walls of the hallway were covered in framed photographs of the weddings of various family members. "This is going to be my life," Ali thought glumly seeing his future mapped out in the photographs on the walls.

Just before reaching the end of the hallway, Ali's mother-in-law stopped and turned round as if remembering something. "Yunus," she cried, finally acknowledging him. "I'm so sorry. I completely forgot you. I'm so absent minded. I was so excited at seeing my new son-in-law and had no thought for anything else. Please forgive me. I can be a forgetful old woman sometimes," she said apologetically. She looked at Yunus and then at Ali again. "You both look so alike, a lot like your father. He was such a tall and handsome man."

"Thank you," Yunus replied, forgiving her absent-mindedness, feeling pleased that she had noticed he looked like his father.

Ali didn't mind being told that he looked like his father, but he wasn't happy to hear that he looked anything like Yunus. As he was unable to think of an appropriate response, he followed them quietly into the lounge.

"Look, who has come to visit," his mother-in-law said jovially to the middle-aged man sitting on the beige leather sofa as if she was surprising him. "Ali, this is your father-in-law," she said introducing him.

Ali's father-in-law got up to greet them. He was smartly dressed in a beige suit that almost blended into the sofa. He was clean-shaven, which was quite unusual for a Muslim man of his age, and was very slim in distinct contrast to his wife. Ali discretely examined his teeth, and was pleased to see that they appeared to look normal, if a little tea stained.

His father-in-law looked very serious despite wearing a smile. He hugged Ali in the strange way that old Pakistani men greeted each other. He placed his head to Ali's left cheek with the first hug, and then moved his cheek to Ali's right cheek while giving him a second hug. Yunus looked on, enjoying the uncomfortable look on Ali's face.

Turning to the coffee table in front of him, he picked up a garland made of fresh flowers. He noticed Ali eyeing them warily. "This is an old custom from Pakistan. If your father had been alive today, I would have been proud to place them on him. Instead your brother takes his place," he said placing the garland around Yunus's neck and then hugged him in the same manner. "It's very sad that you both lost your father while so young," he muttered sadly in Urdu.

"Take a seat my son," he said to Ali pointing to the sofa, and then gesturing to Yunus to do the same.

"Thank you, Uncle," Ali said, uncertain as to how he should address his father-in-law, and promptly sat down. Yunus took the space on the sofa next to him.

"Don't call me Uncle. We are going to be very close when you are married to my daughter. I'll be like a father to you. You must call me Abbu Jee," Ali's father-in-law said sternly.

Abbu Jee meant father. It seemed insensitive of his father-in-law to think that he should be called this especially as their father had passed away shortly after Yunus's wedding. Ali did not quite know how to reply.

Getting a sharp look from Yunus's direction, Ali replied, unsure whether it was what Yunus wanted him to say. "Thank you, Abbu," he said, deciding it was best not to offend him. The words felt strange on his tongue. "How could this man expect me to call him father? He is nothing like my father," Ali thought.

"I am proud to have you in the family, my son," Ali's father-in-law replied.

"I have a present that my mother has asked me to give to Sajda," Ali said, relinquishing the box that he'd been holding.

His father-in-law took the box, opened the lid and smiled in a satisfied manner after he'd examined what was in it. He handed the box to his wife who sat down next to him, and she removed the dress from its box. "It's beautiful," she exclaimed. "It looks like it has been made in Pakistan," she added, recognizing the fine detail. "It's Sajda's favorite color. She will adore it. You must thank your mother. This gift is truly generous of her."

"I'm glad you think she will like it," Ali replied, wondering why his in-laws didn't find it strange that he had not been involved in the choosing of the present.

"We have bought you a present as well. I shall fetch it for you," his mother-in-law said, getting up heavily from the sofa.

"Thank you, but you shouldn't have," Ali said politely.

"It's tradition to exchange gifts," his mother-in-law said admonishingly. "Has your mother not told you this?"

"Rhazia," she shouted, bellowing the name loudly through the open lounge door. "Will you bring down the gift for Ali? Hurry up, child!" Moments later, a young girl stepped into the lounge holding a clothes hanger with a suit displayed on it.

The girl smiled shyly at Ali, before handing the suit to her mother. "This is my youngest daughter, Rhazia," Ali's mother-in-law said, introducing her. Rhazia smiled again and then hurried awkwardly out of the room. She reminded Ali of his own sister, Aneesa, who was just as shy when people came to visit.

"She's very shy, so you have to excuse her," Ali's mother-in-law confirmed apologetically. "She's a good girl. We've brought her up well. She gets shy around men and doesn't talk to them like the other girls her age, just as it should be. We're very lucky that she has turned out so well." She handed Ali the suit. "What do you think of it?" she demanded.

Ali looked at the suit, uncertain whether he liked it. It was dark green, and he was unsure whether he would actually ever wear it. "It's lovely," Ali said, pretending to be pleased with it.

"I'm glad that you like it. When you take it home with you, try it on, and if it doesn't fit, then bring it back. I'll return it for you. I checked the size was correct with your mother, so it should be the right fit," Ali's mother-in-law said to him, pleased that Ali had liked her personal choice of clothes for him.

"Thank you," said Ali respectfully.

"So what are your plans for when you get married?" Ali's father-in-law asked. "What will you do for work? Will you move to Nottingham or will you stay in Birmingham?" The questions rolled off his father-in-law's tongue in an interrogative manner.

"I don't know," Ali said, caught off guard. "I haven't really had the chance to think about it, yet." What he really would have liked to say was that he'd only been told about the marriage yesterday, and that he had been living a gay lifestyle until then.

He looked at his in-laws sitting on their comfortable sofa in their cozy home, and he realized he couldn't treat them like strangers anymore. He'd seen their joy and happiness and suddenly knew that he couldn't let them down. They were good people who wanted the best for their daughter. He represented a lot to them, someone who would be able to offer their daughter the best of both worlds – English and Pakistani – an ideal match.

"Your mother says that you work at the moment and that you have a degree?" his father-in-law asked, seeking confirmation from Ali, just in case his mother had exaggerated.

"Well, I finished my degree two weeks ago, so I've not had time to look for a proper job, yet. I needed a break after my finals. I have been working part-time in a clothing store on the weekends, but I resigned last week as I wanted to concentrate on looking for a job in my field," Ali said, assuring his father-in-law that he wasn't an unemployed layabout that he suspected him of being.

"So you're unemployed! You won't get much money on the dole! How do you plan to support my daughter when you're married?" his father-in-law demanded.

"I don't know. I've only just started to apply for jobs in the research field," Ali said, surprised by the abruptness of the question. "I can probably get my job back with the clothing store. It'll get us by until I've sorted something better out."

"I'm sorry, but I must ask you these questions. I have looked after my daughter all of her life. I want to make sure that you will do the same. A part-time job in a shop won't support my daughter. You must work for my son Omar's friend, Javed. He has a vacancy at his firm, and I'm sure he would like you to work for him. He will pay you more than a job in a clothing store."

"I don't want just any job. I want to work for a pharmaceuticals research company. If I start working full time now, it will distract me from getting a job that I really want," Ali said, dismayed by his father-in-law's suggestion. It was good that he wanted someone who would support his daughter financially, but finding a job for him was insulting.

"Don't worry. It will only be until you get a proper job. Omar is finalizing it for you today. The job will be here in

41

Nottingham, and you can both move into our spare room until you've found a house to buy," he said generously.

"I'm not sure if I'm ready to buy a house. I don't think I want a mortgage just yet," Ali said, trying hard not to show the shock that he was feeling. Things were moving quickly out of his control.

"It's all been organized with your mother. You will not have to worry about a mortgage. As part of the arrangements your mother has agreed to buy a house for you and Sajda. We'll help you to find the right house and afterwards help you to decorate it, too," Ali's father-in-law said generously.

"I don't know, my mother hasn't said anything about this," Ali said taken aback. However, he found it quite easy to imagine that his mother had agreed to this without mentioning it to anyone. Even Yunus looked surprised by the arrangements, which meant she had not confided in him either. He was also probably annoyed that the family had only built him an extension to the house when he got married and not purchased him a house of his own.

"I've already spoken to your mother about it," Ali's father-in-law said. "We both agreed that it's better for you to find work in Nottingham. There are more opportunities for you here than in Birmingham. She agrees there are lots of bad influences for young people there. I've seen Birmingham in the news. It's full of terrorists. There is always a shooting, a riot or someone getting robbed. It is much safer here for you both."

"Birmingham isn't that dangerous at all. They always exaggerate things on the news," Ali said, immediately defending his home city. "In fact, it's going to be as good as London now that they've finished redeveloping the Bull Ring." Ali knew that the real reason his mother had agreed for him to move closer to his in-laws was to get him away from the friends that she thought were a bad influence on him, namely Haseena.

"That is because you're a decent boy, Ali. You don't notice these things around you," Ali's father-in-law said. "It is not right for my daughter to live in such a dangerous city. There are other reasons why you must move here. My daughter is a very modern girl. She has been to college and now works. If she moves to Birmingham, she will not be able to do the same things. The community there is very narrow-minded. They will not understand why she works. They'll say it's because you cannot support her. It's better for you both to live here. Yunus was married to a girl from Pakistan. Yunus did she work?"

"No," Yunus muttered, glaring crossly at the mention of his ex-wife.

"Your wife never worked, and she lived in your mother's house. Why? I think it's because she was from the village. She wanted to have children, look after them and clean the house," Ali's father-in-law said, giving his narrow minded opinion. "Girls born in England want different things. My daughter has been working since she was eighteen. She has a very good job. She has a career. Why must she give this up because she is getting married? These are modern times."

"I've never said that she should move away and give up her career. I didn't even know she worked. All I said is that Birmingham is a nice place," Ali said, upset at being chided.

"You're right. I'm sorry, Ali. I should not speak to you like this. You'll be her husband soon. It will be your decision whether you want her to work or not. I'm just her father, and I forget that my duty ends once she is married," Ali's father-in-law said. "I must ask you one thing. Will you allow my daughter to work?"

"It's up to her. If she wants to work, she can. It's her decision, not mine," Ali said, cringing inwardly, embarrassed that his father-in-law was asking such a question. It seemed that his fiancée's family clearly clung tightly to their Pakistani village values, despite giving the impression that they were modern and forward thinking in their outlook.

"You're a wonderful boy," his father-in-law said, leaning over and hugging him, making Ali cringe further with embarrassment. "I don't like a man who forces his wife to work. I also don't like a man who does not want his wife to work. Like you say, it's her decision, and it's good that you give her choice. My daughter is a good girl. She brings home her wage, gives some money to us and saves the rest for her future. Do you give money to your mother?"

"Yes, sometimes," Ali said. It wasn't as if his mother needed his money, but sometimes he did offer to pay the telephone bill when he was feeling generous.

"That is very good. You truly value your mother. Your mother has told me that you have worked since you were eighteen. You must have lots of money saved," Ali's father-in-law commented.

"I've not really had much opportunity to save," Ali said truthfully. "I've just been trying to pay off my student loan recently."

"A student loan? You have a student loan?" his father-in-law exclaimed worriedly. "Did your mother not pay for your education? Why do you have a student loan?"

"I've supported myself through university. I didn't ask my mother to support me like most people. Studying is expensive. It cost me a lot of money to buy the course textbooks, and the accommodation at the university wasn't cheap either," explained Ali. He thought it best not to mention the cost of late night partying or the boozing.

"Ammi offered to pay his fees, but he refused. Ali likes his independence and wanted to pay his own way," Yunus said, defending his mother. "He is too headstrong sometimes."

"It's good that you wish to pay your own way, but it is wrong of your mother to allow you to get into debt," Ali's father-in-law said sounding grave. "I will talk to your mother. She must pay off your loan before you get married. My daughter has lots of savings, and she must not use it on paying your loan. Debt is not good! We Muslims shouldn't be taking out loans and paying interest."

"My loan isn't that big. I can afford to pay it back, myself," Ali said, annoyed at his father-in-law's suggestion but irritated with himself for bringing the subject to his attention.

At that moment, the doorbell rang. It interrupted what Ali's father-in-law was about to say next. "I'll speak to your mother about this before the wedding," he said, after a pause and recovering from his lapse. "That must be Omar with his friend. Let them in, Begum," he ordered his wife.

"I'm hoping for some good news about a job for you, Ali," his father-in-law said. "Javed's father is a close family friend, so I don't think he will let me down."

Ali wanted to protest, but Yunus gave him another one of his sharp looks, warning him to stay quiet. Ali sat back into his seat and said nothing, annoyed that he was not allowed to put forward his thoughts on the subject of someone finding a job for him.

His mother-in-law bustled back into the room excitedly. "This is Omar," she said introducing the man whose graduation and wedding photographs were displayed among those in the hallway. Omar looked slightly older than in the photographs, but his face was covered in pockmarks, which were not evident in his pictures.

Omar shook Ali's hand limply, almost submissively, before greeting Yunus in the same manner. "This is Javed," he said shyly introducing the man standing next to him. Javed's handshake was very firm in contrast and clearly intended to exert his authority and dominance on anyone he met. Ali deliberately let his hand go limp as Javed squeezed it hard in a handshake, seeing no point in playing power games. That was more Yunus's thing.

"I will let you men talk among yourselves while I make you all tea," Ali's mother-in-law said, after she'd stopped fussing over getting Omar and Javed settled on the sofa. She then left the room quietly, giving Ali a smile on her way out.

"I have a job for your son-in-law, Shah Jee," Javed said smoothly to Ali's father-in-law in a deep voice. He did not seem to have a noticeable accent indicating that he was very middle class.

"Thank you so much. I knew you would be able to help him. He has a degree in Microbiology you know, so this will only be a short-term measure," Ali's father-in-law said proudly.

"Oh," Javed said, pausing as if noticing Ali for the first time. "Where did you study?" he asked, looking Ali up and down unpleasantly as if measuring his worth.

"It was at Wolverhampton University," Ali replied. He was proud of completing his degree, as not many people from his community had been to university.

"I've never heard of it. It must be a polytechnic that thinks it's a university. The standard of teaching in those places is poor. It's unlikely you'll get a job in industry. Why did you bother?" Javed asked him disparagingly without waiting for a response. "You should have stayed at home or got yourself a job at a poultry factory and not wasted your time."

"I was quite happy with the teaching standards," Ali said, trying his best not to sound affronted by Javed's words.

"Is that why you've managed to find a job for yourself?" he asked sarcastically. "Why do you think your father-in-law has come running to me? You're just like the village idiot he married his eldest daughter to, but at least you can read English." He then turned round to face Ali's father-in-law, dismissing Ali completely.

Shaking with anger at Javed's venom, Ali could barely contain himself. The man was an arrogant, nasty piece of work, with a self-important attitude that seemed to have been cultivated by belittling others. Ali tried to stop his face from betraying his hurt look, but it did not matter, everyone else seemed to be behaving as if the exchange had not taken place.

"So what job do you have for him?" Ali's father-in-law asked eagerly, keen for Ali to have a job, and if Ali was insulted in the process, it clearly didn't matter.

"It's a computing job. I need someone to develop the company database," Javed said eloquently, the sharp edge in his voice now gone. "I would ideally prefer someone qualified, but this is a favor, Saab Jee. I won't be able to pay him the full rate, but he will be paid well. If he had a computing degree, it would have been different."

"I've studied a database module at university, so I know how to develop a database," Ali said interrupting.

"Don't interrupt when your elders are talking," Javed said, looking scornfully at Ali. "Has your mother not taught you any manners?"

Ali tried to keep his temper in check. It was rare that someone got away with speaking to him in such a rude manner, but Ali didn't want to upset his father-in-law.

"Who do you think you are, talking to my brother like that? Ali doesn't need to beg for a job from the likes of you," Yunus said, speaking up suddenly in Ali's defense. "If we were in Pakistan, you'd have been working on our lands and cleaning out our cesspit. So be grateful you're in England." Ali breathed a sigh of relief, glad for the first time to hear the caustic words drip from Yunus's mouth, especially as this time, he was not the target.

"You must take this job, Ali," Ali's father in-law said, ignoring Yunus's comments.

For a few moments, Ali considered his options. It felt almost as if he was back at home with his own family, being told what to do. Somehow, he couldn't escape the surreal thought that his life was being chopped into small pieces and slowly being shared out for different people to control.

"No, I don't want this job," Ali said finally. "I've studied science, and I've already explained that I want to work for a pharmaceutical company. I'm sorry if it upsets anyone. I know you're all trying to help, but I'm sure I'll find the right job, myself."

"Well, if the Mirza village idiots are refusing my offer of help then I should leave. I'm not sitting here while they insult me and my generosity," Javed said haughtily, getting up from the sofa.

"Please stay," Ali's father-in-law said, holding onto Javed's shirtsleeve. "Ali will take this job. I shall talk to his mother. He does not mean to insult you."

"Ali is not taking the job," Yunus said aggressively, his voice loud and threatening, startling Ali's father-in-law.

"I should leave. It's obvious that I'm not wanted here, Saab Jee," Javed said snootily, but sounding cowed.

"Stay, Javed. They are young and don't mean to insult you," Ali's father-in-law said, trailing after Javed as he left the room. Omar meanwhile stayed sitting on the settee motionless, watching the scene unfold, preferring to stay in the background and not get involved.

"How dare your son-in-law turn down my offer of help? I have a business to run, and you've wasted my time by inviting me here. Don't expect me to attend the wedding, you peasants!" they heard Javed shout, before he slammed the front door shut as he left.

"You should have accepted his job offer," Ali's father-in-law said to Ali when he returned to the room. "He's not a man to get on the wrong side of. He does not mean to insult people. It's just his way."

"I'm sorry. I would have accepted the job if I knew what it meant to you, but I have to listen to what my brother tells me," Ali said meekly, laying the full blame unfairly on Yunus for his decision.

"Never mind, what's done is done," Ali's mother-in-law said. She had come back quietly into the room and placed a tray neatly laden with a matching teapot, cups and saucers on the

47

Amjeed Kabil

coffee table. "I'll speak to him in a few days time and apologize. He'll have calmed down by then, and all will be forgotten."

"I'd better introduce you to the rest of the family," said Ali's father-in-law signaling to his wife.

"Rhazia, will you bring your sister in?" Ali's mother-in-law shouted out of the door. Seconds later Rhazia appeared with another girl beside her. They were both dressed modestly in Pakistani salwar kameez suits, but their dupattas hung around their necks rather than covering their heads. They both also had short, cropped hair, giving the impression that Ali's father-in-law was a very liberal Muslim.

"These are my daughters," Ali's mother-in-law said. "You've already met Rhazia. She is the youngest."

Rhazia looked to the floor in what appeared to be an attempt to be invisible and murmured an almost indistinguishable hello.

"This is my eldest daughter, Shazia," his mother-in-law continued looking exasperated at her daughter's shyness.

"Nice to finally meet you," Shazia said. "So, are you happy about the wedding?"

Ali was taken slightly aback by the question. A paranoid part of him wondered whether she'd found out about his reluctance to marry and now wanted him to admit it. "I think so," Ali uttered eventually.

"I think so? What kind of answer is that? It doesn't sound like you're very excited about it. Are you sure you want to get married?" Shazia asked, sounding worried.

"Ali's excited about it," Yunus said, interrupting before Ali could reply. "He's just used to being single without any responsibilities, like most guys his age."

"You're probably right, Yunus, but if Ali isn't ready to get married yet, we can wait until he is," Shazia said. Ali's in-laws stared open-mouthed at their daughter's words. What she was suggesting was unspeakable, the wedding invitations had already gone to the printers, and the wedding reception already booked.

"I'm ready to get married. I guess I'm just a little nervous about it," Ali said. The sigh of relief from his in-laws was almost audible.

"Nearly everyone gets nervous about getting married. You should have seen what state I was in before my wedding,"

48

Shazia said laughing flirtatiously. "So what degree have you studied?" she asked, changing the subject as her younger sister slipped into the background joining her brother Omar.

"I studied Microbiology," Ali said.

"What result did you get?" she asked him curiously.

"It was second class honors," Ali replied. At the time, he'd been very disappointed at the result, knowing that he hadn't put sufficient effort into his work until the final year of the degree, by which time it was too late to improve his marks sufficiently to get a first.

"You're the first educated person to marry into this family," Rhazia said, speaking up suddenly. "Shazia's husband couldn't even speak English when he moved in with us."

"Shut up, Rhazia. You should have more respect for your elders," Shazia said crossly, giving her sister a glare, visibly provoked by her sister's comment. "You are such a nice person and seem very honest," she said turning back to Ali. "I think that my parents have made the right decision. You won't believe how many people have come to ask for Sajda's hand in marriage. You are definitely the right choice. I can see that you'll make her happy."

"Thank you," Ali said, not knowing what else to say. His stomach clenched with the guilt he felt at hearing his sister-in-law's words. What if she found out about the lifestyle he'd led? What would she think of him then? Would she still call him honest?

"I am so proud that you are joining our family," Shazia said. "You will be such an asset. We'll all look after you as long as you make sure you take good care of our sister and treat her well. If you hurt her, you'll have us to deal with." She laughed gently to try and hide the threat in her words.

"I'll look after her, and I promise I won't let you down," Ali said, meaning every word. Somehow Shazia had evoked the memory of what he most wanted – to feel he was part of a family and not an outsider. He wanted to be secure and protected, and that's what this family offered.

"I know you will, Ali. Anyway," she said, her voice turning less serious. "I've heard you've turned down the job from that imbecile Javed?"

"Shazia!" her mother gasped sounding shocked. "That is no way to talk about Javed in front of the men." Shazia smirked wickedly in response.

"Yes, I'm sorry about that," Ali said not feeling at all sorry. "It was really Yunus who explained to him that I couldn't take up his job offer."

"Good on you," Shazia said, rewarding Yunus with a smile. "That man is an idiot. I don't know why my parents feel that they have to be so nice to him because of something that his parents did for them over thirty years ago."

"Please don't talk so rudely in front of guests, Shazia," her mother admonished, trying to rein in her daughter's unruly tongue.

"Well, Mother, you know what I think of him. Anyway, is there someone else you would like to meet, Ali?" Shazia asked mischievously.

Ali couldn't help but smile at her teasing. "I don't know. Do you think there is someone else I should meet?" he replied.

"Well, I know someone who is dying to meet you. I'm sure you must be just as curious. Mum and Dad have agreed that you can see her for five minutes in the garden. I'll be keeping an eye on you both throughout, so make sure you behave yourself," she said half seriously.

"Okay," Ali said, suddenly feeling nervous again.

Yunus moved up closer to him on the sofa. "When you meet her try to behave like a fucking man," he whispered into Ali's ear. "If you say anything out of line, I'll make sure that you never walk again." The smile on his face gave everyone else the impression that he was offering Ali some good brotherly advice.

"Well, come on. We haven't got all day you know," Shazia said, opening the patio doors, which led into the garden. "If you wait outside, I'll fetch her."

Ali went into the garden and waited. He felt anxious not knowing what he was going to say to his fiancée. Should he tell her the truth about his sexuality and admit that he'd been forced to agree to the marriage? "What am I going to do?" he thought. All of a sudden, his mind felt like it was in a chaotic maelstrom of indecisiveness. This was his final opportunity to stop the wedding or at least to be honest, but he didn't know how to make use of it. The confusion was exacerbated by the fact that he now knew Sajda's family, and he didn't want to let them down.

The garden was as bleak and depressing as the thoughts racing through his mind. It was covered in large, concrete paving stones where you'd normally have expected a lawn to be. Even the fence was made from concrete slats slotted into concrete posts. A child's football lay punctured and disused in the corner next to a pile of rubble. Among the drabness, two salwars hung on the washing-line breaking up the grayness by flapping in the wind like large red and yellow kites that danced together elegantly, joyously untempered by their surroundings.

Ali tried to wait patiently for his fiancée. He watched the salwars tease each other as they tried to escape the wooden pegs holding them tightly to the line. When Sajda finally appeared, it felt almost intrusive as he tore his gaze away to look at her.

Standing next to her sister, she appeared a couple of inches taller. She looked just like she had in her photograph, except in person she appeared tall, awkward and gawky. Even her shoulders were stooped, giving the impression that she lacked confidence.

He felt just as awkward as she, not knowing what to say. He stood staring for a few long seconds before pulling himself together. "Hello," he finally managed to stutter nervously at her, as Shazia went into the house and stood watch behind the patio doors.

"Hello," she replied, smiling nervously at him.

Ali did not know what to say next, feeling a little tongue-tied. "It's good to finally meet you at last," he said. "I've seen your photograph of course, but you can't know someone from just looking at a two dimensional image."

"Oh, I think you can," she replied.

"I guess," said Ali not wanting to disagree with her. "So what made you agree to getting married to me?" he asked curiously.

"I liked your face. You have an honest face. I saw your photograph, and I immediately felt drawn to you. It was like I'd known you all my life. I had to say yes," she said. "You were born in England like me, so we have the same values. I just know that we will be compatible. So what made you agree?" she asked in return.

It would have been good to have been able to be honest and tell her that he'd been forced to agree, but those words were never going to be allowed to surface. "I thought it was about time that I settled down and married," Ali said. "I also liked your photograph, too," he added.

"So are you happy with all the arrangements?" she asked.

"Yes," Ali replied keeping his reply short. If only he could tell her the truth. The thought of admitting everything to her bubbled treacherously in his mind, but he kept it in check.

"That's good. I'm very happy, too. It's like all my dreams are finally being fulfilled. There is so much for us both to do together," she said longingly. She paused, noticing that Shazia was returning to the garden. "It's been really nice meeting you. Most Pakistani parents wouldn't allow their children to meet like this. We've been very lucky, don't you think?"

"I guess so," Ali said thinking the opposite. "Thanks for meeting me."

"It's time to say goodbye, Sajda," Shazia said, interrupting the uncomfortable conversation. "You've both had your five minutes."

"Goodbye," Sajda said wistfully. "Next time I see you, it will be in my wedding dress." She followed her sister back into the house looking back longingly at Ali, leaving Ali to trail slowly behind, deep in thought.

In those few minutes, Ali had realized that he had nothing in common with Sajda. Their short conversation had been very stilted. She had appeared young and naïve. He'd expected some connection with her at any level, but there had been nothing. No spark, no meeting of minds. Nothing! As he stepped back into the house, he became acutely aware of just how much of his happiness he was sacrificing to keep his mother happy.

Yunus was standing up waiting for him apprehensively as he entered the lounge. "Right, we have to go now," he said.

"Can't you both stay and eat?" his father-in-law asked, sounding surprised that they were leaving so abruptly.

"No, we have to get going. I've remembered that I have a meeting with a client later today," Yunus said regretfully.

"That's a shame. I was about to cook something for you both," Ali's mother-in-law said.

"Well they've both met each other now," Yunus said to her. "What did you think of her? Are you happy?" he asked looking Ali directly in the eyes as if to dare him to say something that he might regret.

Confronted by the question in front of everyone, Ali had no option with his response. "I liked her. Yes, I'm very happy," Ali replied stonily, showing no sign of his apparent happiness on his face.

Sajda's parents both beamed happily, delighting in the misconception that things between their future son-in-law and their daughter had gone so well.

As the time came for everyone to say goodbye, Ali's mother-in-law handed him the suit she'd brought him. "Next time I see you you'll be wearing this suit, and it will be your wedding day," she said, repeating words similar to Sajda's.

Chapter Five

Ali parked his car in front of Haseena's house. It was several days since he had last seen her, and a lot had happened since then. He'd been unable to face any of his friends. Instead, he'd shut himself away in an effort to make a clean break from the past. Today, however, he'd felt worse than ever about his situation and had decided to escape to her house to spend time with someone who actually understood him.

Ali had met Haseena at the clothing store where he'd worked on the weekends. At first, he thought she was like all the other women in the community, but he soon found out she was different, and gradually Haseena became Ali's closest friend and confidant. She was the first person Ali had told that he was gay, and she had given him her utmost support ever since.

Haseena lived on a small inner city council estate in Ladywood, a short walk from Birmingham city center. She'd bought her home from the Council several years ago and was now desperate to sell it, but unfortunately, it was in the worst part of Ladywood, which meant that there had been little interest from buyers since going on the market. The post with the For Sale sign on it was still buried in the front lawn, but it was now looking a bit tatty, having been there for over five months.

Ali got out of his car and walked through the shared alley to Haseena's back gate. He opened it and knocked on the back door before walking in.

"Hi Haseena, it's me," he said, cheerfully announcing himself. Haseena stood hard at work by the kitchen sink, surrounded by dirty dishes with her hands deep in foam. She looked up at Ali.

"So you've finally decided to show up. Have you been avoiding me?" she asked, sounding annoyed.

"Don't be like that, Haseena," Ali said, giving her a hug. "Have you missed me?"

Haseena wasn't what you'd expect from a Pakistani woman in her late thirties. She was very petite, measuring just short of four foot ten inches tall and very slim, too, as she did not suffer the tendency to carry excess weight around her midsection like most of the other Pakistani women in the community. Her face was always carefully powdered with a light foundation, and the subtle use of blusher to her cheeks gave her a healthy glow. Her lips were painted delicately with a dark red lipstick, and her eyebrows were neatly plucked, showing two fine lines above her mascara-enhanced eyes. She looked immaculate and perfect.

Her husband was a white Englishman named Derek. She'd run away with him to Birmingham from somewhere up north to escape her family over twenty years ago. Two years after settling in Birmingham, she'd married Derek in an Islamic ceremony.

Haseena tried to keep her distance from the community in Birmingham, desperate to avoid the constant, petty gossip and internal politics as best she could. Her unusual choice of husband meant that she was well known to the community, but instead of shunning her, some members of the community would occasionally make attempts to include her in their social events, which she then worked hard to find excuses to avoid.

She was very in tune with her cultural and religious heritage and even kept up to date with Pakistani current affairs by reading the Urdu printed *Jang* newspaper every week. She also knew everything there was to know about Islam, despite the fact that she was not very religious and probably had never been inside a mosque in the last twenty years.

Haseena laughed at Ali's attempt to soften her up with a hug, knowing that it was having the desired effect. She could never stay angry with him for long, even when she knew she should.

"You've neglected me," she said accusingly.

"I'm sorry. I've just been very busy," Ali said apologetically.

"Too busy to see me?" Haseena exclaimed. "So what have you been up to that's kept you so busy? Do you want to tell me, yourself, or maybe I can tell you?"

Ali's jaw dropped. "So you've heard then?" he asked.

"I've heard," Haseena replied, her smile drying up quickly. She wiped her wet hands on the apron she was wearing. "Why didn't you come and tell me, Ali? I heard about it at the halal meat shop on Ladypool Road of all places. I overheard that girl, Mafooz talking to the shopkeeper about it. I thought it was just some idle gossip, but when you didn't show up for days, I knew that it was true."

"I'm sorry, Haseena. I just didn't know how to deal with it. I needed some time to sort my head out," Ali said, knowing just how hurt Haseena must have felt hearing something so important about him from someone else.

"That girl, Mafooz. I don't think she likes me," Haseena said. This was probably true of most of the women of the community, who mistakenly marked Haseena as a loose woman for being married to a white non-Muslim man. Ali wondered how they would feel if they knew that Haseena liked to drink vodka and Coke, too. Luckily, they never frequented the types of places that Haseena went to, being far too respectable to even think of going to straight bars and clubs, let alone the gay ones.

"I don't know. She's probably jealous of you," Ali said, trying to reassure her.

"So why are you getting married?" Haseena asked, getting back to the point. "I thought you were clear about your sexuality. You're one of the few people that I know who's not confused," she said, sounding amazed by Ali's decision.

"My family asked me to," Ali said.

"Your family asked you to, and you said yes?" Haseena asked in bewilderment. "But you're definitely gay, aren't you?"

"I was, but I can't be anymore," Ali said. He'd resigned himself to this decision over the last couple of days.

"Stop being silly, Ali. You know that being gay is not a matter of choice. You're born that way. So what did they really say to make you agree to this wedding?" Haseena asked, knowing that there was more to Ali's sudden decision than what he'd revealed so far.

"I don't want to talk about it," Ali said, wanting to avoid reopening the fresh wounds he was trying to heal. Thinking about the way his family had treated him to get him to agree to the wedding still made him feel weak and nauseous.

57

"What happened? Did they force you to agree?" Haseena asked, pressuring Ali for more information. She wanted him to open up and tell her everything, but the brave front he was putting up made him appear remote and distant. He seemed a shadow of his former self, his eyes sore and red from crying, and the dark circles around his eyes indicated that he hadn't been sleeping.

Ali paused for a few seconds as if struggling for air. "Yes, they forced me to agree," he cried finally, his voice hoarse as he burst into tears. Relieved that she was finally seeing some real emotion from him, Haseena pulled Ali into her arms hugging him tightly, as he began to cry uncontrollably.

"It'll be alright," she said gently, stroking his hair.

"I don't know what to do," he blubbered through the tears, gasping for breath asthmatically, as his body shook. "I don't know what I'm going to do," he repeated over and over again, as Haseena cradled him.

As the minutes ticked by, his tears slowly subsided and eventually turned into self-pitying whimpers, allowing Haseena a chance to speak. "You can leave, Ali. I can help you. I can find you somewhere to live. You can run away. You don't have to go through with it."

"I have to," Ali said. "It will kill my mother if I run away."

"It won't kill her. Your mother's been through worse things," Haseena said. "Is that what they've told you? That you'll kill her?"

"Yes, but it's true," Ali admitted miserably. "She's getting old and fragile. I have to try and make her happy."

"They're just trying to emotionally blackmail you. You don't have to do anything. Leave, Ali. Move out," Haseena said, clearly worried for her young friend. She was unsure whether her words would make a difference, but she still had to try to make him see that there was a way out.

"I can't. I have to go ahead with it. If I don't, I'll hurt too many people," Ali said unhappily. "I can't let everyone down."

"Ali, I've been though this myself. I know it's hard to make a break and leave, but you have to. Your family will survive this, but will you? You'll hurt far fewer people if you leave now," Haseena said, trying to persuade him to change his mind.

"I can't leave, Haseena, so let's not talk about it! I just can't do it," Ali said, becoming tearful again.

"Okay, I won't if you don't want me to," Haseena said. "So what does your fiancée think about the marriage? Does she know that you're gay?"

"She doesn't have a clue. None of her family does. I wanted to tell her when I met her, but I couldn't. I don't want to hurt her," Ali said, remembering his meeting with Sajda.

"That sounds all well and good, but how hurt do you think your fiancée will feel when she finds out that you're gay?" Haseena asked.

"She won't find out. I'm cutting all ties with the past and moving on," Ali said.

"It's not that easy. You'll always be looking over your shoulder, always wondering if your past is going to catch up with you. Can you live like that?" Haseena asked.

"I have to try, Haseena," Ali said.

"You won't cope with being married, Ali. You're not the type who could lead a double life. I'm really worried about you. What happens if you can't deal with it? What will you do then? You look terrible now. What will you be like when you're married? You have to leave," Haseena urged desperately.

"I'll cope. I'm not expecting happiness, just stability," Ali said.

"I don't think you will cope. This is a stupid idea," Haseena said. "What if you end up doing something stupid?"

"You don't have to worry. I'm not going to kill myself, not that it will bother anyone in my family anyway. They'll just say I had a mental breakdown, so that it won't bring shame on them," Ali said melancholically.

"Oh, Ali," Haseena said, hugging him again. He seemed so fragile and vulnerable. How was he ever going to cope? "Come to the living room. Let's sit down and talk. My feet are killing me," she said, taking off her apron and hanging it on a hook behind the door.

Ali followed her to the lounge. The mess in the room brought a smile to his face. It was what Haseena referred to as organized chaos. There were some old jazz records that Derek collected, piled high in one corner of the room, while her washing sat on the sofa waiting to be ironed, and a collection of old newspapers lay on the floor in another corner. Ali found some space next to the washing and sat down, while Haseena settled herself on the sofa opposite him.

"I'm sorry. I was just being melodramatic," Ali said trying to convince Haseena. "I'll be fine. Don't worry."

"I hope so, Ali. I really hope so. Right now, you have a choice, even if you don't believe it. It's your life," Haseena said. "Getting married is still your decision, but there will be consequences if you make the wrong choice."

"I know it's my choice, but I've made my decision. I have to stay and see it through. I don't want to hurt my mother," Ali said, picturing his mother's distraught face if he left.

"It's only a week away. Have you thought about what you will do on the wedding night?" Haseena asked, knowing that Ali had never slept with a woman before.

"I'm not sleeping with her straight away," Ali said. "I'll get to know her first, eventually we'll fall in love, and then sex will follow naturally."

"You want to get to know her first? Well that's a start, but I think you're being really naïve to think it's going to work out how you're imagining it," Haseena said. "It's not just your wedding night. It's hers too."

"I know, but I know she'll want the same," Ali said confidently. "Anyway, I've broken up with Steve. I know what this decision means. I'm committed to it, and I'll make sure it works."

"Oh, Ali," Haseena murmured in sympathy. "I was going to ask you about Steve. That's one hell of a sacrifice to make. Giving up someone you love to marry someone you hardly know. I just hope it's worth it."

"It will be. I know you say that I have a choice, but I can't be philosophical about this. I don't have a choice. It's something that I have to do for my family. My happiness doesn't fit into the equation, and I have to make these sacrifices," Ali said despairingly.

"I understand, Ali," Haseena said. She wanted to do her best to support Ali, but she also wanted him to see what he was getting himself into. It seemed he was ignoring the reality of the situation. However, she didn't want to say too much in case she pushed him away, and the last thing he needed now was to feel alienated and unable to speak to her.

"My happiness does not matter anymore. It's about my family's happiness," Ali continued, repeating what he'd said earlier.

"I'm so sorry that you have to go through this. I'm here for you no matter what happens," Haseena promised, trying her best to assure Ali of her continuing support. He needed to know she was there for him. He seemed so weak.

"Thank you, Haseena, I'm lucky to have you as a friend," Ali said, feeling overwhelmed by his friend's words.

"I have to go," he said suddenly noticing the time on the mantelpiece clock. "I was only popping in quickly on the way to pick Ammi up from Soho Road."

"Well, a quick visit is better than no visit at all," Haseena said sadly, knowing that Ali was making an excuse to leave as a way of escaping the bleak atmosphere the conversation had created. He'd probably had days of this already. "You'd better be off as you don't want your mother to be left waiting too long. Not when she's loaded down with all the wedding goodies that she's probably bought."

"Yeah, I know," Ali said grimacing.

"We'll need to arrange a good night out before your big day," Haseena said. "A final goodbye to your favorite club, the Nightingale. What do you say?"

"I'm not too sure. I don't have many days left, Haseena," Ali said, not wanting to let Haseena down, but worrying that it wasn't probably appropriate to go to a gay club before his wedding.

"Don't worry. I'll sort something out," Haseena said with a wicked smile on her face.

Chapter Six

"She's coming! She's booked herself a plane ticket, and she's on a flight to England!" Ali's mother cried, rushing down the stairs at top speed.

"Who's coming?" Yasmin asked, startled by her mother's disheveled appearance.

"My mother, your naree," she cried unhappily. "Her flight arrives in just under three hours. What am I going to do?" she cried pulling at her own hair. "Your Auntie Fazal just called from the airport to say that she's waiting for the flight to arrive. Why did the kuthie not tell me that mother was coming?" Ali's mother asked, cursing her sister in mir-pouri.

"Yasmin, call Yunus at work, and tell him that he must drive us to the airport at once. You must get dressed and come with us, too," she said to Ali who was sitting on the floor in front of the television watching a cartoon in his nightclothes. He'd not really done anything at all for the last couple of days. It was as if he'd fallen into a perpetual state of depression. "You'd better shave as well," she added, without bothering to notice his forlorn and depressed state.

Ali got up without complaining. He'd been spending most of his time sleeping, watching television and keeping out of everyone else's way. It was about time he did something even if it was with the family.

"Start tidying the house up, Aneesa, I want to see it presentable by the time we get back," Ali heard his mother instruct his younger sister. He heard Aneesa moan in objection, but he knew that his mother would make sure that Aneesa had the cleaning underway by the time she left.

Half an hour later, the whole family was gathered in the lounge, waiting to leave. "Have you put all the jewelry in the loft, Yasmin?" she asked her daughter.

"Yes, I've put everything away. She won't be able to get to it this time," Yasmin said. Ali's grandmother was a bit of kleptomaniac when it came to gold jewelry. The last time she'd visited, some of the jewelry had gone missing, and Ali's mother had seen the same jewelry worn by relatives when she'd visited Pakistan. When confronted, his grandmother had denied all knowledge. Ali was quite proud of his grandmother, seeing her as a Pakistani Robin Hood who endeavored to distribute the wealth between family members.

Ali quietly joined Yasmin in the back seat of the car while his mother sat in the front with Yunus.

"How dare she not tell me that she's coming to England! Why does she tell Fazal everything that she is doing and not me? I'm her eldest daughter. I'm the one who sends her money every month. It's my house that she's living in, and it's my land in Pakistan that feeds her," Ali's mother grumbled on the drive to Heathrow airport.

The journey took over three hours with all the congestion on the motorway. When they reached the arrivals terminal at the airport, the information boards showed that the PIA flight from Islamabad had been delayed by several hours.

The arrivals area was heaving with families waiting for the flight. Ali spotted Auntie Fazal sitting on a chair in one of the waiting areas. He contemplated whether to mention the sighting to his mother. He'd not seen his Auntie for several months, as his mother had fallen out with her again. Ali didn't know what the latest argument was about, but it was bound to be something trivial.

Auntie Fazal was the opposite of his mother. She always wore brightly colored clothes that revealed an inappropriate amount of cleavage, and she never left home without at least ten gold bangles on each arm, thick gold earrings and several gold chains round her neck. Ali's mother always said that she was a mugging waiting to happen.

"There she is, the scheming little kuthie," his mother cried upon spotting her sister, before marching over to her angrily.

"How dare you tell me only three hours before the flight arrives that mother's coming to England!" she berated her sister.

Auntie Fazal got up to face her sister. Although she was ten years younger, she'd learned how to stand up to her. "Calm down, Zainub, she only telephoned me two days ago to tell me she was coming. I've not had the chance to tell you until this morning, when I remembered. I've been busy."

"You had plenty of time to mention it to me. I don't think you wanted me here to greet her. If the plane hadn't been delayed, I wouldn't have managed to get here on time. You've been so cunning," Ali's mother said crossly. "What other secrets are you keeping?"

"We all have our secrets, and it turns out that you haven't mentioned your son's engagement or the wedding to mother," Auntie Fazal said, smiling triumphantly at her sister.

"Hmmph," Ali's mother said glancing crossly at Fazal before stomping away loudly. She found a chair and sat down glowering angrily at Auntie Fazal from across the waiting area, while Yunus, Yasmin and Ali joined her on the neighboring seats.

Ali noticed his two cousins, Majid and Sajid, sit down next to Auntie Fazal. They were twins and behaved very strangely, rarely speaking to anyone in Ali's family, but this was probably due to the confusing and volatile relationship between their mother and Ali's.

At times they were allowed to talk to Ali's family, but at other times, they were banned by their mother from doing so, usually following an argument of some sort. They'd once made the mistake of visiting Ali's home when they were not supposed to and incurred their mother's wrath and were not allowed out of the house for several weeks. In the end, Majid and Sajid had decided to err on the side of caution and keep away from the Mirza family altogether. They found Ali's family to be quite intimidating anyway. They, therefore, ignored the Mirza's on this occasion and sat looking bored, waiting for the flight to arrive.

"Ali, you're not to discuss the wedding with your grandmother. If she asks you anything or tries to talk to you about it, you are to tell her to speak to me," Ali's mother instructed.

"Okay, Ammi, I will," Ali said, wondering what was going on. It was unlike grandmother to come to England without notifying his mother first. Maybe she had wanted to surprise them.

The two sisters glanced discretely at each other several times during the wait. They were both very strong willed individuals and that led them to behave antagonistically towards each other. It also didn't help that Ali's mother had been disappointed with her sister's choice of husband, who unfortunately was from a family of sheepherders rather than landowners, as Auntie Fazal had married for love.

The airport arrival lounge was crowded with young Pakistani children racing around, causing mischief and eventually irritating Ali with their loud noise and behavior. He could hear several people complaining about the delay and how it might clash with the timing of their prayers.

The arrival of the PIA flight was suddenly announced over the speaker system, first in English and then in Urdu, following which the screens changed to show that the flight had landed. There was an immediate flurry of activity as people got up and chattered excitedly to each other in anticipation. The Mirza family joined the rest of the families thronging towards the arrivals gate and stood patiently waiting for their grandmother to appear.

Ali was quite apprehensive at the thought of seeing his grandmother again. He hadn't seen her since the age of six. At the time, he'd always doted on her and had very fond memories of her last visit. She used to take him everywhere with her. He winced inwardly as he remembered his favorite trick at that time, which was to steal her false teeth and wear them over his own.

Ali's mother had been fourteen years old when her father had taken another wife without divorcing Ali's grandmother. As was the Muslim custom, men could take up to four wives, but this was rarely done within the Pakistani community. If they did so, they were required to seek permission from the first wife and then to treat both wives equally.

Ali's grandfather had not sought his grandmother's consent to his second marriage and had certainly not treated them both equally. Ali's grandmother had been left to raise her two daughters on her own, and the son she'd been carrying when her husband left her, died within a year of his birth. Ali's grandfather had completely cut ties with his first family, only seeing his two daughters for the first time shortly before he died.

The door to the arrivals section suddenly burst open, and crowds of people started pouring in from the flight from

Islamabad. With them, came the exotic smells and sounds of Pakistan. The aroma of cumin, coriander and other exotic spices mingled with the smell of the sweat of the passengers from their eleven-hour flight and wafted fragrantly around the arrivals lounge.

Trolleys laden dangerously with bulky suitcases and various boxes were pushed precariously through the doors by brightly clad Pakistanis. The awaiting crowd chattered excitedly in different Pakistani dialects each time someone new appeared through the arrivals door. It was this chaotic jumble that greeted the new arrivals, a scene that was not too dissimilar from that which they had left behind in Islamabad.

People shouted excitedly to attract the attention of loved ones. Others grabbed strangers, mistaking them for relatives. People cried joyously as they were reunited with their families, hugging and kissing before melting away.

Ali waited patiently as the crowd slowly dwindled. Auntie Fazal and his mother had drifted towards each other and were now standing together. The two sisters looked very alike except that Ali's mother appeared somewhat older. They both appeared tense at the thought of their mother's arrival.

Ali recognized his grandmother immediately as she came through the arrival gate and yelled out to her excitedly. She hadn't changed a bit. She was a short Pakistani woman, barely five foot tall and very thin. She looked elderly but not frail. She was a little stooped in the way that old people sometimes are. As records of births were not kept in her village at the time of her birth, her age was a mystery, so Ali guessed she must be in her late eighties by now.

She was wearing a thick black winter coat. Ali remembered that she had always found the English summers cold on her previous visits, and this would be her first autumn in England. She wore a bright orange scarf wrapped around her wrinkled neck, which almost touched the floor due to its length. It was a complete mismatch to the coat she wore, which at her age did not matter.

She smiled when she saw Ali and rushed towards him pushing her trolley, which held only one small suitcase. She moved quite quickly through the diminishing crowd for someone her age, shoving people out of her way.

Ali's mother intercepted her before she could reach Ali, giving her a kiss and hugging her tightly. Ali's grandmother didn't return the kiss and bore her daughter's affection coldly. Auntie Fazal pushed Ali's mother aside and kissed her mother several times. She began to wail loudly with tears streaming from her eyes. Some of the travelers turned to watch, smiling in amusement at the display.

Ali's mother looked embarrassed by Auntie Fazal's overenthusiastic display of affection and gave her a nudge to prompt her to stop. As if a switch had been pressed, Auntie Fazal stopped crying and was immediately composed. She wiped away her tears and pulled a small mirror from her handbag and checked her face to make sure that she hadn't ruined her makeup.

"Ali, my beautiful grandson," his grandmother cried, smothering him in kisses as if he was still six. Ali hugged her, taking in her scent. She smelled of cinnamon and mothballs bringing back memories of his childhood. "You belong to me," she said looking at Ali intensely, laying her claim. She barely came up to Ali's chest and seemed to have shrunk over the years. Her body felt brittle and fragile in Ali's arms.

"Yunus," she said hugging him next. "You've grown so big and round. They feed you well in England. I never got to see you when your mother brought you to Pakistan and married you off without telling me. You're divorced already I understand. Your mother should have listened to me." She gave her daughter a meaningful look while Yunus kissed her without responding to her comments.

She gave a quick kiss to Yasmin. "I have a husband in mind for you," she muttered under her breath.

She then turned to Majid and Sajid who were hiding behind their mother and gave them both a kiss on their cheeks. They openly wiped away the spittle that she left behind and gave her a disgusted look, which she thankfully did not notice.

"Where is your husband, Fazal? Why has he not come to greet me?" she asked her daughter. "Is he too frightened of an old woman like me?"

"He's at work," Auntie Fazal said, excusing her husband. "He's a very busy man. If he takes a day off, he loses his bonus. I have our new four wheel drive Suzuki outside waiting to take you to my house."

"I'll be going to your sister's," Ali's grandmother said, dismissing her youngest daughter's offer. "Zainub has managed to turn up to see me arrive, so it's only fair that I go with her. Besides, I have a lot to discuss with your sister."

"I thought you said that you were going to stay with me," argued Auntie Fazal, almost whining.

"Yunus, will you please take my suitcase to the car," Ali's grandmother said, ignoring her.

As soon as Ali's family got into the car and his grandmother had said her goodbyes to Auntie Fazal, her demeanor changed. "You have a lot to answer for," she said angrily to Ali's mother. "How dare you arrange my youngest grandson's marriage without consulting me! What possessed you to arrange his wedding with a girl from that jungalee family?"

"Mother, it was the best match for him. Sajda is educated and she's nearly the same age as him. They were both born in England, too," Ali's mother said.

"What do you mean? I've already given him to someone. I found the best match for him when he was born. I told you then that he belonged to me," Ali's grandmother said, her fists clenched, shaking with rage.

"Who did you have in mind, Mother?" Ali's mother asked crossly.

"You know who it is. He will be marrying my sister's daughter Miriam. I'll not have my grandson marrying a girl whose grandmother begged on the streets," Ali's grandmother said heatedly.

Ali was stunned by his grandmother's words. She actually wanted him to marry her own niece. He wondered whether it was legal in England to marry someone that closely related.

"Mother, you arranged that when he was a baby, and she was five. They were babies! What do you think he is going to have in common with a village girl from Pakistan? I married Yunus to someone from there and look what happened. I'm not making the same mistake twice," Ali's mother said.

"You are wrong. How can you expect your son to know his roots if you marry him to someone from England? You must cancel the wedding immediately. I won't have this family's

69

reputation ruined by your choice of bride," Ali's grandmother said.

"I can't, Mother, and I won't. He's my son, and I'm choosing what's best for him. I'll make the decisions for my family, not you," Ali's mother retorted angrily.

"You went behind my back without consulting me. I demand that you cancel the wedding," Ali's grandmother hissed back.

"I did not go behind your back, Mother. I don't have to consult you on everything that happens. You're thousands of miles away," Ali's mother replied.

Yasmin, Yunus and Ali all listened to the argument in silence. Yunus continued driving, his eyes fixated on the road ahead, while Yasmin fiddled nervously with her hijab. Ali was surprised that neither of them had said anything, as normally they would have been the first to jump to the defense of their mother.

"My grandson's marriage is very important to me. You must marry him to someone in Pakistan. If you don't, all your land will disappear bit by bit. Every year, the other landowners take a stretch of land, and I have to fight to get it back. Who is going to do that when you have no more ties with people in Pakistan and you become too English to go back?" her mother asked angrily.

"I don't know, Mother, I really don't know," Ali's mother said worriedly, conceding that her mother might be right. "Yunus still needs a wife, and I'll start looking for a husband for Yasmin once this marriage is out of the way. There's still plenty of opportunity to solve that problem."

Ali's mother tried to contain her anger. She wanted to put Ali on the straight and narrow before it was too late. If she arranged his marriage to someone from Pakistan, there was more danger of the marriage not working out. If only her mother knew of her son's lifestyle. She shuddered at the thought. It was best not to mention such things to her as she would never understand.

They arrived at the house in deathly silence with no one talking. Ali's grandmother held onto Ali's hand throughout the journey like she used to when he was little. He wanted to pull his hand away from her as he found it just as claustrophobic as his mother's touch. He'd never seen this side to his grandmother before, and it upset him. She had been the one person whom he'd thought he could trust.

"Ali," she whispered as the car stopped outside the house. "I'm your grandmother. You can't marry this girl. Miriam is waiting to marry you back in Pakistan. Meet her. See how you feel. If you don't like her, I'll find you someone else even more beautiful."

Ali groaned to himself. His grandmother was so much like his mother it was unbelievable. He pretended not to hear her and jumped out of the car. His grandmother followed behind, leaving everyone else to scramble after them.

"This country has a horrible smell," Ali's grandmother said sniffing the air. "How can you live with it?" She wrapped her orange scarf tightly around her face to cover her nostrils and mouth, and mumbled through the fabric to order Yunus to bring her suitcase into the house.

Ali grinned at Yunus's scowl. His grandmother always complained about the smell of the English air. She probably smelled the pollution in it. From his trip to Pakistan, he could still remember the stench of the open sewage system in some parts of Islamabad and couldn't see how his grandmother could find the English air to be objectionable in comparison.

While they'd been away, Aneesa had been hard at work cleaning and cooking, and there was a delicious aroma inside the house. Ali's grandmother greeted Aneesa affectionately with a big kiss, after which Aneesa ushered everyone into the dining room, which formed part of the extension to the house.

The room had previously been used as Yunus's private lounge away from the rest of the family when he'd been married. It had its own staircase leading to the large bedroom above so that Yunus and his wife could enjoy some privacy.

"I hope you put extra chili in the food to make it extra spicy," Ali said to Aneesa as she walked past him on her way to set the food out. "If you've made it too perfect grandmother will have you married within days."

"Shut up, Ali," she retorted giving him a cross look.

She hurriedly finished laying out the many dishes that she'd prepared. Ali suspected that she might have had some help from the local takeaway, especially when he saw the perfectly shaped samosas. Aneesa had somehow managed to cook several dishes including chicken saag curry and lamb pilau rice. She'd even made some spicy rice pudding for desert that she'd flavored with cardamom. It was a wonder how she had managed to do it all on her own.

Ali's grandmother said a short prayer in Arabic before scooping up a piece of chicken and chewing it hungrily, making loud cracking sounds with her dentures. She choked suddenly after the first mouthful spitting the food out onto the floor. "It tastes like plastic. Do they not have real food in this country?" she asked. "I shall eat the roti on its own."

She chewed a couple of bites from the chapatti before smiling. "Your roti is very good, Aneesa. Your mother has taught you very well. It's not your fault about the chicken. You made a lovely sauce, but the meat here in England does not taste very good."

"Thank you, Grandma," Aneesa said, glowing with the compliment. She kissed her grandmother and raced off to the kitchen happily, pleased with herself.

"You and I need to talk," Ali's grandmother said to Ali's mother after she'd finished eating.

"Will you all leave the room," Ali's mother said to everyone, putting her plate of food to one side as if readying herself for battle.

"I want them to stay. They should listen to what I have to say as it affects them, too," Ali's grandmother said. "They need to know what they are giving up if you go ahead with this foolish marriage."

"If your grandmother wants you to stay, then you must stay," Ali's mother said. "Who am I to argue?"

"I want you to cancel the wedding. If you don't, I will leave you nothing when I die. All the things I have will go to your sister. My house. The land in the village. My two houses in the city. It will all go to her," Ali's grandmother threatened menacingly.

Ali's mother laughed scornfully. "I have my own property in Pakistan, Mother. You forget my husband had his own land that he left to me. I have houses in the city, and you should see what I have in Karachi. I don't need the barren lands you're offering me. You can threaten all you want. You can give them away to a beggar on the street for all I care!"

"I've made my decision, and I will stand by it. You need to respect that. Just because my husband has died, doesn't mean that you're in control of this family. I say what happens here," Ali's mother continued defiantly.

"If that is the case, then I will disown you. I will not go to this farce of a wedding. I'll stand outside and throw horse muck at the guests as they arrive," Ali's grandmother said dramatically.

"Mother, you will come to my son's wedding now that you are here, or I shall book you on the next flight back to Pakistan. I'll also make sure that no one from this family visits you again. You'll die a lonely and bitter old woman with no one to look after you. It's your choice, Mother, you decide," Ali's mother said, trying to force his grandmother into a corner.

"I have your sister's children to look after me. I don't need you. I wipe my hands clean of you," her mother said, spitting onto her hands and then wiping them on her own cardigan.

"My sister's children don't even talk to you. She's only taught them how to speak English. They don't know a single word in their own language. How do you think they are going to cope in Pakistan? She'll never take them to Pakistan. They are too precious. Has she ever visited you in Pakistan or sent you any money?" Ali's mother asked, knowing the answers to her questions.

"You're just jealous of her," Ali's grandmother gasped knowing deep down that what she was saying was true.

"You can believe what you want, Mother. You have a choice to make. Either you come to my son's wedding or you can get the next flight back to Pakistan," Ali's mother threatened.

"How could you behave like this towards your own mother? I'm old and weak, and all you do is treat me with cruelty. I'm not blind and deaf. I still have a voice, but you just want to silence me. I've struggled for most of my life to get you to England, so that you could have a better life. Is this how you repay me?" Ali's grandmother asked.

"I know what you've done for me, Mother, and I'm grateful. You wanted to do the best for me, but now it's my turn to do the best for my son. Please let me," Ali's mother said, tears slowly rolling down her face.

"It's your decision, Daughter, but don't expect me to be happy. I'll come to this wedding but only because he's my grandson and not because I am happy with your choice," Ali's grandmother said sniffing noisily, sounding a little mollified. "You've ruined Miriam's dreams. She's been waiting a long time for Ali. You must give me Yunus for her instead!"

"We can discuss that another time, Mother. Let's focus on Ali's wedding for now," Ali's mother sighed loudly and hugged her mother tearfully. She had been worried that she would have to carry out her threat and send her mother back to Pakistan, and if she had done that, what on earth would the community have said?

Chapter Seven

It was Sajda's mehndi night, and the Mirza house was empty and quiet. Ali's family had gone to Nottingham en masse to attend the celebrations. Yasmin had even managed to persuade Ali's grandmother to attend, despite her vociferous protests.

Ali had spent the whole day savoring the peace and tranquility of the house. It was the first time since moving back home from the university hall that he had the house to himself, and he definitely appreciated the respite from the usual chaos and noise.

He had tried his best not to think about his impending wedding, so as not to ruin the day with his dark thoughts and had spent most of the day finding escapism in reading. As he lay on the sofa, book in hand, the peace and quiet was suddenly shattered by the noise of a car horn sounding loudly outside the house. Ali got up and went to the window to see who it was. He groaned loudly to himself upon spotting a dressed up and excitable Haseena, waving frantically from the open window of a taxi. She spotted him and gestured to him to come outside.

Feeling annoyed, Ali grudgingly put on his trainers and went out to the taxi without bothering to change from the lounging shorts and the scruffy t-shirt that he was wearing. All he'd wanted from the day was a little time to himself, to enjoy the oasis of calm that had presented itself before the wedding day.

"Ali!" Haseena shouted loudly from the taxi window. "It's your last night as a free man, so get ready and let's go and have some fun!"

"Haseena, I'm too tired to go out tonight. It's my mehndi tomorrow and my wedding the day after. This is the only day I've got to myself. All I want to do is relax on my own tonight," Ali said, sounding irritated and ungrateful.

"Ali, Ali," Haseena drawled. "Your family has gone away for the night, so it's the only chance you'll get to forget about the wedding for a few hours and enjoy yourself. Let's do something fun. Go and get changed. You have five minutes," Haseena ordered looking at her watch.

"I don't want to go, Haseena. Why don't you come inside, and we'll order a pizza and watch a DVD together. I won't have fun if we go out," said Ali, trying to compromise. He knew he was letting Haseena down, but if she'd warned him about this beforehand, then he might have felt differently.

"Put your clubbing gear on and get in the taxi," Haseena commanded. "I'm going to make sure that you have a great time. We're going to the Nightingale."

"I really don't want to go. I can't be bothered getting dressed and making an effort," Ali said.

"I'm going to wait out here for five minutes, Ali. If you're not dressed by then, I'm going to come out of the taxi and bang on your door," Haseena threatened. "Do you really want your neighbors to be disturbed?"

"Okay, I'll go and get ready," Ali said sounding even more fed up than before. He walked back into the house without a further word. The last thing he wanted was the neighbors getting involved and informing his mother the next day. He got dressed in a rush, not bothering to shave, and joined Haseena in the taxi, having changed into a white shirt and his favorite pair of blue denim jeans that had a leather stripe running down the side.

"You look good, but you could have made a bit more of an effort and shaved," Haseena said, taking in her friend's outfit and his two-day-old beard.

"I told you that I wasn't going to make an effort," Ali retorted.

"Can you take us to Essex Street. It's off Hurst Street," Haseena said, turning to the taxi driver who started the engine and began to drive off.

"You look good, too," Ali said, admiring Haseena. She was wearing a black tube top that revealed her flat stomach, displaying a sparkling, silver jeweled piercing in her belly button. She wore a tight black leather mini skirt that came to just above her knees and black high heeled leather ankle boots. Keeping true to her roots, she had stuck a silver bindi to the center of her forehead that sparkled brightly complementing the glitter that she'd applied round her eyes.

"Thank you, darling, I do try my best. I'll be forty next year, so I've got to start making that extra bit of effort to grow old disgracefully." Haseena cackled loudly reveling in the compliment.

The taxi eventually reached Hurst Street, at the heart of Birmingham's gay village. It was nine-thirty on a Friday evening, and the street was already buzzing. Flamboyantly dressed groups of people walked along the pavement moving from bar to bar searching for a place with the latest music to dance to and the cutest men to play with.

The taxi driver stopped on Essex Street about a hundred yards from the nightclub. The street was very badly lit, but Ali could see that there was already a queue built up outside the club.

"That'll be six pounds fifty," the driver said, turning to Haseena.

"I'll get that," Ali said, taking out a ten-pound note from his wallet.

"Shut up, Ali, I'm paying," Haseena said, pushing his hand away.

"Okay, as long as you let me pay to get us into the club," Ali said. They both got out of the taxi and queued up outside with the rest of the clubbers to pay their ten pound entry fee. Before long, they were inside.

The nightclub was like an immense labyrinth, sprawling under several disused or partially occupied office blocks. If you took a wrong turn by mistake, it was easy to get lost inside. When you walked through the club doors, there was a small bar to the left. A corridor then took you to a large bar and the main dance floor, which had bright disco lights beaming down from the ceiling like the stage from *Top of the Pops*. There were also some UV light panels running along the back walls. Men in tight white T-shirts danced in front them giving out an eerie glow from their outfits.

A further set of double doors by the bar took you through to another dance floor. This was mainly used by the lesbians and had a pool table situated in one corner for them to use. Ali had rarely seen a gay man play pool in there. The club also had its own diner that served food until two in the morning. It was a great place to go, but it was rumored that it was moving to another location a few streets away.

The nightclub hosted different themed nights, and tonight, they had posters up for a Bollywood themed night.

"They have your favorite DJ on tonight," Haseena said taking her jacket off and handing it to a large female cloakroom attendant.

"Who? Not DJ Pixie?" Ali asked excitedly, passing his own jacket to the cloakroom attendant who put it with Haseena's and generously charged for the one.

"That's the one. I think she's doing the Bollywood music," Haseena said.

"That's fantastic," Ali exclaimed, his earlier misgivings evaporating. He loved the music at the Nightingale, however, this particular DJ was the best and played some of the funkiest tunes around. A relaxing blend of urban and Indian vibes mixed cleverly to create a beautiful ambience. Ali didn't know the DJ's name and wasn't brave enough to ask her, so had instead nicknamed her "DJ Pixie."

Ali imagined her to be a lost pixie princess who'd forgotten her origins. The DJ was petite like Haseena, with small delicate pixie-like features, a small stubby nose and elfin ears. She had an air of silent mischief about her and seemed to be a bursting cauldron of creativity, hand-making rings for some of the club regulars, mixing records, and creating her own music that she sold through the nightclub. She even managed to find time to paint and display her artwork in local exhibitions. Ali had always been in awe of her.

He followed Haseena through to the main dance floor. "See, she's here," Haseena said, pointing out the DJ to him. "You should say hi to her. If she blanks you then you won't have to worry about the embarrassment. It's not like you'll be coming back after the wedding."

"I don't want to. I want her to remain mysterious and enigmatic in my memories forever," Ali replied laughing.

"Don't say anything then," Haseena said. "It's your loss, wimp!"

"I won't," Ali assured her.

"What do you want to drink?" Haseena asked, as she squeezed herself between two beautiful women to get to the bar. She held Ali's hand and pulled him after her.

"I'll have a lemonade with ice and a slice of lemon. Make sure they don't forget the slice of lemon," Ali said. He liked to eat the lemon at the end of his drink.

"Have a Malibu and Coke instead. You know you love it," Haseena said trying to tempt Ali with his favorite tipple.

"I can't drink tonight. You know what it does to me," Ali said. "I can't afford to have a massive hangover tomorrow." He loved the taste of Malibu, but he tended to react to alcohol very quickly. Half a glass of Malibu and Coke could get him drunk within minutes, with the resulting hangover lasting for days.

"Sorry, you're right. You shouldn't drink. You don't need alcohol to have fun anyway." She gave Ali a hug before turning her attention to the bar. She gave the blonde woman serving behind the bar a flirty look to attract her attention and managed to get served in record time. "It's amazing what my beautiful smile can do for me," she said laughing as she handed Ali his drink.

The dance floor had been given a radical Bollywood makeover. Incense sticks were burning in urns dotted around the room, creating a dense smoky atmosphere with a scent that reminded Ali of the local mosque. Ali shook his head at the sacrilegious comparison. The walls of the dance floor had beautiful embroidered saris in bright colors hanging on them, upon which large hypnotic shadows created by the dancers moved rhythmically.

"It's like a Pakistani whore's boudoir. I love it!" Haseena exclaimed. "Let's pretend we're on a Bollywood movie set. I'll be Aishwarya Rai and you can be Shahrukh Khan," Haseena shouted over the loud Bollywood soundtrack that was being played.

"This is my favorite," Haseena said, sounding delighted as she recognized the starting beats of a song. "It's called *Aap Jaisa Koi* from the film *Qurbani*. It's from well before your time."

"I've heard it before," Ali said. He recognized the song from when his mother used to listen to the Indian music channels on the radio while his father was out. Ali joined Haseena on the dance floor with his drink in his hand, mouthing the words to the song as it played.

It seemed that Haseena and Ali were the only Asian people dancing, which was quite normal, as it was rare to see many other Asians out and about on the gay scene in Birmingham. Ali had heard that there was a club called Kali for gay Asians in London, and it was rumored to fill to capacity every time. It surprised Ali that there were enough gay Asians to fill a whole nightclub when he'd only seen a handful since he'd started clubbing in Birmingham.

Ali danced next to Haseena but before long noticed her moving away deeper into the dance crowd. He couldn't be bothered to follow her, knowing that she would turn up at some point. Slowly, he let himself get lost in the music.

The songs that were being played evoked memories of all the Bollywood movies that he'd watched with his mother as a young boy. It gave him a sense of what he might have given up if he hadn't agreed to the wedding. The music helped him to recognize what the marriage offered – love, children, respect, and strong cultural values. Getting married somehow seemed to be the right thing to do.

Ali sighed to himself. He knew it was unlikely he would ever go to a club like this again after the wedding. When he'd been single, he used to go clubbing with Haseena every Friday and Saturday, and at least once during the week, usually on a student night.

He'd managed to make a few friends on the scene, but the gay scene was ever changing and very fickle, so the friendships never lasted for very long. This was the second time he'd been clubbing in over a year, and he couldn't see any familiar faces. The only constant in the sea of changing faces was DJ Pixie.

"Hey misery guts, what are you thinking about?" Haseena asked, shouting loudly into Ali's eardrum and disturbing him from his thoughts.

"Nothing," Ali said, trying not to jump. "I was just caught up in the music and contemplating life."

"Well, stop it! I've found someone for you to talk to. This is Imran," Haseena said, introducing Ali to what could only be described as a Pakistani man dressed as a woman. "Imran, this is Ali, the friend I've been telling you about."

"Hi, Ali, it's really nice to meet you," Imran said, kissing Ali on both of his cheeks.

Ali tried to hide his amusement. Imran was wearing a beautiful cinnamon red sari, with matching sandals and bangles. A bindi was stuck at the center of his forehead, just like Haseena's, and his face was matted in foundation in an attempt to hide the dark shadow that lay beneath. However, he hadn't bothered to do anything with his hair which was cropped short.

"Let's get some chips and chat in the other room," Haseena suggested.

"That's a good idea," Imran said, in his androgynous voice. He followed Ali and Haseena to the café within the nightclub. It was decorated to look like a fifties American diner with bright neon lights and posters of Elvis Presley everywhere. A small jukebox stood in a corner blasting out a fifties tune that Ali didn't recognize. While the others found a table to sit down, Ali ordered two plates of chips to share and then joined Haseena and Imran at their chosen tables.

"So you're getting married on Sunday, darling?" Imran asked, as Ali put the plates down.

Ali gave Haseena a withering look, knowing that she'd discussed his wedding with Imran while he'd been ordering the chips. "Yes, I am. News travels fast, doesn't it?" Ali said, picking up a couple of steaming chips, which he'd smothered with vinegar, and stuffed them into his mouth.

"Don't be like that, sweetheart. I'm married, too. It'll be eleven years next month," Imran said waving his wedding ring in front of Ali's face as evidence. "What do you think of my gorgeous ring? It has three diamonds set in it. I've just had it valued for five thousand pounds. You know what they say, sweetheart, 'diamonds are a girls best friend.'"

"It's beautiful," Ali commented looking at the ring. However, he couldn't help but find the ring too extravagant and couldn't understand why anyone would spend so much money on a single piece of jewelry.

"So, did you get married in Amsterdam?" Ali asked out of curiosity. "I know that two men can marry each other there. It's called a civil ceremony right? I think they're going to allow the same in England, soon."

"It wasn't in Amsterdam, sweetie. It took place in Pakistan. It was an arranged marriage to my beautiful wife. The most beautiful woman you could ever meet," Imran said.

81

"What?" Ali and Haseena said united in shock.

"You're married to a woman? But you're so gay," Ali said. Realizing what he'd just said, he flushed with embarrassment. He had almost sounded like Yunus. "Well, I didn't mean it like that. I was just surprised. I thought you were married to a man."

"Not to worry, sweetie. A lot of people are surprised when I tell them that I'm married. When my parents first told me that I was to marry I was so unhappy. I couldn't believe what they were doing to me. I locked myself away for days, not wishing to talk to anyone, but my parents managed to persuade me to meet my betrothed. I'm so glad I did. It was love at first sight. From the first moment that I saw her I knew that I'd finally met my soul mate," Imran said, gazing into the distance.

"That's really nice," Haseena said, still looking and sounding puzzled.

"You know the English say that marriage is one of the greatest institutions in the world. It is, but it has to be based on trust. Trust is the basic foundation for everything," Imran said philosophically. "That is why I had to tell her that I preferred men sexually."

"She must have been devastated. What did she say? The poor thing," Haseena said.

"She accepted what I told her. She said 'so what if you like men. It doesn't stop you from marrying me.' Women in Pakistan have such different ideas about sexuality and marriage. They are more realistic and have fewer expectations," Imran observed.

"I'm not sure if I could marry a man knowing that he was gay, and I don't know any other Pakistani woman who would either," Haseena said, disagreeing with Imran's comment.

"She was brought up in a small village, so she was used to seeing hidden sexual relationships between the different men in her community. Most of them were married, or if they weren't, they always ended up getting married," Imran said trying to explain his wife's acceptance of his sexuality.

"That's interesting. So are you both happy?" Haseena asked.

"Yes, we are. My wife and I have so much in common. Shopping, dressing up in saris, and sharing each other's makeup. The list is endless," Imran said.

"That sounds wonderful," Ali said feeling a pinch of envy. He imagined telling his own fiancée about his sexuality, but the picture that came to mind was completely different – a distraught Sajda, two irate families and a cancelled wedding.

"Have you told your fiancée?" Imran asked, as if reading his mind.

"No," Ali said, shuffling uncomfortably in his chair. He reached out for some more chips and stuffed them into his mouth as if to detract from his answer.

"I believe you should tell her. Your fiancée deserves to know the truth about you. You're going to spend the rest of your life with her, and you can't deceive her. It's not fair to her," Imran said.

"My circumstances are different," Ali tried to explain. "I've decided to become straight, so I don't think she needs to know about my past. I'm not planning to ask her about her past, so it doesn't really matter."

"You can't become straight overnight if you're gay, Ali. Listen to me. I couldn't deny that I still had sexual needs despite being happy with my marriage. My relationship with my wife was based on the meeting of two minds and the joy that we both shared in each other's company. It didn't include sexual desire," Imran said. "One day, my wife found me crying in the garden, and we ended up discussing what was bothering me. I explained that I was missing the sexual side of my life, and she told me to go out and date men if I wished. I cried for joy knowing that my wife loved me unconditionally."

"Your wife doesn't mind you dating other men?" Ali exclaimed in disbelief.

"No. What matters to her is that I'm happy and that I love, cherish and adore her. I've been dating a lovely man named Nick for the last four years, and she's welcomed him into our family with open arms. She accepts that I'm committed to him as much as I'm committed to her," Imran said.

"Isn't that selfish? It's like you can have your cake and eat it, too. I would never put up with it," Haseena exclaimed heatedly.

"It works for us. Not only does my wife get to be with me, but she also gets another companion whom she can go shopping with. She's the diva, and he's the real McCoy," Imran said.

"Well it seems very unfair. I mean, what if she wants to have children?" Haseena asked.

"We have children. We have two boys," Imran said.

Ali looked at Imran with more than a little surprise. He couldn't imagine Imran sleeping with a woman. It was too bizarre an act to contemplate. He was probably making everything up for the drama of it.

"Two children? Boys?" Haseena repeated almost to herself.

"Yes, I can see that you're both surprised, but I worked out when my wife was most fertile, and then I had sex with her. It wasn't pleasant, but in the end, we only had to have sex three times, and we've been successful twice now," Imran said proudly.

"Do the children know you're gay?" Haseena asked.

"No, of course not. They're too young to understand. I don't dress in my sari in front of the children, no matter how much I want to. They have been introduced to Nick. He's like a second father to them. They adore him," Imran said. "He lives with us. To people in the community, he's a lodger, a doctor friend who works locally and who lives with us because he has no family of his own."

"I could never be as brave as you," Ali said. "I wanted to tell my fiancée when I met her, but I just couldn't. I was too frightened of what her reaction would be."

"There is no point in being scared, sweetie. You must tell your fiancée before you get married. Give the poor kitten a choice. Let her decide whether she wants to go ahead with the marriage. What if she finds out from someone else that you're gay? How do you think she'll feel then?"

"I can't. I don't want to hurt her. She'll never accept it. Anyway, I've already told you it won't be a problem because once I'm married I'll never go back to being gay!" Ali said crossly.

"Hey, Rani, what are you doing sitting here? I thought you'd be out there dancing," a loud voice said, interrupting the exchange between Ali and Imran.

Ali looked up to see who was talking. It was another Pakistani man. He looked to be in his late twenties, and was dressed in a black pinstripe suit with a black shirt and white tie. His side burns were shaved into pencil thin stripes that ended just below his jaw and just under his lower lip was a small triangle of hair.

"Altaf, sweetheart, I'm so sorry. I don't know how I managed to lose you on the dance floor," Imran said to his friend apologetically. "I found these lovely people to talk to. Altaf, meet Haseena and Ali. Haseena, Ali, meet Altaf," Imran said introducing everyone to each other.

"Sit down and stop towering over us," Imran ordered Altaf. He gave Altaf a playful pinch on his bottom as he sat down. "Oh Altaf, you have the most pert bottom that I've ever had the pleasure of touching," he exclaimed.

"Butt clenches baby, butt clenches. It helps keep it firm," Altaf said laughing, and not the least bit embarrassed.

"Ali's getting married on Sunday," Imran said informing his friend.

"Congratulations," Altaf said turning to Ali.

"It's not congratulations, silly! It's more like condolences. His parents are forcing him to marry," Imran told him.

"Oh, I'm sorry, Ali. I thought you were straight. Sorry. Are you okay?" Altaf asked sounding concerned.

"I'm fine. I've had time to get used to the idea," Ali said.

"Altaf's married you know. He came out in a really big way. Oh, it was such a scandal," Imran said delighting in the salacious gossip that his friend had created.

"It was. You should have been there," Altaf said proudly. "I was working as a model in London a few years ago and had a relationship with a Tory MP. We were together for over two years. One morning I woke up to find reporters on my doorstep. They'd found out about us. The next day, there were snapshots of me plastered in all the tabloids. Did you see them?"

"I think I read something about it," Ali said, vaguely recalling the story.

"It was such a lovely life dating an MP. He paid for everything. I could go to any restaurant to eat, and he'd always pay, no matter what the cost. We went away together on exotic holidays without me spending a penny. He was such a wonderful man. So kind and generous. You would think that an older man can't offer someone of my age anything, but there are lots of financial benefits. There have to be when you're dating an older man, don't you agree?" Altaf asked, as if expecting Ali and Haseena to be in agreement.

"Oh my God, you're like a rent boy," Haseena exclaimed.

"Not at all, I was more like a kept man. I can't afford to sustain a relationship with a man and support my wife as well. The man I date must have something more to offer than good looks and sex," Altaf said.

"So, did your family ever read the papers?" Haseena asked curiously, wanting to know more.

"That was the worst part. They didn't see the articles when the papers came out, but you know what our community is like. Some busybody came across the story and showed the newspapers to my wife and the rest of the family. The wife was understandably humiliated and ordered her brothers too beat me up. I ended up in casualty for over two months because of the injuries. She has a very brutal family," Altaf said, shuddering at the memory.

"That's awful," Ali said.

"I know. You know what pissed me off though? It was the fact that one of the brothers who beat me up was in love with a twenty-year-old boy back in Pakistan, and the other had made a pass at me a couple of years before, the hypocritical bastards!" Altaf said crossly.

"That's typical of most Pakistani men, isn't it? They don't think they're gay if they're married," Haseena said angrily. "So are you divorced?"

"No. The family won't let me do that to the wife. She's turned really nasty since it all happened. If I leave the house, she thinks I'm going to a gay nightclub, so she reports me to her brothers and they go out looking for me. She has got it right sometimes, and they have given me a beating. Look," he said pulling his shirt out from his trousers to reveal a bruised but well developed six-pack. "This is from when they beat me the last time."

"Have you reported them to the police?" Haseena asked.

Altaf shook his head, "No, it's family business. I can't let outsiders get involved."

"Well, you can't allow yourself to be a victim either. You've got to go to the police," Haseena said. She sounded livid at the thought of Altaf's abuse. "Can't you leave?"

"I can't. My family won't allow it. They've threatened to take my children to Pakistan and not let me see them again. I love my children. I wouldn't be able to cope if I couldn't see them. My philosophy is very simple. I accept things as they are," Altaf said. "That way no one gets hurt."

"That's very defeatist. You should leave if you're not happy," Haseena said, giving the same advice that she'd doled out to Ali so many times before.

"I'm fine. I can handle it, but a word of advice to you, Ali. Don't get emotionally attached to anyone outside your marriage, and whatever you do, don't see anyone who's in the public eye," Altaf said.

"Thanks, but I won't be dating men while I'm married," Ali said. "I'm going to be faithful to my wife."

"You say that now, but wait until you're a couple of months into your marriage and you start eyeing up every man that walks past you in the street," Altaf said.

"Personally, I think Ali should leave," Haseena said interrupting. "He should move out and go away, very far away to somewhere they can't find him. That's my advice, but he just won't listen."

"I can't leave. The arrangements for the wedding have all been made," Ali said. "If I leave now, it would destroy too many people."

"You're probably right," Imran agreed. "Maybe you need to go through with it and deal with the consequences later. If you leave now, you'll shame both her and her family, and it's highly unlikely anyone else will want to marry her afterwards."

"She's young. If he leaves now this will be forgotten in a couple of year's time and her family will probably find her someone else to marry in the meantime," Haseena said, contradicting Imran.

"I don't think it's that simple," Altaf said.

"So, how do you two know each other?" Ali asked Altaf, changing the subject. He'd had enough of talking about marriages. He'd agreed to come out to try and enjoy himself, but it seemed that he couldn't escape from the fact that he was getting married.

"We've known each other for a very long time. We met when we were small children in Pakistan. It was my first time in Pakistan, and Imran's family had moved back there from England. I didn't know anyone, and all the other kids would throw stones or be generally unpleasant to me. One day, I was getting beaten up by some bullies and Imran rescued me from them. Since then we've always been friends," Altaf said.

"You're all really depressing me. Can we go and have some fun on the dance floor, please? That's what we're here for, right? It's Bollywood night, and the only brown faces in the place are moping over some chips," Imran cried.

"You're right. I'm meant to be helping Ali enjoy himself, not upsetting him. Let's go and dance," Haseena agreed, getting up swiftly.

The men followed Haseena's lead and got up, leaving the plates of half eaten chips behind. They trailed after Haseena as she led them to the dance floor. Ali stood next to her and tried to dance, hoping to get to the same happy equilibrium that he'd reached earlier. However, he found it difficult to drown himself in the music this time.

His mind kept leaping to the forthcoming mehndi and wedding. "What am I going to do?" he thought to himself. He played the scenario of telling his fiancée about his sexuality through his mind again, and again the outcome was the same, with the wedding being cancelled and a lot of lives being ruined.

He wondered about the possibility of leaving the whole mess behind and running away as Haseena had suggested. The thought of it wasn't even worth contemplating when he considered what he would be giving up – the warmth and luxury of living at home, with his own bedroom and not having to worry about money to pay the bills. "Is that why I really want to stay? For security?" Ali asked himself.

"If I move out, I'll be responsible for everything. I wouldn't have anywhere to live. I'd be poor, and what about my mother and fiancée? It would destroy them both." Ali brushed the thought of leaving home from his mind and turned to Haseena. "Can we go home?" he asked. "I can't enjoy myself anymore. I need to go home," he reiterated. He suddenly felt distressed and overwhelmed by everything that was happening to him.

"Ali, I didn't want your last night to be like this. I'm sorry. Let's just slip away. You won't see Imran and Altaf again, so there's no point in saying goodbye to them. We can sneak out quietly," Haseena said, knowing that Ali was not in the mood to exchange pleasantries and farewells with anyone. She grabbed hold of Ali's hand and pulled him after her away from the sweaty dance floor. Haseena collected their two jackets from the cloakroom, and they both left the nightclub, leaving another chapter of Ali's life behind.

"It's been a very strange night," Haseena said getting into one of the taxis queuing up outside the nightclub. She gave the driver instructions on how to get her home and continued her conversation with Ali. "We never usually see any other Asian people in there, and today we meet two other Pakistani guys who are both married."

"I don't think it was that strange," Ali said disagreeing with her.

"I do. It's like you were meant to meet them to see a snapshot of what might happen if you went ahead with the marriage. You saw two victims in there," Haseena pointed out. "It's a message to you. It's saying don't go ahead with the wedding, or your life might end up like this. You'll end up being a victim."

"Stop talking nonsense! We met two gay Pakistani guys who were out at the Nightingale because it was hosting a Bollywood night. If we'd stayed longer, I'm sure more Asian guys might have appeared. Most Asian guys we meet in gay clubs are married, so there was nothing significant about meeting Imran and Altaf tonight," Ali said crossly.

"You're wrong, Ali. We met them for a reason, but you can believe what you like. I know you're going ahead with the wedding no matter what I say, but I think it'll be the biggest mistake that you'll ever make," Haseena said.

Hearing those words stunned Ali. It was the first time that Haseena had been direct in her opinion. He couldn't think of anything to say and sat back in silence. They didn't talk to each other for the rest of journey, too wrapped up in their own thoughts. When the taxi drew up outside Haseena's front door, she got up to get out of the car.

"Good luck with the wedding;" she said to Ali. "I don't think we'll be able to see each other much after tonight."

"Why?" Ali asked, feeling hurt.

"Well, you'll be married, and you'll have a responsibility to your wife. She won't want you visiting me, will she? It wouldn't be fair to her," Haseena said, widening further the gulf that had suddenly opened up between them.

"You're coming to the wedding aren't you?" Ali asked. "I've made sure that Yasmin sent out an invitation to you."

"I've received the invitation, but I can't come to the wedding. It would hurt me too much to see you getting married. I've sent my apologies already. I'm sorry," Haseena said sadly.

"Please, Haseena, you have to come. I won't be able to cope without you. I need you there to support me," Ali said, almost pleading.

"I can't. I'm sorry. I'm not changing my mind. If you need to speak to me you can call me anytime you want. That's if you change your mind about the wedding," Haseena said.

Ali hugged her, knowing he wasn't going to be able to change her mind. "Thank you for being a wonderful friend to me," he said. Haseena gave him a goodbye kiss on the cheek before stepping out of the taxi.

Ali watched as she walked to her front door. She took her keys out from her handbag and fumbled with the lock before opening the door. Turning around, she waved goodbye and then stepped into the house closing the door behind her.

Ali turned sadly to the taxi driver and gave him directions to his home. "That's probably the last time I'll see my best friend," he thought to himself as he sat back in the seat.

Chapter Eight

"Hello Steve. How are you?" Ali asked.

"I'm fine. It's good to hear from you. How are you feeling?" Steve inquired in return.

"I'm fine, considering everything" Ali said.

"That's good to hear. So what are you up to?" Steve asked.

"Nothing much. It's my mehndi later on. I was feeling a bit down and just wanted to hear your voice," Ali said. He was sitting on the floor of the extension that had been built for Yunus and his wife, making the phone call using Yunus's private phone line.

The room was completely bare. Ali's mother had removed all the furniture from the downstairs rooms of the house and stored the items in the garage for safekeeping until the wedding celebrations were over, so that nothing got damaged by the guests. She had even laid out specially ordered plastic coated fabric on all of the floors for guests to sit on, thereby ensuring that her beloved wilton carpets were protected from any mishaps.

"What's mehndi?" Steve asked. "Is it like a stag night?"

"No, it's nothing like it. Mehndi means henna. It's when they put henna on your hands and feet, and all the women sing traditional songs. It was Sajda's mehndi yesterday, and they're doing mine tonight. Normally the guy has to go to his fiancée's house, and it all takes place at the one event, but because we live in different cities, they've done two separate ones," Ali said, trying to explain a small part of the complicated wedding arrangements.

"So you're going to have henna tattoos all over your hands and feet?" Steve asked laughing.

"It's no laughing matter. I'm dreading it. They're planning to put henna on my feet. What if they see the tattoo on my calf? No one knows I've got one. What am I going to do?" Ali asked worriedly, knowing that people would be horrified to see the Chinese symbol tattooed on his leg.

"Your trouser leg shouldn't slip back that much, so I wouldn't worry about it," Steve said.

"I won't be wearing trousers. I've got to wear a white Pakistani suit. You know, a kurtha salwar," Ali said. "It's very loose fitting. You must have seen one. You could pull the legs of the salwar up on both sides and make it look like a pair baggy underpants if you wanted to, so they'll definitely see the tattoo. I'm going to be so embarrassed," Ali said.

"Just stick a plaster on it and say you've got a cut," Steve advised.

"That's a great idea. I'll try it, but it'll have to be a big plaster," Ali said, the problem now resolved.

"You seem to be coping with everything a lot better than I had imagined you would," Steve remarked.

"I guess it just seems that way, but if you really want to know, I feel completely miserable. I'm just so unhappy." Ali said, his eyes welling up with tears.

"Ali, I'm so sorry. I wish I was there, so you didn't have to go through this on your own," Steve said, sounding upset as well.

"I'm sorry. I'm just being silly. When I talk to you it just makes things harder," Ali said. "I've had Haseena looking after me, so there's no need to worry."

"How is she?" Steve asked.

"She's fine. She arranged a night out for me at the Nightingale last night when my family was away," Ali said.

"That was nice of her. Did you have a good time?" Steve asked.

"It wasn't good, but it wasn't bad either. I just felt as if I was going through the motions. I tried to enjoy myself, but I couldn't get my mind off the wedding, so we left early. When I got back home I just felt so alone. I couldn't stop crying," Ali said. "I feel so drained all of the time. There is no one that I can talk to in the family. They know how bad I'm feeling, but no one mentions it because then they'll have to acknowledge that I'm unhappy."

"Ali, that's awful. How can they carry on putting you through this?" Steve asked in disbelief.

"I don't know. I guess they think that once I'm married I'll be happy. I don't think they realize what they're doing to me," Ali said.

"Do you think you'll be happy?" Steve asked.

"I'm hoping I will. I don't know," Ali said. "Anyway, I'm sorry, I shouldn't be talking to you about all of this."

"You don't need to be sorry, Ali. I'm still here for you. I'll always be here for you no matter what," Steve said reassuringly. "I love you, you know."

"I love you, too, but you'd be so much happier if you moved on with your life. You can't stay around waiting for me," Ali said.

"I know. I can't help it. I can't move on yet," Steve said, sounding as if he was about to cry. "I just love you so much. I miss you."

"I'm sorry, Steve. I never wanted to hurt you like this," Ali said.

"Hush, you have nothing to be sorry about. Where are you ringing from," he asked suddenly.

"From Yunus's phone line," Ali said.

"I can hear an echo on the line. I think someone might be listening," Steve said sounding suspicious.

"There's no one. You're being paranoid. The phone's separate from the main phone line in the house," Ali said. "To be honest, I don't really care if anyone's listening. I've sacrificed a lot for this family. Maybe they need to find out just how much."

"Oh, Ali," Steve sighed.

"Nobody here is interested in me. They are all too busy deciding what they're going to wear. I'm just the spare part that they'll roll out on the wedding day. They don't understand that it's my life that they're destroying. I just hate all of them," Ali ranted angrily.

"You don't really hate them. If you did, you wouldn't be getting married. You could have left if you'd really wanted to. In fact, I think you still can," Steve said.

"It's too late. I can't leave. Everything is so out of my control," Ali said. "Anyway, I don't know when I'll be able to talk to you again. It'll probably be after the wedding now."

"I hope so. I know things will change between us after the wedding, but I hope you'll stay in touch," Steve said sadly.

"I will. I promise," Ali said, wondering deep down whether he'd be able to keep this promise.

"I love you," Steve said.

"Same here," Ali replied reassured by Steve's words. "I'll try and call you soon."

"Goodbye, darling, try and be brave," Steve said.

"I will. I love you. Goodbye," Ali said, as he put the handset down reluctantly. He cradled the phone in his lap for a few moments and began to cry. He missed Steve so much. What were things going to be like once he was married? What if he never saw Steve again? "What am I going to do?" he muttered to himself tearfully. "I should just kill myself. That would teach them!"

Ali imagined his mother finding an empty bottle of painkillers at the side of his lifeless body and blaming herself for the cause of his apparent suicide. "I could write a suicide note and blame all of them," Ali thought. His whole body felt empty, and the pain he was feeling made him feel nauseas. He burst into tears of self pity as the image of his suicide played in his head.

"I should end it all then see whether they can have the wedding without me," Ali thought, before breaking into another flood of tears.

"Why are you crying?" he heard Yasmin's voice say. When he looked up, she was towering over him looking down at him with suspicion in her eyes.

"I'm not crying," Ali shouted angrily at her.

"Who were you talking to on the phone?" she asked, looking at the phone in his lap.

"None of your damn business! All you ever do is go around poking your nose in other people's business. It's like you've haven't got a life of your own," Ali yelled at her.

"What's upset you?" she asked, trying a different tact. Somehow she managed to sound genuinely concerned.

"Leave me alone, Yasmin. Just go away! I can't stand the sight of you!" Ali said furiously, venting his anger and frustration at her.

"Ali, I'm your older sister. I worry about you. Who's upset you? Was it someone on the phone? Did they want you to do something that you didn't want to do?" Yasmin asked.

"There was no one on the phone. Just leave me alone," Ali said beginning to shake with anger.

"I care about you, Ali. I love you. You're my own flesh and blood. I don't like seeing you so upset and hurt," Yasmin said.

"What do you want from me?" Ali screamed at her angrily.

"I want you to be happy. These next few days should be the happiest days of your life. Instead, you've just been moping around as if you're about to die. You haven't involved yourself in anything. I don't understand! It's meant to be your wedding," Yasmin said worriedly.

"You don't understand? Have you forgotten already? You all forced the wedding on me. I wouldn't have agreed to this wedding if I had any choice in the matter!" Ali exclaimed, unable to believe Yasmin's lack of comprehension at what they'd done to him.

"You weren't forced into anything. You were leading a lifestyle that was unacceptable for a Muslim. It's our duty not only as your family, but as Muslims to put you on the right path. What did you expect us to do? Ignore the perverted life you were leading?" Yasmin asked.

"Leave me alone, Yasmin. I've agreed to the wedding, so just let me be. I can't bear to listen to your religious babble," Ali said.

"I don't like seeing you unhappy, Ali. I can tell you've been talking to one of your stupid friends, and they've been trying to influence you. Why else would you be crying? You have to stop listening to them for your own sanity. Your life has taken a different path. They're degenerate. You must leave them behind and stay away from them," Yasmin said.

"You just can't stop lecturing me can you? Look at you! You're nearly thirty, and no one wants to marry you! You've scared off all the men with your fanatical ranting. You wear that hijab everywhere, but you're the only girl I know who wears one. Ammie doesn't even like you wearing it when she takes you out. You're going to end up as a bitter old spinster who'll still be living at home in her sixties," Ali said, tearing into Yasmin furiously.

"Unlike you, Ali, I don't worry about what other people think of me. I've got something precious to hold onto. My faith. It's kept me on the path that God has chosen for me," Yasmin

95

said. "Have you looked at yourself? You have no clue about what it is you want with your life and blunder about blindly. Islam would give you all the answers if you let it."

"Oh shut up. I don't want to hear it!" Ali retorted angrily.

"It's your mehndi tonight. Please try to enjoy it," Yasmin said. "Speaking to your friends seems to upset you. Look at the state of you. You have the rest of your life ahead of you with Sajda. These friendships you have are meaningless. You have to put an end to them."

"What do you know about friendships when you don't have any!" Ali snapped angrily.

"Ali, I know which friendships are right to have and which ones are wrong. I know about that man you're friends with. Steve isn't it? That's not the type of friendship that a man who's about to get married should have!" Yasmin exclaimed.

"I don't know who you're on about," Ali said in denial, not wanting to drag Steve into the mess. It was as if a hole had opened up in the ground in front of him. How had Yasmin found out about Steve?

"Is that why you're in a public phone box nearly every evening making your phone calls? I know all about it. You should have tried to be a little more discrete. Your friendship with Steve has to come to an end! If you don't stop contacting him, I'll make sure that his family finds out about it. I suggest that you end it, or else, there'll be trouble," Yasmin said, threateningly.

"Leave me alone. That's my personal business," Ali said, outraged at the threat. "You know what, Yasmin? Once I'm married, I won't have anything to do with any of you. I'll move to the house in Nottingham, which Mum is buying for me, and I'll make sure that I never see anyone from this family again."

"Ali, I feel so sorry for you. You really don't know the importance of family," said Yasmin, shaking her head with a sigh. "If only Dad was alive today to put you on the right path. Instead the duty has to fall to me."

"I'm going to my bedroom. I can't bear to look at you, let alone listen to you," Ali said getting up.

"Yes, run away when someone tries to talk some sense into you," Yasmin shouted after him. "Just behave like a man tonight, and make sure the guests don't find out what problems you've been causing us."

Ali stomped up the stairs to his bedroom like an angry teenager. When he got to the safety of his room, he banged the door shut loudly behind him and flung himself onto the bed. "Why are they making me do this," he said to himself, shaking uncontrollably at his confrontation with Yasmin.

After a while, his shaking stopped, but his thoughts took a different turn. "I just want to kill myself," he muttered as tears of self-pity began to flow down his face again. He turned himself face down on the bed and began to cry. He tried to muffle the sound of his crying by covering his face with the duvet, so that no one in the house would hear him.

Chapter Nine

The day of the wedding had arrived. Ali's mehndi had taken place the night before, and the events of the previous evening now washed over him like waves in a bad storm as he sat in the car recalling them. The evening began with the arrival of the guests, and the men and women going into two separate rooms. Ali's in-laws had traveled from Nottingham to join in the celebrations, leaving Sajda behind.

Ali was introduced to the best man, his dost – Khamran, under his father-in-laws approving gaze. Khamran had been specially chosen for this role by Ali's mother, who informed Ali that he came from a good Pakistani family. What she didn't say was that she hoped Khamran would be a good influence on him and stop him from being led astray in the future. She had even professed that Ali used to play cricket with Khamran as a youngster, knowing that it was a lie.

After the initial greeting and exchange of pleasantries, Ali and Khamran realized that they had nothing in common as their conversation soon dried up. Kham, as he liked to be known, was the same age as Ali and loved listening to music by The Who, despite strong disapproval from his father. He prayed five times a day, and made sure he attended the Mosque every Friday. He was looking forward to settling down and getting married to a girl from Pakistan in a month's time.

There were no other guests present who were in Ali's age group, which meant that Ali ended up spending most of the evening sitting in painful silence as the older men swapped stories of their own weddings. Their recount of tricks that had been played on them by their own dosts became more and more outrageous as the evening dragged on. Yunus joined in with the conversations, laughing animatedly in the right places, and adding his own tales to the repertoire. Ali felt envious at the ease with which Yunus had managed to fit in. Ali therefore welcomed the intrusion when Yasmin called him to join the ladies in the other room.

The room was full with women sitting and standing in every available space. They were clapping their hands loudly to the beat of a drum that was being pounded by Auntie Fazal who was in the thick of the festivities. Several women chanted a traditional mehndi song in Urdu while others took turns to join in with the chorus.

Ali was seated on a chair in the center of the room, and amidst the raucous cries of the women, his hand was coated in Vaseline to stop the henna dye from staining it. Ali's mother explained that it might look unseemly if Ali went to a job interview with a red hand. However, it didn't stop the women from covering his left foot with the stuff. They then took turns in rubbing coconut oil into Ali's hair until it was dripping onto his clothes.

The whole episode was filmed by a cameraman, who was short, fat, and balding. He sweated profusely with the strain of carrying the camera. Ali's mother had hired him at a bargain price to film the whole wedding ceremony.

Glistening with coconut oil, Ali made his excuses and slipped away to have a shower. He quickly washed away the nauseating smell of coconut before scraping away the henna that seemed to have imbedded itself onto his foot. When he finished, instead of going back to the guests, Ali crept back to his bedroom.

Yunus found him lying on the bed an hour later. Ali ignored his tirade of abuse as he tried to persuade him to come back downstairs to the guests. Tiring of Yunus's ranting, Ali covered his head with the duvet, closed his eyes, and blocked Yunus out. Yunus eventually gave up and left the room to the surprise of Ali who'd expected him to use force to get his way.

"We're here," called out Uncle Kareem from the driver's seat of the car, rudely interrupting Ali's reverie. Uncle Kareem was Ali's mother's stepbrother.

Ali's mother's already fragile relationship with Uncle Kareem had been destroyed overnight a few years ago by the announcement of Yunus's marriage, and they hadn't spoken to each other since. It wasn't unusual for first cousins to marry each other within Pakistani families, so Uncle Kareem had naturally assumed that his eldest daughter would marry Yunus, and he had been completely devastated at the announcement.

In the spirit of reconciliation, he'd approached his stepsister as soon as he heard about Ali's wedding to volunteer his new Mercedes to ferry Ali around on the wedding day and to conduct the wedding ceremony itself. It had given him an opportunity to try and get closer to her and to rebuild some bridges. Maybe a wedding between his daughter and the newly divorced Yunus might still be arranged in the process.

Ali felt conspicuous in the car and was pleased that they'd finally arrived. It felt as if all the other motorists on the road were staring, which was probably true due to the decorations on the car. It had pink paper ribbons running along the length of it and several brightly colored balloons adorning its wing-mirrors. To make matters even worse, the car was part of a convoy that was similarly decorated.

Ali looked out of the window, pulling aside the sehra that was veiling his face. The sehra was a small curtain made of gold tinsel hanging from a red and gold band that had been tied around his head. He looked ridiculous and knew it. Traditionally, the sehra was made from fresh flowers, but this was the cheaper mass produced option favored by the community. It irritated Ali's face and made his forehead itch from where Kham had tied it earlier.

"Do you want me to loosen it for you?" asked Kham, noticing Ali's discomfort. Despite sitting next to each other, they'd hardly spoken throughout the journey. The silence, however, was a comfortable one. They'd come to a mutual unspoken understanding the previous evening that they were both here to perform a duty for their families, and that getting to know each other did not have to be a part of it.

"I'm fine, don't worry," replied Ali. He dropped the sehra back in front of his face, opened the car door and stepped out. The cameraman from the mehndi evening was already standing in front of him pointing the lens into his face as if he was auditioning to be a member of the paparazzi.

"I'll help you," Kham said following after him. He kindly held Ali by his arm and guided him to the house knowing that Ali could barely see from behind the sehra.

It was noisy and chaotic outside the house. Through the small gaps in the sehra, Ali could make out small groups of young children playing. They yelled excitedly upon noticing

Ali's presence and watched as he was led into the house. To Ali's bemusement, the house was sparkling with Christmas fairy lights. It had been completely covered with the stuff, as every window, door and even the roof danced with rainbow colors.

When they entered the main room, Ali resisted the urge to push aside the sehra so as to see clearly. "Ma sha Allah. The bridegroom is finally here," he heard a man's voice exclaim loudly.

"Sit next to your brother," Kham said maneuvering Ali to a chair and then taking a seat on the other side of him.

"You made it," said Yunus giving Ali a friendly pat on the shoulder, as Ali recoiled from his touch.

"I'm so proud of you, young man," Uncle Kareem said jovially, shaking Ali's hand before striding away.

Ali gave his uncle's disappearing form a withering look from behind the sehra. Uncle Kareem looked the perfect picture of Islamic respectability. He'd grown his beard long and was wearing religious garb similar to that which an Imam would typically wear.

It was a far cry from the image that his uncle presented five years ago. He'd driven the latest car, wore designer suits, and owned a string of restaurants in the south of England. However, everything came crashing down around him when his wife discovered his affair with her best friend's daughter who was only sixteen.

As his wife began divorce proceedings, Uncle Kareem turned to drugs for comfort and lost all of his money chasing the high that only drugs could bring him. Then he suddenly rediscovered Islam and began to practice to become an Imam. Three years later, his past sins were now forgotten, and he was back with his wife who'd been persuaded by the community to take him back.

"Let me see your face?" Ali heard a voice grate shakily, before a wrinkly hand reached and pulled the sehra aside to look at him. It was a wizened old man with a walking stick in his hand, looking unsteady on his feet. He hovered, hunched over in front of Ali. His eyes were brimming with tears. "You look so much like your father," he said forlornly.

"Thank you," Ali said, pleased by his comment.

"Your father would have been so proud today," the old man said. "Did he ever talk about me?"

"I don't remember him mentioning you," Ali said unsure who the elderly man was.

"He used to talk about you a lot," Yunus said interrupting.

"He was such a kind man. I miss him dearly," the old man said. He stroked Ali's face with his gnarled hand and then hobbled away to sit next to a group of men his age, and stared mournfully at Ali from across the room.

"He's our great-uncle. Try and be more respectful," said Yunus crossly.

"I didn't know," Ali hissed back at him. "I've never met him before!"

Ali took the opportunity to take in his surroundings without the sehra clouding his view. The lounge had been transformed since his last visit. It had been cleared of most of the furniture like his mother's house; however, a few chairs and a two-seater sofa remained behind. The room was decorated appropriately for a party with crepe paper streamers hanging from the center of the ceiling in a multitude of colors creating the image of a maypole, but without the dancers.

It was a crowded and noisy room, and everyone was in deep conversation with each other barely noticing Ali. The men either sat on the floor or stood chatting. Little boys wearing silk waistcoats and tiny bow ties played among them, adding to the din. The only people Ali recognized were his twin cousins Majid and Sajid who sat together in a corner isolated from everyone else.

Ali glanced sideways at Yunus, who was wearing a new suit that Ammi had brought him. The white carnation on the lapel matched the carnations that Ali and Kham both wore. He smiled warmly when he noticed Ali looking at him, but the smile wasn't for Ali's benefit. It was for the cameraman who was filming them.

"Cover your face. They're going to start the ceremony," Yunus said sharply, as Uncle Kareem returned to the room with Ali's father and brother-in-law in tow.

"Who is going to speak for Sajda?" Uncle Kareem asked, beginning the Nikah.

Amjeed Kabil

"I'll speak for her," Ali's father-in-law said stepping forward.

"Ali, do you wish to accept the marriage to Sajda Hussein, daughter of Farooq and Balquees Hussein?" Uncle Kareem asked.

Ali took a deep breath. This was the deciding moment that would govern his fate for the rest of his life. If he said no, maybe life would be better. Refusing the marriage in front of witnesses might finally break the stranglehold grip that his family had on his life. "Yes, I do," Ali said his voice echoing nervously in the hush that had fallen in the room. He wasn't so brave as to defy his family openly after all.

"Does Sajda Hussein accept Ali Mirza as her husband?" Uncle Kareem asked Ali's father-in-law, who quickly left the room.

"She accepts," he said, returning a few seconds later. He sounded out of breath having rushed away to repeat the question to Sajda.

"Repeat after me line by line," Uncle Kareem said in a low voice before he began to recite the wedding prayer in Arabic from memory. Ali repeated each line word by word. The words tumbled from his dry mouth in steady procession leaving him feeling numb and empty. Each word he uttered cemented him deeper and deeper into a marriage he did not want like a well sprung trap.

"Ali, will you sign the Nikah Document?" requested his Uncle handing a pen to him. Ali took the pen, signed the document without reading it and returned it to his uncle who then countersigned it. Uncle Kareem then left the room to perform the same ceremony with Sajda in the next room, with the cameraman trailing behind filming every step.

Ali sat in silence.

"You're now married, young man," Uncle Kareem said returning. He shook Ali's hand as if confirming Ali's thoughts. "Congratulations."

It was real and it had happened. He was now a married man. He felt stunned by the knowledge. He was trapped!

His father-in-law gave Ali a hug and welcomed him to the family. Omar, his brother-in-law, who had hovered in the background came forward and shook his hand. When Yunus

104

attempted to give a hug, Ali shrugged him away and gave him a cold handshake.

"Do you think it's okay if I take the sehra off?" Ali asked Kham.

"I don't know," replied Kham. "I'd leave it on just in case."

"I'm taking it off. It's really annoying me," Ali said ripping the sehra off and handing it to Kham. At that moment, the door dividing the women from the men burst open, and a large gaggle of women came pouring in. They were dressed in traditional clothes, bright in color ranging from turquoise to bright green, and all with heavy gold jewelry around their necks and wrists to proudly display their wealth.

"My beautiful son, I'm so proud," Ali's mother cried happily as she swept him into her arms. "You've made me so happy." She handed him a roll of ten pound notes. "Here's five hundred pounds. Don't give her more than that," she whispered without any further explanation, as he was pulled off the chair by the gaggle of women.

It was then that Ali saw Sajda for the first time that day. She was being led into the room by her mother and two sisters. A group of women chanted in Urdu in the background to the beat of Auntie Fazal's drum.

Sajda had her face to the floor as if weighed down by the clothes she wore. She was dressed in a traditional lehnga suit and a red embroidered dupatta covered her head. A gold pendent covered in jewels hung in the center of her forehead, held by a gold chain that ran beneath the dupatta, along the parting in her hair. As she approached Ali, she continued to keep her gaze to the floor and sat down carefully on the chair that Ali had been forced to vacate.

"It's going to cost you to sit next to my sister," Rhazia cried as she raced to sit in the remaining chair next to Sajda. "How much do you think it's worth?"

Remembering what he'd seen at a wedding that he'd been to in the past, Ali made a deliberate effort to stop his mind going back to his previous gloomy thoughts and began to play his part as the bridegroom. "Ten pounds" Ali offered, waving a ten-pound note in front of Rhazia's face.

"Ten pounds!" Rhazia exclaimed in mock anger grabbing the note from him. "What an insult!"

"You're just a kid, ten pounds is a lot of money for you," Ali said. "You wouldn't know what to do with it if I gave you any more."

"I know exactly what to do with money," Rhazia exclaimed. "I'm a shopaholic!"

"One hundred pounds?" Ali offered counting out the money.

"I'll take that!" Rhazia said, quickly snatching the money out of Ali's hands with a giggle. "It's not enough though. More!" She gestured with her hand.

"Pull her off the chair," a woman shouted from the gaggle that now surrounded them both.

"How am I going to support your sister if I give away all my money?" Ali asked humorously.

"Let him sit down. Can't you see the groom is pining to be with his beautiful bride," yelled another woman.

"Triple it, and you can have the chair to rest. You must be growing tired," said Rhazia, having noticed a sharp stare from her mother who didn't want her daughter to appear greedy in front of the guests.

"Done! As long as you promise that you're going to let me have the chair," Ali said. He counted the money out and wafted it in front of Rhazia, this time making sure it was out of her reach.

"It's all yours," said Rhazia, as she got up and collected the money and joined her sister Shazia who stood by her side.

"Did you get all that on film?" Ali heard Shazia ask the cameraman as Ali sat down on the chair.

"Yeah, it's all on there love," he heard the cameraman reply gruffly before turning his attention back to the filming.

Ali's mother checked to make sure that the cameraman was filming and then opened the jewelry box which she'd been holding and placed it on Sajda's lap to reveal four solid gold bangles inside. She waited a couple of moments to make sure that the cameraman had done a close-up shot. She then took them out and put them onto Sajda's left wrist one by one, proudly displaying the expense she'd incurred on behalf of her daughter-in-law.

It was Ali's turn next as his mother-in-law took hold of his hand. She turned around to face the camera and smiled before brutally forcing a gold ring that was obviously too small onto his wedding finger. She spat on Ali's finger to lubricate it and finally managed to slip it on leaving Ali's finger red and swollen. She then gave him a kiss and stood back to allow other people to present Ali with gifts.

Ali's grandmother handed him a thick roll of money. He wondered how she could afford so much until he unrolled the notes and discovered with a smirk that she'd given him several hundred rupees rather than pounds, which totaled less than three pounds in value! Meanwhile, Auntie Farooq took a modern approach and left a large gift-wrapped box in front of Ali's chair after giving him a kiss.

Kham's family surprised Ali by giving him an expensive Rolex watch before the rest of the guests followed with their offerings. Most of them gave money, while a few left gift boxes by the chair, all of them checking to ensure that it was captured on film so that the community saw their generosity when the film subsequently did its round.

"Can you get up to leave," instructed Yasmin with a whisper in Ali's ear as she materialized from the crush of people. She noticed the pile of money sitting in Ali's lap. "I'll take that," she said. She promptly picked up the money and put it into her handbag.

Ali's mother told him to hold Sajda's hand as he stood up. He followed her instruction and took Sajda's heavily jeweled hand into his own and led her out of the house to the waiting car outside, closely trailed by the cameraman and the guests. While the cameraman took several more shots of the married couple, the guests took great delight in throwing rice over them.

Ali climbed into the back seat of the car with Sajda while uncle Kareem held the door open. He sat back in the seat and closed his eyes briefly as his uncle shut the car door and got into the driving seat. As the car started to move, Ali opened his eyes again. He wondered what to say to his beautiful bride, but no words came to mind.

Uncle Kareem peered into the rear view mirror trying to catch a glimpse of the newly married couple. "They are young.

They have plenty of time to get to know each other and fall in love," he thought wisely as he sighed deeply at the silence. "Tomorrow I'll talk to his mother about Yunus and my daughter."

The reception was taking place at a hotel in the Nottinghamshire countryside. As they reached the hotel and approached the long drive, Ali couldn't help but feel impressed with the grandeur of the building that had been hidden from view behind a canopy of poplar trees. It was a Victorian building, four stories high with numerous glass windows in an old rectory style. Surrounding it was an immaculately trimmed lawn with a large man made lake in the center brimming with autumnal water flowers.

The peaceful and tranquil surroundings gave way to scenes of chaos outside the building. Ali and Sajda's families were already waiting outside the hotel with the guests milling around them, as the cameraman tried to capture the vivid imagery of a Pakistani wedding reception in a country location. They all cheered loudly as the car came to a stop in the busy courtyard and Ali and Sajda got out.

The grandeur of the hotel became even more apparent as Ali entered with Sajda, followed by everyone else. The room for the reception had several crystal chandeliers hanging from the ceiling reflecting light generously into it, and beautiful oil paintings hung in ornate wooden frames on every wall. A wood fire burned under a large mantelpiece casting a glowing radiance around the room. The room had been filled to capacity with circular tables that had been carefully laid out with fresh napkins and cutlery for the several courses of Pakistani dishes that were now to be served.

Ali and Sajda were escorted by an usher to two chairs at a table in the center of the room, which was raised off the floor by a two-foot platform. Sajda's family took the chairs to the right of Sajda, and Ali's family took the remaining seats to the left of him.

A heart shaped wedding cake with three tiers sat on the table in front of Ali. It was deliciously coated in rich, sumptuous, white icing and finished off with a handmade sugar rose on its top tier. The cameraman filmed the cake from several angles before turning his attention to Ali and Sajda.

"Cut the cake," instructed Yasmin from where she was sitting, as she passed a cake knife to Ali.

"Cut a piece and put it into her mouth," the cameraman advised, as Ali stood up to cut the cake. After cutting a small slice, he leaned over to feed it to Sajda, who opened her mouth coyly. She struggled slightly with the piece finding it too big, but eventually managed to swallow it. When it was her turn to cut the cake, she mischievously cut a large slice and stuffed it into Ali's mouth smirking at the floor as it spilled out.

"Yasmin, cut the rest of that layer for the guests, and then put the remaining layers away," Ali heard his mother whisper as he sat down. "We can share the rest between our own family."

The rest of the reception sped by in a blur for Ali. The succession of people who came to offer their congratulations and give monetary gifts to Ali and Sajda at the table seemed endless. Just when the reception hall emptied and Ali thought it had come to an end, the hall was immediately filled with more guests ready to eat, offer gifts and take yet more photographs.

Ali watched as his mother chatted merrily to several women in one corner of the room, while Yasmin and Aneesa seemed to be the center of attention among a group of girls elsewhere.

"What's wrong with me?" Ali thought miserably, his smile masking the pain as another guest took a photograph of him. He felt isolated and almost disassociated from everything that was happening around him. The isolation was made harder by his attempts at conversation with Sajda who ignored him with a bashful look on her face, playing the blushing bride perfectly.

"Are you happy, bro?" Yunus asked coming up to Ali and startling him from his thoughts.

"No," Ali mouthed to him unable to bite back his resentment.

Yunus's face looked stunned at what seemed to be a revelation to him. "Get up! We'd better get going. All the guests have finished eating," he said coldly. "I'll be driving you back home!"

Auntie Fazal led a chorus of women in singing a traditional wedding song, as everyone followed Ali and Sajda out of the reception hall. Just as they reached the car, Sajda suddenly tore her hand out from Ali's and flung herself into her fathers arms sobbing uncontrollably.

Ali stared at her, unsure what was happening. Had she felt the undercurrents of his unhappiness and could no longer deal with it, or had someone told her about his past? The thought of discovery made him feel sick. He looked at his mother for reassurance, but she was looking at Sajda shrewdly.

"There, there, you'll be back tomorrow," her father said gently as he hugged her tightly.

Her mother then gathered Sajda into her arms giving her several kisses in an effort to comfort her. "Go now," she said, leading her to the car and seating her inside. Ali got into the car after her and sat down beside Sajda bewildered by the exchange. Sajda sniffled a few times, but as soon as the car started and was out of view from the waving guests, the tears stopped just as suddenly as they had started.

Ali sat back tiredly in the car seat. "This is it. The start of my new life," he thought sadly as the car began its journey back to Birmingham.

"It was a really good day," Yunus commented loudly. "You two make a really lovely couple."

Ali gave him a filthy look knowing that Yunus was watching him in the rear view mirror, but he noticed Sajda blush shyly. Yunus fell back into silence again knowing that Ali was in no mood to talk to him. He drove slowly and with care trying to create a good impression.

The whole family was waiting outside the house as the car pulled into the driveway. Ali's mother greeted Sajda enthusiastically and ushered her excitedly into the house barely acknowledging Ali who followed behind. As he entered, Ali stifled the instinctive urge to run upstairs to his bedroom and cocoon himself away reclusively.

"Would you like some tea?" Ali's mother asked after she'd settled everyone down in the lounge.

"Yes, please," Sajda replied shyly, her voice barely audible. Yasmin rushed away immediately to make it without even being instructed by Ammi in an effort to create a good impression.

"It's good to have you here," Ali's mother said, as she sat down next to Sajda. Ali's grandmother cast a dark angry look in their direction and muttered under her breath before turning back to the gas fire in front of which she was sitting.

The room was quiet until Yasmin came back carrying a tray laden with tea and Pakistani sweetmeats. She served the tea to everyone, but Ali refused the proffered cup and saucer, unable to face drinking anything.

"Ali, can you help your brother unload Sajda's things from the car," said Ali's mother. "We just about managed to fit her suitcase in the boot, but it's very heavy," she warned.

The suitcase was as heavy as Ammi had described. It took both Yunus and Ali to lift the suitcase out of the car boot. "You shocked me with what you said earlier, Ali," Yunus said breathlessly breaking the silence between them just after they'd brought the suitcase into the house, heaved it up the narrow stairs and into Ali's bedroom. "Tell me you're happy."

"I can't. If I said that I'd be lying to you," Ali said simmering with anger.

"You've been smiling all day. You've sounded so happy. I don't understand," said Yunus sounding perplexed. He looked at his younger brother unable to grasp what was wrong.

"It's an act. You and the rest of the family destroyed me today. I hate you!" Ali said angrily, trying to keep the melodramatic tone out of his voice.

"We didn't want you to end up being a queer bastard. Did you expect us to sit back and let you play with your perverted friends?" Yunus asked, reflecting the same anger back at Ali.

"Fuck off and leave me alone! You got what you wanted!" Ali said trying not to shout too loudly.

"I'll never leave you alone, you stupid fuck! I'll always be here!" Yunus said, then without any warning, he grabbed Ali by the throat and squeezed hard making him choke. "I want to hear you say that you're happy."

"No, leave me alone," Ali said struggling to breath. He attempted to pry Yunus's fingers away from his throat.

"Tell me you're happy," Yunus said.

"Leave me alone," Ali gasped in pain, unable to breath now. Maybe if he stopped struggling and he let Yunus strangle him it could all end now.

"Tell me you're happy," Yunus repeated.

"I'm happy," Ali managed to whisper feebly, unable to break away from Yunus's tight grip.

"If I ever hear you say otherwise, I'll finish the job!" Yunus said letting go. "Make sure you fuck her tonight," he said as Ali collapsed to the floor his face red and hot. He could still feel Yunus's grip on his throat as he tried to get his breath back. He eventually reached for the inhaler that he kept in his bedside drawer, took several puffs from it, and waited for his breathing to return to normal. He looked up to face Yunus wondering how his brother could behave so violently towards him, but he'd already left the bedroom.

Ali picked himself up and lay down on the double bed that had replaced his single one. He stared up at the ceiling trying his best not to cry. "What am I going to do?" he thought gloomily. "My life is horrible," he muttered.

Taking a few deep breaths, he got up from the bed and went back downstairs to the lounge to join his new wife and the rest of his family with a bright cheerful smile painted on his face.

Chapter Ten

"It's my wedding night, and it was meant to be the best night of my life, but it's not turning out the way it's supposed to," Ali's new bride said accusingly. "We're meant to make love to each other, but you've not even touched me. You've ignored me since we got into bed together!"

"I'm sorry," Ali replied. "I'm just really tired. The camera flashes from all of the photographs that people were taking has given me a migraine." He lay in the double bed facing away from his wife, feeling numb and empty, and in a state of shock.

"That shouldn't stop you. You're a man. What is it? What's wrong? Don't you find me sexy? Why aren't you even facing me?" Sajda asked almost petulantly.

"Of course I find you sexy," Ali said, trying to comfort his new wife. Somehow he knew that he didn't sound very convincing, but hoped she believed his words. "I want to get to know you first before we do anything. This is only the second time that we've met. I hardly know you, yet. We need to spend some time getting to know each other a bit, that's all."

"Ali, that's a silly notion. It's what English people say. We're Muslim, and once you take a bride in Islam, she belongs to you. She becomes your property to do with as you please. I'm yours. I belong to you. You can do anything you want with me. Anything! We don't need to wait and get to know each other first. Why don't you try touching me," Sajda suggested earnestly.

Ali turned round to face his wife. "I don't want to do this," he thought to himself miserably. The reality of the wedding was now hitting him hard. He hadn't envisaged that the night would be like this. What he'd failed to consider was that Sajda might have her own expectations for the night.

"I'm not ready to do anything, yet. I need to know someone properly before I can," Ali said, trying desperately to escape from committing himself to anything sexual. "Let's take some time getting to know each other. We could date each other, find out what we like and don't like. Let's develop things slowly. We don't have to rush. We have all the time in the world."

"Forget about that, Ali. I'm here now. We can get to know each other right now," Sajda said suggestively. "You know people say that I have the most beautiful body. Why don't you hold me and find out whether it's true."

Ali moved closer to Sajda's small form, which was hidden under the duvet. He leaned over reluctantly and put his arm around her waist. As he held her, all Ali could feel was extreme despair and anguish. He knew that Sajda was feeling unhappy and let down, and he wished desperately that he could make things right, but there was nothing he could do to make things better other than to give in to her demands.

Sajda pushed herself into Ali's arms and held his hand. "Every married girl that I know has told me that their wedding night was the best night of their life. I can't even begin to describe mine," she said.

"I'm sure they've lied to you," Ali said. "I bet they were all too tired to do anything but sleep."

"They're my closest friends. Why would they lie? Tonight's been such a disappointment. I've waited for this moment for most of my life. You agreed to marry me, yet you don't want to touch me. Why?" Sajda asked, making sure that Ali understood her frustration. She moved Ali's hand gently to her breast.

Ali sighed and pulled his hand away. "Today has been a very long day," he said. "Why don't we make love tomorrow night when I'm less tired. Let's try and make it special, something that we can both enjoy. Maybe you're right and we don't need a long time to get to know each other. Maybe just talking to each other tonight will be enough."

"You're right," Sajda said. "We shouldn't ruin it. I'm not like the other Pakistani girls. I've been saving myself for my wedding night. When I was at college, I had lots of guys asking me out, but I knew it wasn't right. I knew the perfect person would come along. What's another night? Let's wait until tomorrow, but can you give me a kiss tonight?"

Ali sighed inwardly in relief. His body felt wracked with pain and guilt. Part of him wanted to kiss Sajda and hold her in his arms and tell her that everything was going to be all right, but the other part rejected what was happening to him, finding every moment distressing and not wanting to share such closeness with anyone. "I just want to kill myself," he thought to himself finding relief in the words and knowing that he'd somehow managed to postpone the inevitable.

The romantic notion that he might get to know Sajda better and fall in love with her was no longer a possibility. The wedding night had become a nightmare. He realized that he'd made the wrong decision. Things were so out of control. "I shouldn't have married," he thought. It was too late now though. He was going to spend the rest of his life with the woman next to him, and there was nothing he could do about it.

Ali tried to catch his breath. He felt trapped and asthmatic, as if caught in a lift that was stuck between two floors with no sign of rescue. Trying to calm himself down, Ali slowly counted to ten and managed to get his breathing back to normal. He leaned closer to Sajda, who had turned her face to him, and gave her a quick kiss on the cheek.

"Ali, I'm married to you. You can do whatever you want to me, but you kiss me on my cheek as if I'm your sister," Sajda said. "You can touch and kiss me wherever you want. I told you that I belong to you."

Ali turned back to her and gave her a lingering kiss on her lips despite feeling no desire for her. He felt his chest tightening and his breathing became asthmatic. He felt a strong urge to go to the bathroom, but held Sajda for a few more moments trying to find the right timing to leave the bed.

"I need to go to the bathroom," he said eventually, getting out of the bed. He didn't turn the bedside light on in case he saw a hurt look on Sajda's face. Ali opened the bedroom door, and looked back at the silhouette of his wife lying on the bed in the now unfamiliar room. Her eyes glinted in the dark as she watched him.

"Do you want any water or anything?" Ali asked her.

"No, but thank you for asking," she said to Ali. He could hear the sadness and worry in her voice. Her husband's behavior had told her that something was wrong, but she had no idea what the problem was.

Ali crept to the downstairs bathroom quietly, making sure he didn't make any noise to wake the family. The house was quiet, and everyone seemed to be asleep. All probably content and happy in the belief that Ali's wedding had gone smoothly and that his life had now been sorted out.

He went to the bathroom, sat down on the toilet and urinated. When he'd finished, he held his head in his hands in anguish. "Why is this happening to me?" he muttered to himself despairingly. "I hate myself."

He felt the urge to scream and wail loudly at the injustice of it all, but instead he cried silently making no noise at all in case someone overheard him.

Sajda, his poor wife, had been expecting something memorable from her wedding night, but all he could give her were vague promises that he wasn't sure he would be able to keep. All her romantic ideas of the wedding night had been ruined. She had even tried to initiate sex with him, but Ali had completely rejected her. The thought of this brought fresh tears to Ali's eyes. "I've ruined her life and mine," Ali thought sadly to himself.

He got up off the toilet seat and went to the washbasin, turning on the tap to wash his hands. He glanced at his face reflecting back at him from the mirror over the washbasin. "I look haggard," he thought. His eyes gave away the trauma that he'd been through. They looked bleary and red from the lack of sleep and the crying, but most of all they had a pained and haunted look about them.

Ali turned on the coldwater tap and tried to soothe his sore eyes by patting cold water onto them with his hands. "I should just end it all," he thought to himself. The pain he was feeling was unbearable, and there seemed to be no end in sight. His head seemed overloaded with misery, and there was only one way that Ali thought he could stop it.

He went into the kitchen, took out a large stainless steel knife from the rack and walked back to the bathroom with it. He felt the edge of the knife with his index finger. He gasped as it bit into his finger making a fine cut and drawing blood. It was very sharp. "I can't take anymore," he thought to himself.

Ali closed his eyes and rested the cold blade on his wrist. He imagined his family finding his lifeless corpse on the bathroom floor next to a pool of blood in the morning. He knew that it would hurt every one of them terribly. It was as if he'd finally have his revenge for the hurt they'd all caused him.

However, the sudden image of his wife lying in his bed stopped him. "What about my wife?" he thought. She might start worrying that he'd not returned from the bathroom and come looking for him. She'd be the one to find his body in the bathroom and cry in horror, wondering whether it was something that she'd done that had caused him to kill himself. It would completely destroy her, being made a widow on her wedding night.

"I can't ruin her life. It's not fair," he thought, but the sensation of the cold steel against his wrist felt good and inviting. Ali scratched himself, brushing the blade sideways along his wrist. It was soothing. The mental pain he was feeling diminished as he felt the sharp physical pain on his wrist take hold.

He put the knife down and using his finger nails scratched his wrist again and again, causing large red welts to appear. The pain on his wrist felt real. This was pain he could deal with. It took away the pain in his head that he had no control over and gave him something physical that he could concentrate on. His wrist felt sore and stung painfully, but Ali felt better. He went back to the kitchen and returned the knife to the rack.

He then went to the kitchen cupboard where his mother kept all the medicines and looked for the bottle of painkillers. Having found it, he took out two pills for his headache, which he washed down with a glass of water. Taking two puffs of his inhaler to ease his breathing, Ali crept back up the stairs to his bedroom, guiltily holding onto his left wrist.

"Ali, you're back! You've been gone over half an hour. I was getting worried, thinking that something bad had happened," Sajda said tearfully.

"It's okay. Don't worry. I'm back," Ali reassured his wife as he got back into the bed.

"What's wrong, Ali? It's like you don't want to be with me. You don't want to kiss me. You don't want to make love to me! Do you not like me? What have I done wrong? I just want to do my duty to you as a wife," Sajda cried in distress.

"You have done nothing wrong. It's just me. It's a problem with me. I need to know you before I can get any closer to you. I don't really know anything about you. All I know are

117

details of when you were born, what you do for work, and about your family, but nothing about you as a person," Ali said trying to find a way to make a connection with her.

"When your family came to ask for my hand in marriage, my life changed completely. It suddenly felt as if I finally belonged. I felt special for the first time in my life. I was so proud to have been chosen by you," Sajda said.

"That is nice, but tell me about you," Ali said. "What do you like doing? What are your goals and ambitions?"

"Well," she said, cuddling up closer to Ali for some warmth, "you know about my job. I'm a trainee manager in human resources. I really love working there, and I've made lots of friends, but I don't have to work there if you don't want me to."

"So do you want a career?" Ali asked.

"I would like one, but it doesn't matter if I don't go back. I'm on a week's holiday at the moment, but I won't work if you don't want me to," Sajda said submissively, as if seeking permission to work.

"It's your choice whether you want to work or not. Things are different with our generation. Most Pakistani women your age want to work," Ali said.

"Now that I'm married, I belong to you. It's your decision whether you want me to work or not. I'm happy with whatever you decide. I'm not like all those other Pakistani women who want a career. I know where my place is," Sajda said.

Ali was shocked by her words. He had assumed that Sajda had a modern outlook on life, but she almost mirrored his sister Yasmin in her views. For some reason, Ali had believed her to be very independent-minded, but it was more a picture of her he'd created himself. She had been raised in virtually the same family environment as he, but seemed to have accepted the values around her without question.

"I don't mind you working," Ali said. "It's your choice. I want to support you in everything you want to do. You don't have to ask my permission. So what else do you like? Do you like movies? Theatre?" Ali asked.

"I've never been to the theatre. I go to the cinema once a month with the rest of my family. You have to be careful about what you are seeing though at the cinema because of my nieces and nephews. They make such dirty movies these days, even when they say that they are PG," Sajda said.

"I don't mind movies," Ali said. Sajda's views and attitude seemed to be the same as Yasmin's without knowing it.

"So do you want to have children right away?" Sajda asked. "Or do you think we should wait a few months?"

"I'm not sure. I've not thought about children at all," Ali said, remembering what Steve had said to him. If he had children, Steve would no longer wait for him, but life with Steve already seemed a distant thought.

"I think we should have children straight away," Sajda suggested. "That is what everyone will be expecting from us, and we should have them young, so we can get on with our lives afterwards."

"You're probably right," Ali said, trying not to think about it. Instead, he concentrated on the pain on his wrist.

"We can start tomorrow night, maybe?" Sajda asked.

"Yes, tomorrow night will be good. We will be less tired, so it will be better," Ali agreed half-heartedly, knowing that tomorrow night he would have no excuse and would have to consummate the marriage.

"We will be at my mother's house tomorrow. It will be very special, making love at my parents' house where I grew up. It will be good for you to see where I have lived all my life. I can't wait for tomorrow night," Sajda said excitedly.

"Shall we try to sleep? It's three in the morning," Ali said, looking at the clock on his bedside table.

"You're right. We should sleep. We can't have you tired tomorrow night," Sajda said giggling. "Could you hold me while we sleep?"

Ali put his arms around her and closed his eyes. He felt her breathing gently in his arms. There was no spark or sexual attraction. What was he going to do tomorrow? For anyone else, tonight would have been the best night of their lives, but for Ali it was one of the saddest.

Chapter Eleven

Sleep did not come easily to Ali. He found it uncomfortable lying next to the unfamiliar form of Sajda, and his asthma was persistently getting worse. He tried to control his panicky breathing without using his inhaler in case he awoke her.

At some point, the room had started to get lighter, and he could hear the birds chirping noisily outside. He desperately wanted to escape from the bed and to start to do something active, but he feared it would appear suspicious if he left the bed so early. He felt his wrist. The stinging had gone, but it still felt sore.

Ali looked at his wife lying in the bed beside him. There was a gap of a foot between them. She slept lying on her back, her face pointed toward the ceiling, her breathing regular with her chest moving in rhythm. Ali knew that she had pretended to fall asleep, but eventually all pretence had fallen to one side as real sleep had finally taken her.

Ali could not deny that she was very beautiful, but she held no sexual attraction for him. She was the wrong sex. He noticed that her face was still coated in the makeup from the wedding day, but it still looked surprisingly fresh. Her arms were stretched to her side outside of the duvet, and her heavy gold bangles glinted in the early morning light.

Ali watched her quietly. "I can't kill myself. I could not hurt her like that," he thought unhappily remembering his feelings from the night before. She looked young and vulnerable, and sleep seemed to have washed away the hurt of the wedding night away. Ali felt a strong urge to hold her, but he stopped himself. "What am I going to do?" he thought to himself, feeling confused. "I don't want to make love to her. All I want to do is hold her and make her feel better," but he knew that this would not be enough.

"This is my wife. I'm finally married," he thought again to himself. "I'm gay and I'm married." Feeling his breathing becoming strained, Ali took out his inhaler and hid his face under the duvet before using it quietly, so as not to disturb Sajda, and waited for the medication to take effect.

He pulled his head out from under the cover and glanced at the clock. It was eight in the morning.

Ali contemplated whether he should wake Sajda and ask her if she wanted breakfast but decided against it. Without making a sound, he crept out of the bed. He found his clothes, using the light coming in from the sides of the curtains, and dressed quietly, so he wouldn't awaken her.

Ali went downstairs to the lounge and sat down on the sofa deciding whether he should go to Haseena's. All he wanted was to be hugged by someone whom he felt genuinely cared about him.

He heard some noises in the kitchen next door and went to investigate. It was his mother.

"Sit down and I'll make you some breakfast," she said, glancing at Ali before returning to what she was doing.

"I'm not hungry, Ammi," Ali said, watching her knead the dough for chapattis.

"Was everything fine last night?" she asked. "I heard you go downstairs."

"Everything was fine, Ammi," Ali said reassuring his mother, before returning to the lounge and sitting back down on the sofa again. He considered his options for a few moments. The more he thought about it, the more he wanted to go and see Haseena. It felt like she'd ended the friendship the last time he'd seen her, but he needed her now more than ever.

"I'm off to the cash point to get some money!" Ali announced to his mother through the kitchen door and then rushed out of the house before she could say anything or follow him.

Ten minutes later, Ali was knocking loudly at Haseena's door. Haseena opened the door wearing a nightdress. "Ali, for some reason, I knew it was going to be you. Thanks for waking me up at this time," she said giving him a big hug and letting him into the house. "What are you doing here so early?"

"I just needed to see you," Ali said hugging her again, relieved that she still appeared to be his friend.

"How are you feeling?" Haseena asked, studying his face.

"Terrible. It's horrible. I just want to kill myself," Ali burst out. Haseena tightened her hug, feeling sympathy for what her friend must have been through.

"I don't know what to do. I just don't know what to do," he blubbered through the tears streaming from his eyes and wetting Haseena's nightdress.

"It's okay." she said gently. "It's all right now. Let it all out." Haseena stroked his head as if he were a ten-year-old child. She'd known this was going to happen, but Ali had not wanted to listen to her. The words "I told you so" crept into her mind, but she dismissed them quickly knowing that they were highly inappropriate.

"Do you feel better now?" she asked, when Ali's crying had subsided. He made some whimpering noises, still hugging her tightly. "My nightdress is wet," she said pretending to complain. "Come on, get off me."

"I'm sorry, I know you said things would be different when I got married, but I just didn't know what to do," Ali said, trying to apologize for intruding on Haseena.

"You have nothing to be sorry for. You're my best friend, and I'm here for you whatever happens," she said hugging him again. "So what happened? Did you sleep with her?"

"No, we shared the same bed, that's all," Ali told her. "I'm such a horrible person. I ruined her wedding night."

"Oh Ali, you're not a horrible person. The situation is just horrible. You can still leave. It's still not too late," Haseena advised her friend, hoping that this time he might actually listen.

"I can't, Haseena. She's in love with me. I can't leave her," Ali said.

"She's not the one for you, Ali. You've not consummated the marriage. So it's still not too late," Haseena said.

"I can't, Haseena. I just can't," Ali said.

"Where does your family think you are?" Haseena asked, knowing that she wasn't getting anywhere.

"I've told them that I've gone to the cash point to get some money," Ali replied.

"Well you can't stay here for too long. I don't want to get into trouble with your family," Haseena said.

"I know, I'm sorry," said Ali.

"I'm just worried what they might say if they found out you've come around to mine. It'll just appear strange to them," Haseena said.

"I've told her that I'd sleep with her tonight," Ali said, telling Haseena what was on his mind. "I don't know how I'm going to get out of it. It's too soon. I wanted to get to know her first, but she wouldn't have it."

"I don't know what to tell you, Ali. You're married now and you're going to have to deal with the consequences yourself. I don't know how to help you anymore. The only choice you have is to leave. If you don't, you'll have to go through with it tonight," Haseena said, aware that there was no easy solution for him.

"I know," Ali murmured. "I'm sorry. I shouldn't be burdening you with all of my problems. You're right. I don't have any other options. I'll just have to do it with her tonight."

"It's your decision, Ali, but remember you still have a choice," Haseena said sadly. "You'd better get going, or your family might start looking for you. I know you like my company better than your wife's, but you're a married man now."

"You're right," Ali said. "Thanks for listening to me. I'm sorry for being such a pain."

"You're no trouble at all," Haseena said, giving him a kiss, "I'll see you soon." She waited on the step and waved goodbye to him as he got in his car and drove away.

When Ali got back home, the smell of fried eggs and freshly cooked parathas was hanging in the air, and everyone seemed to have finished eating their breakfast. Sajda was sitting on the sofa in the lounge with his grandmother and seemed to be chatting with her quite pleasantly. She looked up, her face lighting up when she realized that it was Ali who'd entered the room. Ali smiled back at her. He felt awkward standing there, wondering whether to sit next to her or to go to his bedroom.

Luckily, his mother came in from the kitchen to interrupt the awkwardness of the situation. "I was getting worried that something had happened to you," she said sounding concerned. "I thought you said that you were going to the cash point up the road."

"It was out of money, so I had to go to the bank in town," Ali lied.

"I could have given you money. Not to worry though," his mother said. "We need to leave soon for your in-laws. Do you need to eat before we go?"

"I'm not hungry. I'm ready to leave whenever you are," Ali said.

At that moment, Yunus walked into the room. "You're back then," he said hugging Ali warmly. "You should have asked me. I would have given you some money." Ali almost reacted at the false display of generosity, but then noticed that Sajda was watching.

"It was too early. I didn't want to disturb you," Ali said politely.

Yunus leaned up close to him. "You shagged her last night, didn't you?" he whispered.

Ali did not respond, shocked that Yunus would mention such a thing while his wife sat only meters away.

"Well, you don't have to tell me. I know you shagged her. You're a fucking man now. Respect," he said patting Ali on his back.

"It's none of your business. Leave me alone," Ali whispered angrily.

"Zainub, why haven't you taught your children Urdu? All I hear them speak is English," Ali's grandmother said crossly in Urdu. "Do they know nothing about their own language and culture?"

Realizing that this was going to be the start of a long debate, Ali saw an opportunity to escape and took it. "Ammi, let me know when you want to leave. I'll be in my bedroom," he said giving a guilty glance in the direction of his wife before racing up the stairs.

"We're ready," he heard his mother yell after him, but it was over two hours later before anyone was actually ready to leave. Ali had meanwhile taken the time to fill a small suitcase with his clothes for his stay with his in-laws. The suitcase still held remnants from his trip to New York.

Stuck in with his passport were the stubs of his flight ticket. It had been Ali's second trip abroad, the first being to Pakistan. New York was a short getaway just before Steve left for Strasbourg. Ali had already moved back home by that point and had lied to his mother about where he was going. A week's work experience is how Ali had described it to his mother.

Ali ripped the ticket stub into small pieces and hid it in his pocket wondering why he'd forgotten to destroy the evidence of his trip. He zipped up his suitcase, leaving his passport in the side pocket, and carried it to the car, placing it carefully alongside Sajda's case.

"Now that you're married, the seat next to you is for your wife. My place is in the back," Ali's mother said, making the announcement about her change in status, as she got in the back seat of his car with his grandmother.

"Thank you, Ammi," Sajda said smiling happily at her elevated status and sat in the front passenger seat as if she were being given a special place of honor.

The rest of the family, Yasmin, Yunus and Aneesa all came out to wave them off as Ali started the engine and headed along the now familiar route to Nottingham.

"I shall buy you a new car. You need a bigger car now that you're married. A family car would be more suitable, especially as you're going to have children," Ali's mother said, breaking the silence half an hour into the journey.

"I like my car. I don't want to change it," Ali said, upset at his mothers plan for him to start a family.

"It's an additional wedding present to you both," Ali's mother said. "You must allow me to buy it for you."

"Can we discuss it some other time," Ali said not wanting to get drawn into an argument in front of his wife.

"Of course," Ali's mother said, sitting back in her seat smiling, knowing that she'd get her own way in the end especially now that she had Sajda as an ally.

The rest of the car journey passed in silence. At times, Ali thought of saying something just to end the silence, but he felt too traumatized to do so. It was as if he were disassociated from everything that was happening around him, like going through the motions, but no longer being actively involved.

The smell from his mother's Arabian perfume smothered him, making him feel claustrophobic. He wound down the car window to get some fresh air. As he did so, his wife dropped something in his lap. It was a folded up piece of paper.

Taking one hand off the steering wheel, Ali picked up the paper and unfolded it. "My darling Ali, I can't wait for tonight when you'll finally make me a woman. Yours forever, love Sajda" was scrawled on the paper in black ink. Ali felt a sinking feeling at the pit of his stomach. "What am I going to do tonight?" he thought. Knowing that he needed to respond in some way, he turned to look at his wife and smiled, trying his best to hide his anxiety. She gave him a longing gaze in return.

Ali checked in the rear view mirror to see whether his mother or grandmother had noticed anything, but they were too busy whispering to each other secretly.

Sajda's entire family was waiting outside to greet them when Ali drove into the driveway of her parents' home. He parked the car on the drive and stepped out.

"Welcome, my son," his father-in-law cried excitedly, placing a garland around Ali's neck and embracing him. He then sidled up to Ali's mother and grandmother and did the same.

"This is a very happy day for all of us, Zainub," he said to Ali's mother. "Our two families are now joined. We are so blessed."

"We are very blessed," Ali's mother agreed.

"Welcome back, Sajda. We've all missed you so much," Ali's father-in-law said giving Sajda an embrace as if they'd been parted for several weeks rather than just one night.

She in return gave her father a timid smile before her mother pounced on her and gave her several kisses all over her face. As her mother turned her attention to Ali to greet him in the same manner, Sajda returned to stand submissively behind Ali.

"Come into the house and let's sweeten our mouths," Ali's mother-in-law said to everyone after she'd finished giving him several kisses, leaving his face sore.

They all followed her and sat down around the coffee table which had been neatly laid out with fresh samosas and drinks. Ali hadn't eaten since the wedding day and feeling ravenous grabbed one of the samosas and ate it hungrily.

His grandmother meanwhile picked up several samosas and deliberately bit a chunk out of each one before returning them one after the other to the tray.

Several conversations had already started. Ali's mother was in deep discussion with his father-in-law, while his mother-in-law was trying in vain to engage his grandmother in conversation. Sajda had disappeared to another room with her sisters, and he could hear their giggling from the next room. Ali felt invisible. It was as if he'd fulfilled his obligation and was no longer necessary.

"I'm going to town to pick up a few things," he said in his mother's general direction.

"I'll tell Sajda that you want to take her to town. It won't take her long to get ready," his mother-in-law said, hearing but misunderstanding his intention.

"No, don't disturb her. She seems busy with her sisters. I just need to get a couple of things and have a look around the shops. She'll probably get bored. I'll take her out some other time," Ali said, not wanting to take his wife along.

"You're such a thoughtful man," his mother-in-law said. "I'll be cooking a dinner for everyone at six. So get back by then."

"Don't worry, I'll be back in plenty of time," Ali said. He gave a guilty look in his mother's direction before hurrying out, knowing she would have wanted him to remain at his in-laws' house. No doubt she would mention it later.

Ali got in his car and started the engine. He couldn't remember the way to the city center, so he drove randomly but was lucky enough to come to a road sign directing him to the Broadmarsh Shopping Center. It wasn't long before Ali was parking his car at the center's multi-storey car park.

He explored the town center looking around the shops. It was a clone town, with identical shops to those in Birmingham. He wandered around aimlessly looking in the shop windows and going into the clothes shops, it helped clear his mind.

He caught his own reflection several times looking back at him from a shop window and couldn't believe how unhappy and withdrawn he looked. How could anyone believe that he was actually happy? He wondered what the other shoppers made of his miserable façade, but they were oblivious to him. He was just another face in the crowd with problems.

Ali picked up a copy of a new Bollywood CD, and decided to post it to Steve when he got a chance. He paid by credit card, knowing that he was close to his limit, and worrying that the transaction would be refused. He breathed a sigh of relief when he was asked to sign the credit card receipt, and left the store smiling, clutching his purchase in his hands.

It was five o'clock and getting dark already. He knew he should go back. Very reluctantly, with a heavy feeling in his stomach, Ali made his way to the multi-level car park and located his car and sat in it for a few minutes without moving. Eventually, he paid the parking fee and left the car park driving slowly in the busy traffic back to his in-laws and his wife.

He felt a sudden urge to eat, more out of comfort then out of hunger. Spotting a small newsagents, he parked his car and bought himself two eight bar multi-packs of Kit Kat before continuing his drive, munching on the chocolate as he drove.

The house was still twinkling brightly with the fairy lights when Ali parked his car opposite. The house gave off a warm and welcoming aura that seemed like an invitation to join the family, but this wasn't what he wanted. The depth of his unhappiness almost seemed to overwhelm him as he sat in his car watching the shadows behind the net curtains. "What am I going to do?" he thought to himself for what seemed like the hundredth time.

He took out the new Bollywood disc from its cellophane wrapper and put it into his car's CD player. He then started to munch on the chocolate bars. It was when he fumbled for another bar and couldn't find one that he realized he'd eaten all sixteen. They still hadn't filled the deep routed emptiness inside him.

He needed to talk to someone who understood him, someone who had the knack to make him feel better. Haseena. But he had already been to see her too many times. What if he drove her away with his constant inability to do anything positive about his situation?

Throwing his insecurities aside, Ali started his car and went looking for a phone box to call Haseena. He eventually found one on a main road not far from the house. Getting some change out from his wallet, he got out of the car to make the phone call.

He dialed Haseena's number hoping she was in and that she'd pick up. "Hello, Haseena," he said trying to sound cheerful and happy when she answered the call.

"You seem very happy, Ali, which means you're not!" she said seeing through his façade.

"Honestly, I'm happy," Ali said, not sure whether he wanted to admit to her how he felt in case he drove her away. He just wanted to hear her voice and to feel comforted.

"Bullshit! You wouldn't be ringing me if you weren't upset," she said. "You're not okay. You don't sound fine at all. You sound like you're still in shock," Haseena said.

"I don't want to burden you with my problems all the time," Ali replied. "I just wanted to talk to you about normal stuff. "

"Ali, you're not burdening me at all. I'm your friend. You don't have to hide how you're feeling from me," Haseena said, trying to reassure him.

"I know. I'm sorry. I just feel so down in the dumps right now. I wanted to talk about other stuff. Something that would get my mind off my problems," Ali said, finally admitting that he was depressed.

"Well, why don't you leave? It's not too late," Haseena advised.

"We've discussed this. I can't. I'm not running away. I've made my decision. I'm staying. I'll be fine," Ali said.

"I'm worried that you might do something stupid if you stay. I've never seen you this depressed before. I'm so worried about you," Haseena said, hearing the melancholy in his voice.

"Don't worry, I won't do anything stupid. I'm too much of a coward for that," Ali said.

"You're not a coward. You're the bravest person I know. You've put aside your own personal happiness for your mother's sake. I don't know anyone else who'd do that," Haseena said.

"Well, I don't feel that brave. All I want to do is to kill myself, and I'm too much of a coward to do it," Ali said, his words slipping out before he had a chance to stop them.

"Don't talk nonsense, Ali! Don't you dare do anything stupid like that," Haseena warned.

"I wouldn't. I'm only joking. Honestly. I'll talk to you later when I'm feeling more positive," Ali said wanting to get out of the phone box for some fresh air.

"No! I want to talk to you for a bit longer," Haseena said worrying about Ali's state of mind, knowing that right now she was too far away to be effectual.

"I'm all right, Haseena. I'll talk to you later," Ali said.

"No wait, Ali, listen to me," Haseena said, but it was too late. He'd already put the phone down.

Ali got out of the phone box, feeling overwrought. His head seemed to be in a spin. The calm that he'd found earlier while shopping had evaporated. The reality of going back to his in-laws hit him hard. Tonight, he would have to consummate his marriage and then there was no going back.

He got into his car and started the engine. Glancing at the clock on the dashboard, he noticed that there was only an hour left until dinner was to be served. Ali put the car stereo on and turned the volume high before sitting back to drive.

It wasn't long before Ali looked at the clock on his dashboard again. He then did a double take in shock. Somehow an hour had gone by since he'd started driving. Looking out of the windscreen and taking note of his surrounding for what seemed like the first time, Ali was horrified to find that he was back in Birmingham. He'd driven all the way back to Birmingham!

"Oh my God! What am I going to do?" he thought to himself in panic. "How could this happen? What's happening to me?" He parked his car, took out his inhaler and took a few puffs of it. His head was spinning, and he felt very dizzy as if he was about to be sick.

"I've run away!" he thought in realization. He counted to ten before taking some more deep breaths to calm himself and managed to stop himself from hyperventilating. He started his car again, knowing that the only safe place to go was Haseena's.

"I've run away," he thought again to himself. "What will my family say when they find out?" That's when he started to feel really scared.

When he got to Haseena's house, Ali considered parking his car outside, but feeling worried that his family might come

Amjeed Kabil

looking for him, he drove his car half a mile away and parked it on a secluded street.

He walked back to Haseena's and knocked on her front door, which she opened swiftly.

"Ali!" Haseena exclaimed in surprise. "What are you doing here? I thought you were in Nottingham with your wife," she said sounding baffled as she ushered Ali into the house.

"I've run away," Ali said calmly trying not to shake.

"What?" Haseena exclaimed. "When we last spoke, you said you'd made your decision."

"I know. I just don't know what happened. One minute I was driving back to my in-laws, and the next minute I look up and one hour's gone by, and I'm in Birmingham. I don't even remember driving back. I don't know what's happening to me!" Ali said, unable to recall anything about his journey, worried for his own sanity.

"It must have been a subconscious thing. Deep down, you must have known that you had to get away, and your mind reacted," Haseena said, finding an explanation.

"What am I going to do? I didn't plan to run away," Ali said, starting to shake suddenly.

"Sit down, Ali," Haseena said, guiding Ali to the sofa. "I'll make you a cup of tea. It's okay. You're just in shock." She looked down at the shaking figure of her friend, surprised by the sudden turn of events.

Ali's face seemed drained of all color. "I've got to go back. I can't stay here," he said still shivering.

"Ali, you've come this far. You've left now. Be brave. There'll be consequences, but I'll be here to help you to deal with them. You're not alone," Haseena said, trying to encourage him to remain strong.

"My wife's suitcase is in the car. I have to take it back," Ali said.

"Leave it. We'll sort the suitcase out later. Let me make you a cup of spicy Indian tea to calm your nerves," Haseena said.

"Okay," Ali agreed. He shivered again despite the fact he was sitting in front of Haseena's gas fire.

Haseena rushed to the kitchen to make Ali a cup of tea. She knew it was going to be a long night.

132

Chapter Twelve

They heard the noise of angry voices outside Haseena's front door and then there was a loud knock. "Quick, get up the stairs. Don't make a sound," Haseena whispered to Ali urgently. "I'll check to see who it is. It might be your family."

Ali began to race up the stairs, but stopped halfway when he heard Haseena scream, "How dare you barge your way into my house!" Ali didn't try to go any further up the stairs, worried that he might be heard. Instead, he perched himself on a step, trying hard not to shake like a leaf, and attempted to listen to what was happening in Haseena's lounge.

"How dare you come into my house without being invited! Who do you think you are?" Ali heard Haseena say.

"What are you going to do about it, you stupid bitch?" he heard Yasmin's familiar voice reply. "What have you been saying to my brother to turn him against his own family? How dare you persuade him to run away?"

"I don't know what you're on about. I've done nothing of the sort. I haven't seen him for days," Haseena exclaimed pretending to be surprised by the news.

"It's your influence that's caused all of this. Don't think we don't know. You and your fucked up ideas! Who the bloody hell do you think you are? We're his family. He should listen to us, not you," Yasmin raged. "I know he's here. I know he's come running to you with lies about us."

"I don't know what you're accusing me of. I thought you married him off, yesterday," Haseena said, still denying all knowledge of Ali's getaway.

"You know exactly what I'm talking about, you evil bitch! He's run away, leaving his poor wife behind. You must have told him to. You're the one who fills his head with stupid shit. He was fine until he met you, but then he became a stranger to his own family," Yasmin yelled accusingly.

"My fucked up ideas? I have nothing to do with this. You only have yourselves to blame. You all forced him into a marriage knowing that he's gay. You should have left him to lead his own life. What did you expect?" You have to take responsibility for what's happened, not go blaming other people," Haseena shouted back.

"Don't you dare insult my brother. He's not gay! He knows what we think of gays. They should all be put on an island and shot. He just suffered a lot of stress with university, thought he liked men, and you've just encouraged him to believe he's gay!" Yasmin insisted.

"He's gay, your whole family knows it, and you've all been trying to cover it up ever since you found out," Haseena responded. "I've never heard of stress turning anyone gay. You're born that way."

"Listen bitch, what do you know? You haven't got a clue about your own culture. You've married a white man, as you can't have children and still have the nerve to go around calling my brother gay," Yasmin shouted. "Don't you realize Ali was meant to be our route into the Nottingham community. He was to open doors for us, and we want him back."

"How can you expect me to know where he is? I only hope he's safe and not about to do anything stupid because of what you've forced him into," Haseena said, trying to sound convincing. She knew that if Yasmin found Ali on the stairs in his fragile state she wouldn't be able to stop her from persuading him to return to his wife.

"I know you've got something to do with this," Yasmin said. "My mother's worried about him. His wife is crying at home because he's not returned from his shopping trip. If you had an ounce of decency about you then you'd tell me where he is," Yasmin pleaded.

"I've told you. I don't know where he is," Haseena said.

"You're lying. You're hiding him," Yasmin screamed.

There was a scuffle and the door leading to the staircase suddenly jolted open, startling Ali, but then shut just as suddenly.

"How dare you! Get out of my house!" he heard Haseena yell. Yasmin's attempt to get upstairs to search for Ali had been thwarted by Haseena.

"I'm not leaving until you let me check your bedrooms. I know you've got him hiding up there," Yasmin shouted.

"I've had enough. Get out, or I'll call the police," Haseena threatened.

"I'm not leaving without my brother," Yasmin replied.

"Your brother isn't here. If you don't leave now, I'll call the police," Hasena warned. Ali heard her pick up the phone.

"Okay, I'm leaving, but I know he's here, and when he comes out we'll be waiting. You won't be able to hide him forever. When Yunus gets back from work, I'll make sure that he pays you a visit," Yasmin said.

"Are you threatening me?" Haseena asked angrily. "I should warn you that Derek will be back soon, and he doesn't like anyone threatening me."

"Well, pass on a message to my dear brother," Ali heard Yasmin say loudly, as if making sure that anyone hiding in the house would hear her clearly. "Tell him we all love him very much and that he has responsibilities to his wife who is heart broken. Tell him that we will do everything in our power to get him back."

"Tell him yourself when you see him. I'm not your slave," Haseena said crossly, knowing that Ali had heard every word that had been said in the room.

There was a loud bang as the front door banged shut and then a hush descended in the house.

When Haseena opened the door leading to the staircase she found Ali hunched on the stairs, shivering as if he was in a state of shock. "It's going to be okay," she said hugging him. "If she had gone up the stairs, I would have called the police. I wouldn't have let her take you away."

"I'm really sorry, Haseena. I didn't mean to drag you into this. I'd better go back. I don't want to cause you any more problems," Ali said, sounding helpless.

"You're not going back, Ali. I'm your best friend, and I'm here for you no matter what," Haseena said.

"Thank you," Ali said, sounding relieved.

"I'm your friend, and this is what friends do," Haseena said, brushing his hair gently with her hand. "I'll go and draw the curtains in the lounge. Then I'll call you."

Haseena went back down the stairs and into the lounge. She peered discretely out of the gap in the curtains to see if anyone was outside and noticed a taxi parked on the street corner. She waited a few minutes to see whom it was waiting for, but no one appeared. She suspected that it was someone keeping a watch on the house.

"I hope Derek gets back soon," she thought worriedly. He was on call tonight and had been called out on a plumbing job just before Ali had arrived.

"Come down, Ali, it's okay," Haseena shouted after she'd finished drawing the curtains. Ali's disheveled form appeared in the doorway to the lounge. He paced the room nervously for a few moments before sitting on the sofa next to Haseena.

"I'm really sorry about what Yasmin said about you. I know she didn't mean it. She was upset," Ali said, ashamed at his sister's behavior.

"Don't worry, Ali. I know what people say about me. They're so narrow minded that they think I only married Derek because I couldn't find a Pakistani husband as I couldn't have children. I've heard all that crap before, so please don't worry," Haseena said.

"I'm sorry," Ali said, apologizing again.

"Stop worrying about me, Ali. Let's sort somewhere out for you to go. The last thing I want is Yunus barging his way in here and finding you," Haseena said. "Oh, I've just thought about something. Where have you parked your car?"

"It's really quite far. I parked it on George Street," Ali said.

"That's good. Your family won't find it there. Now what are we going to do with you?" she asked herself out loud.

"I don't know. I didn't plan to leave," Ali said feeling lost. "I don't know how I'm going to sort myself out."

"Well, you'll have to leave the country for a while. They'll find you if you stay in Birmingham. Why don't you visit Steve in France while all the fuss dies down," Haseena suggested.

"I'm not sure," said Ali. "I can't dump myself on him. He's busy with his studies. He won't want me there. I have to sort this out myself."

"You're in no fit state to sort this out yourself, Ali. Steve loves you and will be there to support you. You can't go through this without him," Haseena said. "What are you afraid of?"

"I don't know. Well, what if he doesn't want me there?" Ali said.

"Of course, he'll want you there. You're just feeling insecure right now. Give him a call and tell him that you're going over," Haseena said.

"I'm not sure. I don't want to be a burden on him," Ali said.

"Phone him, Ali. See what he says and don't just rely on what you think he might say. Take the phone upstairs and call him," she said, picking up her cordless phone and handing it to Ali.

"I can't use your phone, Haseena. It's expensive to call France," Ali said.

"I can afford it. Go on. Call him," Haseena replied.

Ali took the phone from Haseena, went up the stairs and sat on the landing. He pulled out the antenna from the phone, dialed Steve's number and waited for the ringing tone. It rang for a few seconds and to Ali's relief was picked up by the receptionist at Steve's hall of residence. He gave her instructions in French to put him though to Steve's room.

He just didn't know what Steve's reaction to his news would be, and he couldn't help but feel insecure.

The phone rang several times before being picked up. "Fabien?" Steve's voice asked.

"Steve, it's me, Ali. Who's Fabien?" Ali asked jealously, taken aback.

"Oh, how are you, Ali? I'm so glad you've rung. Fabien's a friend I've made here," Steve said.

"I know the names of all your friends, and you've never mentioned him before," Ali said suspiciously.

"I met him at a party yesterday. So how was the wedding?" Steve asked, changing the subject quickly.

"I have to tell you something," Ali said.

"What is it?" Steve asked.

"I've left home," Ali said.

There was a long silence at the other end of the phone. "What?" Steve asked eventually in disbelief.

"I've left home," Ali repeated again. "I've run away."

"That's wonderful," Steve said, after the news slowly sank in. "What happened?"

"I don't know. It was all very sudden. I just got up and left," Ali said.

"So what are your plans? What are you going to do now?" Steve asked.

"I need to get away from Birmingham. I thought I could come over and visit you in Strasbourg while it all blows over," Ali said haltingly.

"I don't know if that's possible. I'm really busy with my studies right now. I don't really want any disruptions," Steve said.

"I won't disrupt your studies. I just need somewhere to stay while I sort myself out," Ali said, trying not to show the hurt in his voice.

"Ali, I don't know if it's going to be possible. I'm in university accommodation, and they don't allow guests to stay overnight," Steve said worriedly.

"I don't know what else to do, Steve. You're the only person that can help me. I can't stay here. My family has already been to Haseena's looking for me. They'll find me if I don't go somewhere far away," Ali said.

"Okay, Ali, Okay! I guess I'm going to have to sort something out for you," Steve said grudgingly. "Have you got any money?"

"No, not much," Ali replied.

"How come, Ali? If you're coming to France you'll need some money," Steve said.

"I didn't expect to run away. If I'd done it consciously, I would have planned it a lot better. It just happened," Ali said, bewildered by the lack of support from Steve.

"What are you going to do for money when you get here, then?" Steve asked.

"I'll get a job," Ali answered.

"You hardly know any French, and you think you'll get a job?" Steve exclaimed.

"I'll find something. I can do something manual," Ali replied.

"Well, if you really have to, then I guess you can come and visit me," Steve said finally. "Give me a call and let me know your flight details when you have them."

"Thanks, Steve," Ali said feeling relieved.

"I'll speak to you soon," Steve said and hung up the phone before Ali had the chance to say anything else.

Ali got up from where he was sitting feeling worried. "Maybe he's met someone else," he thought, after considering Steve's apparent reluctance for him to visit.

The telephone rang in Ali's hands just as he started to walk down the stairs. Ali answered it immediately.

"Don't forget to bring your credit card with you," Steve said.

"I won't," Ali said, surprised at Steve's instruction. Steve then promptly hung up the phone leaving Ali shocked by this sudden request.

"How did it go?" Haseena asked him as he walked back into the lounge.

"I'm not sure if he wants me there," Ali said, trying not to sound upset. "He even called me back to tell me to bring my credit card with me."

"You know Steve's very practical about money," Haseena said.

"I know, but this was very different," Ali said.

"Ali, you finished with him a few weeks ago to get married, and then you call him up out of the blue to tell him that you're running away to be with him. He just needs time to get used to it. Be patient with him," Haseena advised.

"He seemed different. He didn't say he loved me. He always says 'I love you' at the end of our telephone conversations, but he didn't today," Ali said worriedly.

"Steve loves you, and if you're worried that he doesn't, then the only way to find out is to fly out there and see him," Haseena said.

"I know you're right," Ali agreed.

"I've just thought," Haseena said suddenly. "Have you got your passport with you?"

"Yes, I think so. I'm sure I left it in the suitcase. I can't remember taking it out when I packed to go to Nottingham," Ali said, sounding uncertain.

"Not to worry. I'll go and check your suitcase later," Haseena said. She pondered to herself for a few moments. "Ali, I don't think it'll be safe for you to stay here tonight in case Yunus decides to pay a visit."

"I don't have anywhere else to go. What am I going to do?" Ali said sounding immediately distressed again.

"I have a friend who might be able to put you up for the night. She owes me a few favors. I'll give her a call and ask her," Haseena said. "Then, as soon as Derek gets back, we'll make a move."

"Thank you, Haseena," Ali said gratefully. "I don't know where I would be without you."

"I'm sure you'd be fine," Haseena said. "Why don't you lie down for a bit on the sofa and have a rest while I go upstairs and make that telephone call. Tonight is going to be a long night, so you will need all the rest you can get."

"Okay," Ali said, as Haseena left the room, shutting the door behind her. Ali took off his shoes and lay back on the sofa. The leather felt sticky against his face as he rested his head against it and shut his eyes. He knew Haseena was right. It was definitely going to be a very long night.

Chapter Thirteen

"Wake up!" Ali heard someone say. "Ali!" the voice repeated sharply. Ali was jolted quickly from his dreamless sleep and opened his eyes to find Haseena towering over him. He tried to get up off the sofa but felt too weak and slumped back. The sweat on his face had attached his cheek to Haseena's leather sofa, and it made a sound when he eventually peeled his face off it and sat up.

"I'm sorry, but I had to wake you up," Haseena said. "I phoned my friends Anne and Mick, and they've agreed to look after you tonight." She went over to the window and peered out through the side of her curtains.

"The taxi's still waiting on the corner of the street. It's not moved since I checked last," Haseena said, whispering. "I've sent Derek out to see how safe it is for us to leave."

Feeling upset, Ali rocked gently on the sofa trying to comfort himself. He attempted not to cry and just about managed to succeed.

"It'll be okay, Ali. They won't get you," Haseena said, coming over to Ali and giving him a hug. "You're my closest friend, and I'll make sure nothing bad happens to you."

The door to the lounge opened, startling both Ali and Haseena. It was Derek.

"Hello. I see you're finally awake," Derek said, greeting Ali. "It's good to see you again. I can't remember when I saw you last." Derek was still dressed in his overalls. He was a tall imposing man with a shaved head and a stocky build.

"It's good to see you, too," Ali said, smiling shyly as Derek took his hand and shook it vigorously.

"The house is definitely being watched. There's a taxi on the corner of the street and another one further up the street," Derek informed them both.

"So what are we going to do about getting Ali out of the house without being seen?" Haseena asked.

"I have an idea," Derek said with a big smirk on his face. He raced up the stairs, pounding the steps with his big boots as he went. Ali and Haseena heard the sound of wardrobe doors being flung open and then the noise from his boots as he came back down the stairs.

"I've found a disguise for you to wear," Derek said coming back into the room with several items in his hands. "Here, put these on." He handed Ali a large Afro wig, a baseball cap and a beige trench coat.

"Clever idea," Haseena exclaimed, kissing Derek on his cheek lovingly.

"They'll know it's me," Ali said, feeling unhappy at the thought of wearing such a ridiculous disguise.

"Put it on, Ali, and let's see how you look," Derek said. "It's not meant to be a proper disguise, just something that'll make them doubt it's you."

"Okay," Ali grudgingly agreed. He put the wig on with Haseena's help and then pushed the baseball cap down onto the wig. He then tried on the trench coat, which was far too big for him. The bottom of it even touched the floor. Ali turned round to face Derek who immediately burst out laughing.

"I look stupid," Ali said. "It's never going to work." He went and peered at his reflection in the mirror above the mantle piece and found himself laughing at the absurd disguise. "I look like Krusty the Clown!"

"That's the first time I've heard you laugh in weeks, Ali," Haseena said smiling. "If it doesn't work, at least it's made you laugh."

"Let's go for that drive then. You will walk with Ali, Haseena. Hold his hand, walk him to the back seat of the car and then get in the front passenger seat. Ali, when you walk make sure you keep your head down to the ground and walk fast. When you're both in the car remember to lock the doors behind you. It doesn't have central locking," Derek instructed militarily. "Right, let's go."

Derek opened the front door and stepped outside. Haseena gave Ali a quick kiss for comfort and followed Derek out holding Ali's hand tightly. She tried not to look at him again in case she laughed at his disguise and shut the house door behind her before locking it.

Ali kept his head stooped and followed Haseena. The wig was uncomfortable and made his head itch. They walked past the taxi to Derek's car, which was parked right behind. Ali expected someone to spot them but was surprised that they were not noticed. Haseena opened the door for him and shoved him into the back seat.

"Lock the door," she whispered to him and got into the front passenger seat.

Suddenly, there was pandemonium. The door of the taxi was flung open, and a fat Pakistani man came racing out of it. They could hear him shouting incoherently at them before lurching at Derek's car with a baseball bat.

"Start the car Derek! Start the car!" Haseena screamed in panic as the man battered the baseball bat against the windscreen.

"Bastard! Bastard!" Derek shouted as he started the car up quickly. He reversed it and then drove out avoiding the man narrowly as he came hurtling back at the car with the baseball bat raised.

"They're going to get me," Ali yelled in fear. "I don't want to go back."

"It's okay, Ali. Calm down. They won't get you," Haseena said reassuringly.

"The bastard's cracked my windscreen," Derek muttered angrily. "I've a good mind to get out and give him a good hiding."

Ali watched from the car as the man got back into his taxi and raced after them. The other taxi that had been waiting joined it in pursuit.

"What are we going to do, Derek?" Haseena asked, trying to hide her dismay from Ali.

"Let's take them for a long drive. What do you think? Through the back streets of the Jewelry Quarter first, then Aston, then down to the Spaghetti Junction. If we manage to lose them by then, we can head back to Anne and Mick's in Newtown," Derek said.

Ali sat back in the car feeling relieved that Derek had a plan. He was shocked by the brutal attack on Derek's car. It had been so close. How far was his family willing to go to get him back?

Derek drove the car speedily out from the estate and onto Ladywood Middleway, the dual carriageway that split the estate into two. The two taxis followed in pursuit. Derek headed for the Jewelry Quarter trying to lose them in the badly lit back streets, but they continued to keep pace.

"You need to do something to lose them, otherwise we'll be driving around forever, and I don't think my nerves can take it," Haseena warned.

"You got any ideas?" Derek asked.

"Yes, go out of the Jewelry Quarter and over into Aston. There are some speed bumps there, so that should slow them down," Haseena said.

"I'm onto it," Derek said crossing over the traffic lights at the junction, leading out of the Jewelry Quarter and into Aston.

"When I give you the signal, turn quickly into the next street," Haseena instructed. "Now!" she yelled a couple of seconds later.

Derek immediately swerved his car. Its wheels made a squealing noise as he turned the steering wheel suddenly, driving the car into the narrow side street. "Quickly turn in between those two trees and switch the lights and engine off," she instructed pointing to a pair of trees masking the entrance to a small industrial unit.

Derek followed her instructions and entered the small driveway leading to the industrial unit. He then turned the headlights and the engine off and sat back in his seat.

They all waited patiently for the taxis to arrive, and it wasn't long before the first taxi flashed past in its hunt for Derek's car. Moments later, the second one went by, too. Ali sighed in relief.

"That was very close," Derek said mirroring Ali's own thoughts. He counted five minutes on his watch as they all sat silently in the car. He then started up the car and raced out from the small driveway and back along the route they'd previously taken. He kept checking the mirror to see if they were being followed, but it seemed that Haseena's plan had worked.

"I think it's safe for us to take you to Anne and Mick's," he said, sounding relieved.

"Can I take my disguise off now?" Ali said remembering how ridiculous he still looked.

Haseena looked back at him from her seat and laughed. "No keep it on. It suits you."

Ali took the Afro wig off, flung it at her, and joined her in hysterical laughter.

"We're here," said Derek interrupting their laughter. Ali looked out of the car window to see that they were parked in a car park of a large tower block.

"You wait in the car, Derek. I'll just go up quickly with Ali," Haseena said giving Derek a kiss before opening the car door and getting out.

"Thank you," Ali said gratefully.

"That's okay, lad. I'm just glad I can help," Derek said gruffly. "I'll see you tomorrow."

Ali got out of the car and followed Haseena to the tower block entrance. She pushed the button on the buzzer to one of the flats. "It's Haseena," she yelled loudly into the intercom system, but there was no response. The intercom looked broken, and this was confirmed when Haseena tried opening the security doors to the building to find that they were already wedged open.

Ali followed Haseena into the building and recoiled immediately at the smell of urine that greeted them as they entered the lobby. The walls were covered in graffiti, and broken lights dangled from the ceiling.

"I used to live in this very block when I first arrived in Birmingham. It seems to have gone down hill since then, though," Haseena commented.

They went to the lift and got inside, pressing the button for the fourteenth floor. Haseena knew from Ali's silence that he was shocked by the state of the place. Ali had led a somewhat sheltered existence in her eyes and had probably never been inside a council tower block before. She wondered what he thought of the smell of excrement in the lift as it hurtled shakily to the fourteenth floor.

The lift jerked noisily to a halt, and the doors opened, allowing Ali to follow after Haseena.

"It's not the best tower block to live in, so they've added their own security," Haseena explained as they reached the flat. She reached a hand through the black iron bars of a large security gate that had been added to the front of the doorframe and rang the doorbell. It chimed to the theme of *Star Trek* noisily.

145

"That reminds me. Mick's a *Star Trek* fan, so just pretend you like the bloody stuff," Haseena advised him.

A very gaunt and pale looking man opened the door. He beamed happily through his thick spectacles upon seeing Haseena. "Come in, Haseena" he said, embracing her happily.

"Derek's waiting for me in the car, so I can't come in," Haseena said apologetically.

"No problem," Mick said. "Say hi to Derek from me and remind him that we need to arrange the tickets to the record fair in Grimsby soon."

"I'll let him know," Haseena said. "This is my friend Ali by the way."

"Ah, Ali, so pleased to meet you," Mick said, shaking Ali's hand vigorously.

"Don't forget that I need your car keys, Ali," Haseena said reminding him.

Ali fumbled in his pockets worrying that he might have dropped them somewhere, but was relieved to find his keys in the pocket of his jeans and handed them to Haseena.

"I'll double check your suitcase for your passport, and I'll try to get someone to drop off your wife's suitcase with your family," Haseena said sorting out the things that were niggling Ali. "I'll see you in the morning." She gave him a kiss and hurried off.

"Come in and sit down," Mick said inviting Ali into the flat.

The lounge was in surprising contrast to what lay outside. It resembled a penthouse suite. It was immaculately painted in shades of white and had wooden floors throughout. The walls had various original pieces of art on display illuminated with special halogen lighting. These were suddenly disrupted by one wall that was covered with plaques and photographs from *Star Trek*.

"Do you like the artwork?" Mick asked, noticing Ali's appreciative gaze at the paintings. "It's all original."

"It's really nice," Ali said, admiring an oil painting of a figure trapped in the middle of a pirouette. "They must be very expensive."

"Not really. It's all Anne's own work," Mick told him. "She's an artist. She's even had some of her paintings displayed in a London gallery recently."

"Wow," said Ali sounding impressed.

"She's been having a difficult time with the pregnancy, so she hasn't painted for a few months," Mick said, opening a door at the far end of the lounge that led into a sumptuous bedroom.

A four-poster bed draped in lilac stood in the center of the room. A large, black pregnant woman lay in the center of the bed, surrounded by numerous scatter cushions. Mick went over and sat next to her on the bed and held her hand lovingly.

"It's good to see you, Ali. How are you bearing up?" Anne asked, her voice sounding tired.

"I'm fine," Ali said. Anne's sympathetic and caring voice nearly threatened to bring tears of self-pity and anguish to his eyes again, but Ali bit them back. He felt embarrassed and hoped that she hadn't noticed.

"That's good to hear. It must be a terrible time for you. I'm just glad that Mick and I could help you out," Anne said kindly. "You're free to stay here for as long as you need to."

"Thank you so much," Ali said gratefully.

"It's nothing," Anne said, her eyes flickering tiredly.

"I'll get Ali sorted out for the night, and then I'll come to bed," Mick said to his exhausted wife.

"Nice meeting you, Ali," she said tiredly before closing her eyes to sleep.

"I'll get the sofa ready for you," Mick said taking Ali back to the lounge and shutting the door quietly behind him. He pulled the coffee table that was in front of the beige sofa out of the way. "It turns into a bed," he demonstrated before pushing down the back of the sofa and unfolding it into a small bed.

"It's perfect," Ali said.

"I'll grab some bedding for you to use," Mick said as he left the room. He returned loaded with a duvet and pillows. "Here, I'll leave you to put these on the sofa," he said handing them to Ali.

"Thanks, Mick," said Ali.

"I'll say good night to you. It would have been nice to chat into the early hours, but with Anne not being well I can't," said Mick worriedly.

"I understand. Don't worry," Ali said.

"I'll see you in the morning. If you get peckish help yourself to any of the food in the kitchen, and if you can't sleep there are some videos on the bookshelf that you can watch," he said, heading for the bedroom.

"Goodnight," Ali called after him.

Ali made the bed, turned the light off and got in under the duvet covers without changing out of his clothes.

The sofa turned out to be very uncomfortable with the springs digging into Ali's back. The heating was turned off, too, which made the flat very cold. Ali felt glad that he'd left his clothes on although he still felt cold despite the layers. Ali found it hard to settle down to sleep. He could make out large unfamiliar shadows in the room as his eyes adjusted to the darkness.

"I can't live like this," he thought miserably, staring into the darkness. "I don't want to end up like this, living in a council flat alone. I should go back. I can tell them I had a breakdown." Ali shook himself, trying to jolt himself out of the comforting thoughts of returning home. "No, I've got to carry on. It will get better."

"It will get better," he muttered again to himself before closing his eyes.

The room was bathed in sunlight when Ali opened his eyes again. It took a few seconds for him to realize that he'd been asleep. Ali struggled to sit up, but his body ached from sleeping on the cramped sofa bed. When he finally did manage to sit up, he noticed some movement from the corner of his eye. It was Mick.

"You're finally awake," he remarked. "I was about to wake you. Haseena phoned about five minutes ago to say she's on her way. Do you want some breakfast before she gets here? I'm just about to cook something for Anne."

"No, I'm not hungry right now," Ali said, unable to face eating anything. "Is it okay if I get freshened up?"

"Yes, go ahead. You know where the bathroom is. I've put a towel out for you," said Mick.

In the bathroom Ali got undressed and jumped into the shower. He turned it on and then retreated in shock as a spray of cold water hit him. He waited a few moments and then got back under the water, which was now warm. He lathered himself with shower gel, luxuriating in the feel of the warm water against his skin.

He got out of the shower, turned it off and dried himself on the towel that had been left out for him. As he didn't have anything else to wear, he got dressed in the same clothes as he'd been sleeping in.

Haseena was already standing in the lounge talking to Mick when Ali came out of the bathroom. "What took you so long?" she asked. "You've got a flight to catch," she said, not bothering to greet him.

"To Strasbourg?" Ali asked.

"Of course, it's to Strasbourg. Where else would you be escaping to? Are you ready?" she asked hurriedly.

"Yes, I'm ready," Ali replied.

"Well we'd better leave, then," said Haseena. "Thanks for putting Ali up for the night. Can you say goodbye to Anne for me. Tell her I'll pop round next week to see how she is."

"I will do. Good luck, Ali," Mick said shaking Ali's hand.

"Thank you," Ali said as Haseena hurried him to the door.

When they got to the lift they got in and Haseena pressed the button for the ground floor. "I'm sorry for rushing you, Ali, but we have to get you on that flight today. Your sister visited again last night with Yunus. It wasn't very pleasant," Haseena informed him.

"Oh no. I'm sorry. What happened?" Ali asked worriedly.

"I'll tell you some other time," Haseena said not wanting to tell him that she'd ended up having to call the police to get them removed from her doorstep.

The lift came to a stop, and Haseena hurried Ali to the car where Derek was waiting. "Come on get in," he said. "We don't have much time. I'll drop you off at New Street station. You'll need to catch the train from there to Birmingham International for the airport."

Ali got quickly into the back seat while Derek started the car. Haseena quietly took the passenger seat next to Derek.

"I've booked the flight ticket for you," Haseena informed him.

"How much do I owe you?" Ali asked, worried about the cost, not knowing how much money he had left in his bank account to pay for it.

"Let's not worry about that now. When you've sorted yourself out, you can pay me back," Haseena said.

"Thank you," Ali said, feeling relieved.

"Derek's already put your car in storage at his mate's garage," Haseena told him.

"What about my passport? Did you find it?" Ali asked.

"Well it would have been silly booking your flight if I hadn't," Haseena said humorously. "It was in your suitcase like you said."

"What about my wife's suitcase? It was in my car boot. It's got all her jewelry in it," Ali said.

"It's sorted. Mick is going to drop it off at your parents' later tonight," Haseena assured him.

"What would I do without you, Haseena?" Ali asked rhetorically.

"God knows," Haseena said, turning round to smile at him from the front seat.

"We're here, lad," Derek said interrupting them, as he parked the car at the crowded drop off point outside the entrance to New Street station.

Haseena promptly opened the car door and jumped out. She went to the boot of the car and pulled his suitcase out.

"Good luck, lad," Derek said turning round and shaking Ali's hand.

"Thank you," Ali replied before opening the car door and getting out. Haseena handed him his suitcase.

"Your passport and flight tickets are in the side pocket," Haseena told him. "I've also put some euros in there as well. The ticket's open return, so you can come back anytime if you need to. You'd better hurry. You don't have long left for your flight to leave." She hugged Ali before returning to the car and getting in.

She watched as Ali hurried to the station entrance. He looked back at the car and waved before disappearing into the station.

The station was very busy. Ali pushed his way through the crowd to the platform entrance and checked the information board. The train to Birmingham International was leaving in three minutes from platform seven, giving him no time to buy a ticket. Panicking, Ali raced down to the platform lugging his heavy suitcase behind, not even bothering to use its wheels.

He managed to get onto the train just as the guard blew the whistle and the doors shut. Ali found himself an empty seat and sat down, putting his suitcase on the floor in the gangway, and prayed that there was no guard on board to check for tickets.

Chapter Fourteen

Ali arrived at the Air France check-in desk with only fifteen minutes to spare before his flight's departure. He handed his ticket and passport to the female attendant sitting behind the desk, knowing it was very unlikely that he'd be allowed onto the plane this late. He crossed his fingers hopefully.

The attendant checked the passport making sure the photograph matched Ali's face. "You're too late. The flight's already been boarded," she exclaimed when she checked the ticket. "I'll see if there's any way we can get you on the flight though." She picked up the telephone on her desk and spoke quickly into it for a few seconds as Ali waited anxiously.

"There's a small delay, and the boarding gate is still open, but we're going to have to run for it," she said handing him his passport, ticket and boarding pass.

She stood up and picked up Ali's suitcase. "Follow me," she said, leaping into a sprint. Ali raced after her clutching his documents tightly. He gasped for breath as his asthma flared up due to the unexpected exertion. It seemed like ages before they came to a stop at a security gate.

"We have a late passenger," she informed the security guard. "I've got a bet that I can get him onto the flight."

"I reckon you might win," he said to her, taking Ali's suitcase and shoving it onto the conveyor belt for the x-ray machine. "You're not running away are you?" he asked jokingly as he checked Ali's passport and boarding pass.

"No, of course not," Ali said, taken aback by the question. "I'm visiting a friend."

The guard motioned for Ali to go through the metal detector. It didn't make a sound as Ali walked through. The attendant was on the other side having already gone through, herself.

"Come on, we're not there, yet," the attendant said taking Ali's suitcase off the conveyer belt and sprinting off again.

"It's departure gate sixty-four, so there's not far to go," she said, with Ali following after her breathlessly as they ran past departure gate fifty.

"Late arrival," she said to the two male air stewards who were waiting at the boarding gate when they finally reached it. "You'll have to carry his suitcase on board," she told them.

"Thank you very much," Ali said gratefully, turning to her.

"It's my pleasure, sweetheart," she said pleasantly. "You look like a guy with the weight of the world on his shoulders. I hope everything works out for you in Strasbourg." She then leaned over and gave Ali a quick kiss on his cheek. "Hurry up, or you'll miss your flight."

"Follow me," one of the air stewards said in a strong French accent, not allowing Ali time to think about the kiss. The steward led him through the gate and directly into the aircraft. "I'll store your luggage at the front. You can collect it when you disembark from the flight."

He showed Ali to his seat, which was in the economy section. Ali could only count another eight people seated in economy. "Enjoy your flight, sir," the steward said and walked back to the front of the cabin. He pulled a curtain behind him to separate the business class section from the rest of the cabin.

The plane's engines started up as Ali gripped onto the sides of the seat nervously. He stared out of the cabin window, ignoring the safety demonstration, and watched the runway as the plane started to gather speed. It suddenly increased its velocity very noisily as Ali watched the ground slip away from the plane. He let out an anxious sigh of relief.

This was only the third trip that Ali had taken by plane. The first trip had been with the family to Pakistan. The second, which was more memorable, had been to New York with Steve. That flight had been so different. He'd felt happy and excited. This time he couldn't help but feel alone and insignificant.

Ali tried to hold back his tears. "I should never have married," he thought. "I should have run away earlier."

Ali's thoughts turned to Sajda. "What about my beautiful new bride?" he thought despairingly. "I've completely ruined her life. I'm so weak running away. Perhaps it might have worked if I'd given it more time." He thought about his grandmother who'd be mystified by what he'd done, not understanding why he'd run away.

The picture of his distraught mother entered his mind, and he tried to dispel it guiltily. He thought about the anguish and hurt she would be going through knowing that she was probably feeling humiliated and ashamed by his actions.

Ali's thoughts jumbled chaotically in his mind. "I've let so many people down. Why am I such a failure?" he thought angrily as he started to cry silently. He wiped his eyes on his sleeve. It didn't matter anymore. He was still wearing the same clothes he'd slept in the previous night, and he could smell the stale sweat. So what did it matter if he wiped his nose on his sleeve as well?

"I hate myself," he thought savagely, wiping his nose. He paused momentarily, hearing the chiming sound of the plane's seat belt sign turning off, and then continued with his crying.

He was suddenly disturbed by a man peering at him through the curtains of the business class section. Ali quickly wiped away his tears and perked up, pretending to be fascinated by the clouds outside the cabin window and embarrassed that he'd been caught crying.

A few seconds later, Ali felt a tap on his shoulder and looked up. It was the same man who had peered at him through the curtains. "May I sit next to you?" he asked. "I'm bored in business class. I would love to sit with you and enjoy your company," he said speaking English with a trace of an accent that Ali could not place.

"Yes, of course, you can," Ali said, hesitantly, not really wanting the man's company but finding it difficult to refuse the offer in case he sounded rude. "Won't you get into trouble with the air stewards?"

"The flight's under booked. I don't think they'll mind with less than twenty people onboard," the man replied. "I'm so lucky to find such a pretty boy on the same flight as me to share my journey with."

"Thank you," said Ali, feeling a little taken aback by the man's words.

"So why are you traveling to Strasbourg? Is it business or pleasure?" the man asked, taking hold of Ali's hand and stroking it gently.

"I'm visiting a university friend," Ali said, pulling his hand out from the man's grasp.

"Do I make you uncomfortable by holding your hand?" he asked, sounding surprised.

"Yes, I'm not used to a man holding my hand." Ali said. He wanted to add the words "in public" to the sentence, but didn't feel comfortable revealing his sexuality to a stranger.

"I'm Italian. We Italians are a very passionate people. We like to hold hands and touch our friends. We are very tactile," he said excusing his behavior. "You are very pretty. I wish to hold your hand. It makes me happy," he said grasping Ali's hand again.

"Well it makes me uncomfortable," Ali said. He worried that someone might see them holding hands and come to the wrong conclusion.

"You are such a pretty boy. Do you have a hairy chest?" he asked.

"I'm not telling you that!" Ali exclaimed.

"If you weren't wearing that high necked jumper I would have been able to give you the answer myself," he said.

"Well, I'm not telling you," Ali said, feeling irritated by him. He examined him momentarily. The man was quite stout, with dark hair that had a round bald crown rising through the center. He looked about forty five years old, and his face was coated in a layer of sweat, giving him the appearance of sleaziness.

"What is your name?" he asked.

"Ali Mirza," Ali responded.

"It's good to meet you, Ali Mirza. My name is Benigno," he said, shaking Ali's hand but then not letting go. "Your friend, is he a pretty boy like you?"

"Well, he seems very nice," Ali said.

"You have such beautiful hands," Benigno said. "They are so soft. So what will you do together in Strasbourg?"

"My friend is going to show me around. We'll probably go sight seeing," Ali told him.

"I would like to show you the city, too. It is a very beautiful city. I would like to take you to dinner at my favorite restaurant by the cathedral," Benigno said.

"I'm not sure if I can. I'll be quite busy. We'll have to see," Ali said.

"I can take you and your friend. It is the most expensive restaurant in the city," Benigno said grandly.

Ali tried to think of an excuse, but fortunately at that moment the seat belt sign went on. "I think you have to go back to your own seat when the seat belt sign shows," Ali reminded Benigno.

"You are such a tease," Benigno said, getting up. "I'll be back soon. I can't stay away from a lovely pretty boy like you for too long." He leaned over and gave Ali a kiss on his forehead before getting up.

"I must have 'GAY' stamped on my forehead," Ali thought to himself miserably as the stocky figure trundled back through the curtains into business class.

The seat belt sign stayed on for several minutes before being switched off again. "Oh no," Ali groaned to himself as the curtains twitched and Benigno's hands came through.

"Have you missed me my pretty boy?" he asked striding down the walkway to sit down next to Ali again.

"Not really," Ali said, sounding embarrassed at the thought that someone might hear him being called a pretty boy.

"You were looking for me. I could tell. You missed me. A pretty boy like you shouldn't be left alone for too long, or he'll get himself into trouble. I wouldn't want you to get into trouble," he said slipping his hand back into Ali's.

"I've never got into trouble. I'm a married man," Ali reminded Benigno, pointing at the wedding ring on his finger, and pulling his hand out from Benigno's grasp.

"Don't you like me?" Benigno asked sadly. "I just want you to be my pretty friend."

"It's not that I don't like you," Ali assured him. "You keep holding my hand, and it makes me uncomfortable."

"Do you want me to stop holding your hand?" Benigno asked.

"Yes, I would love you to stop holding my hand," Ali said, flabbergasted that he was being asked the question.

Amjeed Kabil

"There you are," Benigno said, releasing Ali's hand. "Now, will you go out to dinner with me?"

"I can't. I'm staying with a friend," Ali said.

"I shall take you both out. You will love it," Benigno said, trying to impress Ali.

"I can't afford to go to an expensive restaurant. I'm traveling on a budget," Ali said.

"You don't have to worry about money. I'm willing to pay anything to be in your company. I can take you both out for a meal every night of your stay," said Benigno lavishly.

"That's very kind of you, Benigno, but I can't accept. It wouldn't be right. If I can't afford something then I'd rather go without. I don't like taking things from people I don't know," Ali said, trying his best to turn down Benigno's generosity as politely as he could.

"I'm Italian. We Italians like to share our wealth. If you don't join me for dinner, I'll be lonely and sad on my own in Strasbourg. Please say you will join me for dinner even if it's just for one night?" Benigno asked.

"Can I think about it?" Ali asked. "I will need to ask my friend. I can't promise anything. It depends on what he says and whether he's already made plans."

"I look forward to it, my pretty boy," Benigno said happily.

"I'm feeling really tired," Ali said feigning sleep. "Is it okay if I try and sleep for a while?" he asked trying to find an excuse to get rid of Benigno.

"Yes, of course. I'll sit here and watch you sleep," Benigno said enthusiastically.

"I can't sleep with someone watching me. Can't you go back to your seat, and we can talk later," Ali said in exasperation. "I'm sorry. I don't mean to be rude, but I'm really tired."

"Yes, my pretty boy. I will talk to you later," he said cheerfully. He gave Ali's leg a quick stroke before getting up.

Ali closed his eyes. "You have beautiful long eyelashes," he heard Benigno say. Ali opened his eyes again, but by then Benigno had left.

Ali found himself drowsing peacefully but was eventually woken up by the pilot announcing the descent into Strasbourg airport.

158

Suddenly, all his insecurities about seeing Steve came flooding back. He tried to block them out, but he couldn't help but wonder if Steve really wanted to see him. "I'm being paranoid," Ali thought, pushing the insecure feelings away as best he could.

Ali looked out of the cabin window to distract himself. The plane was going through some thick vapor clouds and small icy particles stuck to the window pane creating minute snowflakes that mesmerized Ali.

Suddenly, Ali saw the runway lights on the ground as the plane adjusted its flight path. The ground came closer until Ali felt the impact and the thud of the plane's wheels hitting the tarmac.

The plane came to a halt on the runway as the pilot announced the arrival. The cabin doors were flung open a few minutes later, and the steps maneuvered into place. Ali stayed seated while the few passengers on the flight got off the plane. He lingered in his seat until he was sure that everyone had left the plane and then made his way to the exit door at the front where he collected his suitcase from the steward.

Ali deliberately walked slowly toward the terminal building lagging behind the other passengers in an attempt to avoid Benigno. However, Benigno had spotted him already. "Ali! Ali!" Benigno shouted, waving at him frantically, trying to get his attention.

"I've been looking out for you," he said as Ali reached him. "What took you so long?" he asked Ali as he grabbed his hand.

"I had to pick up my suitcase," Ali said, trying unsuccessfully to pull his hand out of Benigno's grasp.

"I can't wait to show you around Strasbourg," Benigno said excitedly.

"I've told you that I'm not sure if I can meet you. It depends on my friend," Ali reminded him. He tried again to pull his hand free from Benigno's as they reached passport control.

"I need to get my passport out, and I can't when I'm pulling my suitcase with one hand and you're holding the other," Ali said trying not to sound too annoyed.

Benigno immediately let go of his hand. "You're a shy boy. I think you don't want me to hold your hand because you are shy. I like shy boys," he said.

Ali separated from Benigno and showed his passport to the customs officer behind the glass screen. He then walked hurriedly through to the baggage reclaim area, seeing it as a fantastic opportunity to escape Benigno.

"Wait, Ali!" Benigno shouted as he raced after him having had his passport checked.

Ali paused briefly waiting for Benigno. "I have to rush off and meet my friend," Ali told him.

"I know. It's sad that our journey together must end. I'll miss you, my pretty boy," he said forlornly, hugging Ali to his chest. "Please have my business card. It has my cell phone number on it. Call me anytime."

"I'll try if I get the chance," Ali said taking the business card.

"You must do more than try. I want to see your pretty face again and spoil you," Benigno said.

"That's very kind of you. I promise I'll try and see you at some point during my stay," Ali said trying to assure him with his insincere promise. It was unlikely that he'd see Benigno again, so it didn't matter what promises Ali made to him.

"Thank you, thank you, my beautiful friend," Benigno said ecstatically. He hugged Ali again and kissed him noisily on both cheeks. "I look forward to seeing you again."

"Goodbye!" Ali said, not looking back and heading out into the arrivals area knowing that Benigno's gaze was following him as he left. He considered throwing away the business card he'd just been given but instead slipped it into his jacket pocket in case he ever needed it.

Ali's gaze passed over the crowd of people waiting at the arrivals gate trying to locate Steve among the people holding large cards with names on them. However, Steve was nowhere to be seen.

Ali waited impatiently, glancing at his watch every few seconds. "Maybe he's caught up in traffic," he thought trying hard not to let his insecure feelings get the better of him. He moved away from the arrivals gate in case he bumped into Benigno and wandered into a small international newsagents at one end of the terminal to buy himself an English newspaper to read while he waited.

Ali picked up a copy of *The Times* newspaper but worked out that he'd be paying the equivalent of three pounds for it. He eventually settled for the *The Mirror*, which was a pound cheaper. It seemed a luxury buying an expensive newspaper when he had so little money. He felt cheated as it only cost thirty pence in England.

Ali found a chair and sat down to wait for Steve. He began to read the paper, but he couldn't concentrate on the stories, worrying that he may miss Steve if he walked past. Half an hour later, Ali was busy trying to digest some of the stories in the sports section, when he suddenly caught his name being mentioned on an announcement over the speaker system in French.

The announcement was thankfully repeated again in English. "Will Mister Ali Mirza please report to the information desk."

"It's Steve," Ali thought excitedly, cheering up suddenly. "He probably couldn't find me." He got up, leaving his newspaper behind on the chair and hurriedly followed the signs to the information desk. When he arrived, he was frustrated to find that Steve wasn't there.

"Do you speak English? My name is Ali Mirza. You've asked me to report to the information desk," Ali said to the female clerk behind the desk not bothering to wait to find out whether she spoke English or not.

"I have a call waiting for you," she said smiling pleasantly, and handed him a phone.

"Thank you," Ali said, taking the phone. "Hello," he said into the phone sounding puzzled.

"Ali, it's me," Steve said.

"Where the heck are you, Steve? My flight landed at four. I've been hanging around waiting for ages," Ali said angrily. "Why aren't you here to pick me up?"

"I'm really sorry, Ali. I've had to make some arrangements for your stay, and I lost track of the time. If I give you my address will you get a taxi?"

"Is it expensive? I don't have that much money," Ali said, not wanting the few euros he had to dwindle away.

"It shouldn't be more than thirty to forty euros," Steve assured him. "You did remember to bring some euros didn't you?"

"Yes, I've got about ninety," Ali said, having earlier counted the euros that Haseena had given him.

"That's not very much. Did you bring your credit card with you?" Steve asked.

"Yes I have, but I don't think I've got much credit left on it," Ali said.

"Oh, Ali, that's terrible. What are you going to do for money?" Steve asked glumly.

"I'll find a job," Ali said trying to sound positive. Part of him wanted Steve to offer to look after him, but that did not seem likely.

"I guess we'll have to sort something out. Have you got a pen and paper, so I can give you the address?" Steve asked.

"Give me a second," Ali said. He made a writing gesture with his hand to the receptionist who understood and gave him a pen and a sheet of paper. Steve gave Ali the address spelling out all the difficult words.

"Have you moved?" Ali asked curiously noticing the address was different.

"Yes. I'll explain things when you get here," Steve said.

"Can't you explain now? I don't like surprises," Ali said wondering what was going on.

"It can wait, Ali. We have lots to discuss when you get here," Steve said.

"What do you mean 'we have lots to discuss'?" Ali asked anxiously.

"A few things have changed, Ali, but we can discuss that when you get here. I don't want to get into it on the phone," Steve replied.

"Okay," Ali said almost petulantly and trying not to sound cross with Steve.

"I'll see you in a bit then," Steve said hanging up abruptly.

Ali handed the phone back to the receptionist and made his way to the taxi rank. "Whatever he tells me, at least I'll get some answers when I get there," he thought.

Chapter Fifteen

Ali pressed the buzzer on the intercom system for the fourth time. There was still no answer. He'd made sure that the taxi driver had dropped him off at the address given to him by Steve before he'd let him leave.

Worried that he might have made a mistake, Ali walked to the end of the street and double checked that the street name on the sign matched the address he'd jotted down. They were identical.

"What's going on?" Ali asked himself. "I should go home. Steve obviously doesn't care about me. What am I still doing here?"

Ali walked back to the doorway of the tall apartment block to try one last time. However, just as he was about to press the buzzer, the door swung open and a young, dark haired French man stepped out. Ali tried to walk past him to get into the building, but the man grabbed him by the wrist.

"Ali?" he asked.

"Yes," Ali said. "Who are you?" he asked feeling confused, and pulling his wrist out from the man's strong grasp.

The French man didn't reply and instead looked Ali up and down as if evaluating him, then finally gave him a look of disappointment as though Ali had failed to measure up.

"He's waiting for you in the apartment. It's on the fourth floor," he said giving Ali a filthy look before hurrying off into the street.

Feeling completely baffled by the man's strange behavior, Ali walked into the apartment building to find himself in a beautifully decorated lobby with a marble floor and a large crystal chandelier hanging from the center of the ceiling. The lobby opened into a private courtyard that contained a small fountain. A glass door elevator was situated in one corner of the lobby and next to this was a wide staircase with a red carpet leading to the apartments above.

Ali took the elevator and got out at the fourth floor. There was only one apartment on the floor. Ali knocked on the door and waited. The door was shortly opened by Steve. Forgetting all his worries and insecurities, Ali rushed into Steve's arms giving him a hug, but something was wrong. Ali looked up at him expecting to be kissed, but Steve held back, appearing cold and reserved.

"Is everything okay?" Ali asked, feeling worried. Steve did not reply. "Aren't you at least a little pleased to see me?"

"Sit down, Ali. We've got lots to discuss. Let me just bring your suitcase inside." Steve picked up Ali's suitcase and pulled it into the apartment, shutting the door behind him.

Steve's home was a luxurious, loft apartment. It had high ceilings and a large lounge diner. The floors were real wood, and the walls were decorated in fashionable neutral colors. "How can you afford this apartment?" Ali asked, bewildered.

"It's a long story. Sit down and I'll explain," Steve said inviting Ali to sit on the cream sofa.

"What's going on, Steve?" Ali asked trying hard to hide the panic he was feeling.

"Would you like a drink?" Steve asked, ignoring the question.

"I'm not in the mood to drink anything. I just want to know what's going on. I've not come all this way to be ignored," Ali said, his face contorted angrily with emotion.

"I didn't expect you to leave your wife, Ali. I didn't expect you to come to Strasbourg," Steve said.

"Just tell me what's going on, Steve. Why have you gone cold on me? What's changed?" Ali asked.

"Ali, the day that you got married I thought I'd lost you forever. Your life had been neatly sorted out, and I'd just become part of your past. I was hurting so much, and I needed to make a break with my past, too. I needed to move on," Steve explained.

"You needed to move on? But you told me that you'd wait for me. You said you'd wait a whole year, Steve. Why did you lie to me?" Ali asked.

"I didn't lie to you. I really meant it. The day of your wedding, I could barely cope. I was feeling so upset, wondering what was happening, how you were getting on with your wife, whether you'd slept with her. I realized that I couldn't go on feeling like that for a whole year waiting for you," Steve said.

"What are you trying to tell me?" Ali asked.

"I don't know how else to tell you this, Ali. I've moved on with my life. You coming here like this has been a complete shock. It's not something I expected," Steve said.

"You've moved on with your life," Ali said in disbelief. "I've left everything behind because of you, and now you're telling me that you've moved on with your life?"

"You left everything behind because you were unhappy. It wasn't because of me," Steve replied. "I never asked you to leave."

"Why didn't you talk to me about this when I was still in England? Why did you wait until I got here?" Ali said angrily, reeling from Steve's words.

"I don't know. I just couldn't tell you something like this over the phone. I'm sorry," Steve said.

"So is it over between us?" Ali asked quietly, wanting to hear Steve say the words.

"Ali, it was over months ago when I came to Strasbourg. I've not seen you for over four months for God's sake," Steve said callously.

"What do you mean it was over months ago? You've never told me that it was over. Every time I've telephoned, you've always told me how much you loved me," Ali retorted angrily.

"I do love you. I mean I did love you, but things changed when you got married," Steve said.

"You've led me on," Ali said in disbelief. "You don't fall out of love with someone over night."

"Ali, I love you, but I'm not in love with you." Steve said. "I want to see you happy."

"You love me, but you're not in love with me?" Ali repeated miserably. "See me happy? You've made me destroy an innocent girl's life and ruin my family's reputation. I left everything behind because of you. How could you do this to me? You bastard!" Ali yelled angrily.

"Calm down, Ali. Stop getting hysterical, or I won't talk to you," Steve said coldly.

"How do you expect me to behave?" Ali exclaimed.

"I know it's a shock for you. I'm really sorry. I didn't expect you here today. I would have told you eventually," Steve said.

"Is that supposed to make me feel better? So are you seeing anyone else?" Ali asked.

"Yes, I'm sorry," Steve replied sheepishly.

"Why didn't you tell me that yesterday? I would have gone back to my wife if you'd told me sooner, you selfish bastard!" Ali yelled angrily. "How long have you been seeing him?"

"Not long, a few weeks maybe. He asked me to move in with him, yesterday," Steve said.

"So, while I was running away, you were playing happy family with your new boyfriend. Why couldn't you tell me? Why?" Ali asked furiously. "Why did you pretend for so long?"

"I was scared. I was worried you'd do something stupid," Steve said.

"Oh, so you didn't tell me out of concern for me," Ali said sarcastically. "You know, you're right, I have done something stupid. I've left everything behind for a worthless bastard like you!"

"What did you expect me to do? You were getting married. I tried my best to wait for you," Steve said.

"You didn't even last a day. All I expected from you was some honesty. Was that too much to ask for?" Ali asked angrily.

"I'm sorry, Ali. I truly am. I want you to know that I'm here for you as a friend," Steve said. "Fabien says you can stay here until you've got yourself sorted out. The spare bedroom is ready, and you won't have to pay rent."

"What planet are you on Steve? Do you really think I'm moving in with you and your new lover? You can piss off! I don't need your help!" Ali retorted. "I hate you!" All the anger and hurt he felt came boiling out of him. He gave Steve a hard slap on his face, leaving a red welt behind.

"I deserved that, Ali," Steve said tearfully. "Go ahead and hit me again. I deserve it."

"I'm sorry I did that, but I'm not doing it again. I really don't want to stoop to the same level as you," Ali said angrily.

"I'm really sorry, Ali. I never meant to hurt you. I'm really sorry," Steve repeated tearfully.

"It's too late to say sorry. I need to go," Ali said.

"Where are you going to go? You don't know anyone here. Stay in the spare room until you've sorted yourself out," Steve said.

"No. I don't want to stay here. I can book myself into a hotel," Ali said, wondering how he was going to afford it.

"Stay here tonight. Please," Steve pleaded as if to relieve himself of some of the guilt he was feeling for Ali's situation.

"I can't stay," Ali said. He would love to have stayed, but the thought of seeing someone else with Steve made him feel sick. Ali picked up his suitcase and headed to the door.

"Let's talk, Ali. It's late and dark outside, and you can't go out in the state you're in. Just stay tonight," Steve said grabbing him.

"Don't touch me," Ali said angrily pulling himself out of Steve's hands. "I'm going. Good bye!" Ali yelled, opening the door and leaving the apartment, banging the door shut loudly behind him.

He headed down the stairs dragging his suitcase behind him on its wheels without bothering to pick it up and let it hit every step on its way down.

It was cold outside. A large part of him felt that he should have swallowed his pride and stayed the night. He wanted to cry. It was as if he'd been punched in the face by the person he'd most trusted in the world.

He'd never thought that Steve would let him down like this. Ali paused to catch his breath. He looked back, but Steve hadn't even bothered to follow him to try and persuade him to stay. Ali wanted to burst into tears. "No, I'm not going to cry," he thought taking control of his emotions. "I need to be strong." Trying to maintain an inner calm, Ali considered his options.

He did not have much money left, probably less then fifty euros, which was never going to be enough for a hotel for the night. He also knew he was over the limit on his credit card, rendering it useless. He could go to the airport and wait there until the flight the next day. Then he remembered Benigno's business card.

Ali searched his pockets frantically for Benigno's card and was relieved to find it in his jacket pocket. His next task was to find a phone box. This was not easy. After walking up empty and badly lit streets for over an hour with his suitcase wheeling noisily behind him Ali finally chanced upon a phone box. After entering the phone box, Ali was frustrated to find that it only took pre-paid phone cards. The phone box next to it was the same.

"What am I going to do?" Ali thought to himself with tears welling up in his eyes. He felt so tired and alone. "I'm not going to cry. I'm not going to cry," he said loudly to himself. "Think rationally. What would you do if you were in England? That's it!" The solution had come to him.

He dialed the freephone number for the operator. "Do you speak English?" he asked when the call was answered.

"Yes," the operator's voice crackled over the line.

"Oh, thank God," Ali exclaimed. "I need to make a reverse charge call to the following number please." Ali read the number for Benigno's mobile phone.

"One moment, sir. I must confirm with the owner of the number whether they will accept a reverse call charge. What is your name, sir?" the operator asked.

"Ali Mirza," Ali said giving his name.

"Hold the line for a moment sir." The line clicked noisily and went silent. Ali crossed his fingers, hoping that Benigno remembered him. "Sir, the reverse call charge has been accepted. I'm putting you through, now," the operator said. The line went dead.

"Hello. Hello," Ali shouted down the line in panic, worried that the call had been terminated accidentally.

"Hello, my pretty boy," Benigno's voice replied after a few moments.

Ali sighed to himself with relief. It was the first time that he had welcomed Benigno's words no matter how sleazy they sounded.

"Hi, Benigno. I'm really sorry to make a reverse charge call. I will pay you back. The telephones all seem to take phone cards, and I only have cash on me. I hope you don't mind?" Ali asked.

"It's okay, my beautiful boy. I would be willing to pay hundreds of euros to hear your voice. So are you coming out to dinner with me?" Benigno asked eagerly.

"Well, I need to ask a favor," Ali said hesitantly, feeling embarrassed at what he was about to ask.

"Anything for a pretty boy like you. Anything. Just ask, and I will grant you any favor you ask for," Benigno said grandly.

"Well, I've had a big falling out with the friend that I was visiting, so I was hoping that I could stay at yours for the night. If you don't mind that is. It will only be for one night. I'm flying back to England tomorrow," Ali said.

"Yes, of course you can stay the night, my pretty boy. You can stay as long as you want," Benigno said.

"You're not expecting anything in return are you?" Ali asked, cringing at his own words, but unable to find another way to say them.

"Anything in return? What are you suggesting, my pretty boy. All I want is your company and a chance to look at your beautiful face and those beautiful brown eyes," Benigno said, trying to set Ali's mind at rest.

"Okay, but nothing more?" Ali asked a little suspiciously.

"Nothing more than that. I promise." Benigno said. "Do you have my address?"

"I think so. Is it the one on your business card?" Ali asked peering at the card again.

"Yes, that is the address. If you're coming by cab just give the card to the driver," Benigno instructed him.

"Okay. I shall see you soon," Ali said.

"I am looking forward to it you beautiful boy. Don't change your mind, now," Benigno said before hanging up.

Ali got out of the phone box wondering how he was going to find a taxi. Seeing the spires of a cathedral in the distance, Ali knew if he followed the road he'd find himself somewhere in center of the city where there would hopefully be a taxi available.

Strasbourg was a beautiful city that Ali would have explored under better circumstances. The walk into the city center along the tree lined roads and the river would have been enjoyable if he'd not been worried about the uncertainties of what was going to happen with his life.

His mind was focused on getting to Benigno's, but kept going back to the thought of returning home and living the life that had been mapped out for him. It took Ali half an hour to finally arrive in the city center. He felt embarrassed and paranoid that people were watching him as he wheeled his suitcase through the cobbled streets.

The city was crowded with tourists even though it was now late evening. There were small stands with people selling chestnuts and bakeries with waffles being sold from carts on the street. The smell made Ali hungry, and he tried to ignore his stomach rumbling. The place had a lively and friendly atmosphere, which made him feel like an intruder with his deep level of unhappiness.

Ali finally found a taxi rank near a busy thoroughfare and got into a taxi. He took out Benigno's business card and pointed at the address on the card to instruct the driver.

The driver said something in French. "I can't understand," Ali replied in English.

"Ah, you are English. I take you there," the cabbie said in pigeon English. "It is near Parliament. Nice."

The drive didn't take that long, and once they got to their destination, Ali got out, taking his suitcase with him and paid the driver.

The cabbie had dropped him in a leafy suburban area, outside an apartment block similar to the one Steve was living in with his new boyfriend. Ali felt sick at the thought. The building had lots of large stone balconies, which were festooned with elaborate designs carved into the stone. The style was vaguely gothic.

Ali could almost imagine Benigno flying off the balcony in a vampyric flight. The chubby image of Benigno with a cloak and large canines brought a smile to Ali's face.

Ali pressed the buzzer for Benigno's apartment.

"Come in, my pretty boy. I am on the fifth floor. Come right up. You have such a beautiful face," Benigno's voice said longingly from the intercom. Ali noticed that it had a small camera built into the unit. Ali smiled and waved into it.

He walked into the building once Benigno had buzzed the door open to let him in. He felt very guilty knowing that he was using Benigno to get a free place to stay for the night.

Ali reached the apartment and knocked on the door "Hello my pretty boy! How are you?" Benigno cried excitedly as he answered the door. He hugged Ali tightly as if they were long lost friends. "Come in. Let me take your suitcase."

Benigno picked up Ali's suitcase and pulled it into the hallway. "I'll leave it by the coat stand," he said putting it down. "I'm in the middle of cooking a meal for us, a tasty Italian pasta dish with fresh home made sauce that was my mother's recipe. I decided it was much better than going out for dinner," Benigno said.

"That sounds delicious," Ali said hungrily. He hadn't eaten all day.

"Talk to me while I cook," Benigno said leading Ali to the kitchen. Ali took his jacket off and hung it on the clothes stand before following him into the kitchen. The kitchen was huge with a large six-ring stainless steel cooker as the main feature. An elaborate wrought iron dining table sat in the center of the room with beautifully designed handmade chairs.

"So, what's your story, Ali. Tell me what's happened," Benigno requested as he looked over the steaming saucepan of pasta being boiled

Ali considered what to tell Benigno. He had nothing to lose by being honest. "I was forced into an arranged marriage by my family and I ran away," he said.

"Oh, my dear boy," Benigno said, looking shocked and pausing from what he was doing. "I didn't know things like that still happened. No wonder you looked so unhappy on the flight. That's what drew me to you. I wondered why someone so beautiful was walking like he had the weight of the world on his shoulders."

"My friend, the one who I had the disagreement with, is my ex-partner. I was hoping for a reconciliation, but he had already moved in with another man," Ali said. His own words stung him bringing him back to the harsh reality that Steve was no longer there for him.

"I'm really sorry to hear that, Ali, but you have me. I'm your friend while you are here. You're not alone," Benigno said warmly. He looked at Ali and turned back to his cooking again.

"Thank you, Benigno, that's very kind," Ali said, feeling gratitude at Benigno's kindness.

"Right, the food is ready. You can set the table. The cutlery and the plates are in the cupboards over there," Benigno said pointing to one of the kitchen cabinets.

Ali silently laid the table out, and they both sat down together to eat. The pasta tasted delicious. Ali ate the food that had been put out for him ravenously, devouring the meal in minutes.

"You must have been very hungry," Benigno commented looking at Ali's empty plate. "Would you like some more?"

"I wouldn't mind," Ali said staring greedily at the pasta bowl. "It's delicious, the best pasta I've ever tasted."

"Help yourself. I will only throw away what we've not eaten, so it's best to finish it all," Benigno said.

"Thank you," Ali said piling some more pasta onto his plate and digging into it with his fork.

"It's getting late. We should go to bed," Benigno said when they had finished eating.

"What time is it?" Ali asked.

"It's just gone past eleven," Benigno said looking at his watch.

"I didn't realize it was that late," Ali said. "Is it okay if I have a shower first?"

"Yes, use the en-suite in the bedroom. It's the first door on your left in the hallway. There are some fresh towels in there as well."

"Thank you," Ali said.

The shower was luxurious and warm. Ali found a bottle of orange scented shower gel on the shower cubicle floor, which he used to lather himself. It smelled divine and helped wash away the dirt and grime that he'd gathered during the day.

The hot water spraying on him was blissful. Ali closed his eyes enjoying the sensation of the warm heat massaging his tired and sore muscles. His mind wandered slowly to thoughts of Steve, and he wanted to open himself to the feeling of despair he'd been bottling up since Steve's rejection, but stopped himself quickly. "Cry later," he told himself firmly.

Ali got out of the shower and dried himself on the white towel that had been put out for him. It was so nice to be clean and fresh again. Wrapping the towel around his waist, Ali silently crept out of the bathroom to get his suitcase and hurried back in case Benigno came across him. He didn't want to be seen by him with just a towel round his waist.

Ali opened the suitcase, to find the pajamas that he had planned to wear at his mother-in-law's house. He put them on.

Looking at the contents of the suitcase, he couldn't believe how much his life had changed since packing it. Ali closed the suitcase and returned it to the coat stand in the hallway before joining Benigno in the kitchen.

"You look beautiful," Benigno exclaimed.

"Thank you," Ali said feeling embarrassed.

"Well let's go to bed," Benigno said. "I only have one bed, so you'll have to share it with me."

"It's okay, I can sleep on the couch," Ali stuttered worriedly.

"Don't be scared, Ali. I just wish to share my bed with you because it is comfortable. I want friendship from a pretty boy like you and perhaps a kiss one day. I wouldn't do anything that you don't want to do," Benigno said assuring Ali of his good intentions.

"I'm not very good at sharing a bed. It's easier for me to sleep on the couch," Ali said.

"I wouldn't dream of it. Trust me, my pretty friend. I don't have any ulterior motive."

Ali tried to trust Benigno, but he followed him to the bedroom feeling tense and worried that Benigno had some hidden sexual motive in inviting him to share his bed.

The bedroom was beautifully decorated in an Indian theme. The bed linen was of terracotta and orange color with bands of gold embroidery. Over the bed, hung a print in a silver frame showing a photograph of rows upon rows of different shades of spices in large earthenware bowls, and the curtains were made from sari fabric.

"My bedroom is ethnic for my ethnic friend," Benigno said. "I brought everything from India when I visited last year."

"It's beautiful," Ali said gawking at the splendor.

"So, are you getting into the bed or are you just going to stand there," Benigno asked getting into the bed.

"I'm getting into the bed," Ali said, and got in shyly.

"Good night, pretty boy," Benigno said, and without another word turned the light off.

"Good night," Ali said, putting his head onto the pillow and trying his best to get to sleep. He felt very uncomfortable lying in bed with Benigno and tried not to make a direct comparison to his wedding night. "What if he tries something,"

Ali thought. Each time he was about to nod off, he jerked himself awake with fear of being molested by Benigno.

"Go to sleep," Ali heard Benigno whisper as if sensing his concern. "Nothing is going to happen, you silly boy."

With those words, Ali felt all of his anxiety slip away and fell into a heavy and exhausted sleep. When he woke up, he found that he was cuddling Benigno. For some reason, he did not mind it. It felt comforting.

Ali cuddled him for a bit longer seeking comfort and warmth from him. His mind went back to the wedding day and then to Steve's betrayal. "I am not going to cry," he muttered to himself. "I have to stay strong. I will not cry."

Ali dragged himself out of the bed quietly, trying not to wake Benigno in the process and went to the bathroom and showered. Finding his shaver in his suitcase, he shaved before getting dressed in a clean outfit from his suitcase.

Ali went back to the bedroom, but Benigno was no longer there. He went to the lounge and opened the door. Benigno was already there sitting at a small table on the balcony terrace drinking coffee.

"Come join me," he said noticing Ali. "Have some breakfast."

Ali sat down enjoying the cold breeze that drifted across the balcony. He poured himself a glass of warm coffee. Staring hungrily at the plate of croissants, he helped himself to two. "Thank you," he said to Benigno, biting into the croissant.

"Thank you for sharing my bed with me, pretty boy," Benigno said. "What are your plans for today? Would you like to spend the day with me?"

"Benigno, I would love to, but I have to go back to England, today," Ali said.

"You don't need to rush back, yet. You are welcome to stay here as long as you want. Treat my home like it is your own," Benigno said.

"I have to go back. I've got to try to sort out the mess that I've made of my life," Ali said earnestly.

"I understand," Benigno said sadly. "You must promise me that you will stay in touch and visit me again once you have sorted your life out."

"I promise, Benigno. You are a wonderful friend. I am so glad that I've met you," Ali said.

"Is it okay to use your phone to check my flight time and to call one of my friends in England?" Ali asked.

"Go ahead," Benigno said generously.

Ali called the airline company first, confirmed his seat on a flight leaving in two hours time. Then he dialed Haseena's telephone number and prayed that she was in.

"Haseena, it's me," he said hearing her voice on the line. It was so nice to talk to her again.

"Ali, I've been worried sick about you. I was expecting a call from you yesterday. Are you alright?" Haseena asked sounding worried.

"I'm fine. I was right. Steve did not want me in Strasbourg with him. He'd already moved in with another man," Ali said despondently.

"Oh my god. Are you alright, Ali?" Haseena cried down the line.

"I'm fine, Haseena. I'm trying not to think about it. I'm coming back to England," Ali told her.

"You can't, Ali. Your family has been harassing everyone to discover your whereabouts. I've heard that they've even hired a private detective to look for you," Haseena said urgently.

"Oh my god. What am I going to do? I can't stay here," Ali said.

"You can't come back to Birmingham. You're going to have to try and go somewhere else. Do you know anyone outside Birmingham whom you can stay with?" Haseena asked.

"There's a guy named Pete. He's in Leicester, but I've not been in touch with him since I left university. I think I have his address in my address book," Ali said

"Okay, go to Leicester," Haseena ordered. "What time is your flight getting in?"

"It's going to be about one o'clock in the afternoon," Ali said.

"Get the train from Birmingham to Leicester. It's a direct one. I'll meet you at the train station there. I'll drive your car over and catch the train back," Haseena said, planning everything meticulously.

"What time are you going to meet me?" Ali said noticing that she'd omitted the most important detail.

"Three o'clock. Don't worry if you're late. I'll wait until you arrive," Haseena assured him.

"Thank you for being so good to me, Haseena," Ali said.

"You're my friend, Ali. I'm here for you no matter what," Haseena said. "I have to go. I've got the police at my door," she said suddenly.

"Oh my god. What do they want?" Ali asked.

"I don't know. I'd better answer the door. I'll see you in Leicester, bye," Haseena said hanging up.

Ali put the phone down feeling anxious and upset. Since he'd arrived at Benigno's, it felt as if he'd been cocooned for a short time without having to deal with the turmoil engulfing his life. Reality was difficult to escape from, as Ali's thoughts turned to returning to England.

"Stay with me, Ali. Let me look after you. I can make you happy," Benigno said seeing Ali's gloomy face.

"I'm sorry, Benigno, but I can't. I need to sort things out in England. I promise I'll visit you when I've sorted myself out," Ali said, assuring his new friend again.

"I shall miss you," Benigno said embracing him in a warm hug.

"I'll miss you, too," Ali said.

"Come on, get ready," Benigno said letting go of Ali. "I'll drive you to the airport and wait with you," he offered kindly.

"Thank you," Ali said gratefully. "I'll just go and re-pack my things in my suitcase." Ali hurried back to the bedroom and quickly packed his shaver and pajamas back into his suitcase, then met Benigno minutes later for his ride to the airport.

Chapter Sixteen

"Oh, Ali, I'm so glad to see you," Haseena said kissing him. "I've missed you so much."

Ali wrapped himself wordlessly around her petite form in a hug. He wanted to cry and tell her how he was feeling, but he knew that if he let go of the tight reins he'd put on his emotions his whole world might collapse around him. He needed to be strong and not think about things which he wasn't yet ready to deal with.

The flight to Birmingham had been on time, but the train to Leicester had arrived over an hour late. Haseena had waited patiently for him by the ticket office, knowing he would turn up.

"Let's have a coffee," Haseena said, taking her silent friend to the small coffee bar opposite the ticket office. She ordered two coffees while Ali found a table for them.

"Here's your coffee," Haseena said, handing one of the two mugs that she was holding to him.

"Thanks, Haseena," Ali said, taking the coffee, sipping a mouthful and relishing the taste.

"I'm sorry about Steve. I never realized he was such a bastard. How are you feeling?" she asked as she sat down on the chair opposite Ali. She stroked his hand gently as if that might take away some of the hurt. Anyone looking at the pair might have mistaken them for lovers if they'd not known that Ali was gay.

"I'm trying not to think about it. I'm not ready to deal with it, yet," Ali said "I've got too many other things to worry about at the moment."

"Oh, Ali, I'm so sorry," Haseena said.

"I'll be fine, Haseena. Don't worry about me," Ali said to reassure her, although inwardly wondering if there was any truth in his words.

"Okay. Let's not talk about Steve. Do you think you're ready to deal with a few letters?" she asked him.

"What letters? From whom?" Ali asked curiously.

Haseena rummaged through her handbag and pulled out a small bundle of letters, which she handed to Ali. "These arrived for you at my house. I think it's your family sending them, knowing that I'll pass them on to you. The one on top arrived by recorded delivery, so I'd say that's important. Open it first," Haseena suggested.

Ali opened the letter, wondering what his family would say to him. He pulled out several bright green pieces of writing paper. A couple of white sheets of paper that had been stapled together also fell out from the same envelope onto the floor. Ali picked up the document and looked at the letter. At first, he didn't recognize the handwriting and had no idea who might have sent it to him, but the identity of the author soon became clear as Ali began to read the letter.

"You cheat. You bastard,

"I've learned that you're gay. That you're a gandoo bastard. People who have known you for years have said that you had a partner, a MAN for over two years. You've deliberately betrayed us. Your family were shocked when I told them. They had to hear it from us that you're a gay bastard. This information was so easy to find once we started looking. It seemed everyone knew.

"If we had an idea or inkling before the marriage that you were such a dirty gay bastard I wouldn't have let you get near my family, or my daughter. The whole of the Pakistani community from Birmingham, Nottingham, and the village in Pakistan condemn you and your satanic actions. None of them have heard of the type of action that you've taken.

"You are in hiding now. You're a rat!

"This is your punishment from Allah. That you are a gandoo! You unbeliever! You forgot Islam, our religion, that's why you've got this punishment in this world. It will be the same in the next world for you. A good Muslim would never do what you've done. They believe in Allah.

"You're an unbeliever, impatient and fled as you were gandoo. You thought to have a go with a marriage and left home because you were not a real man. You didn't realize that you would hurt a respectable family.

"When you come out of your rat hole we'll find you. In this short space of time we have found out so much about you.

It will be so easy to track you down and hurt you like you've hurt my family.

"We gave back all the jewelry and gifts from you to your mother. It's a great insult to us! We gave you a lot! Wasted a lot of money! Money that should be spent on the funeral of a big gandoo bastard like you!

"If we ever find out you have come back home you will need to explain why you have destroyed my daughter's life. To think that we welcomed you with open arms and put a garland round your neck. We should have wiped our dirty shoes on you and put shit round your neck.

"There is a piece of paper enclosed. It is a Talak document, a divorce paper. Sign it three times you shit and post it back.

"May god punish you! You've lost your culture, your respect, your dignity, and your identity. You unbeliever! You were brought up in a bad environment."

"What does it say?" Haseena asked seeing the pained expression on Ali's face.

Ali handed the letter to Haseena. "Read it, yourself. I can't bear to look at it again," he said tearfully. "I've hurt so many people." Reading the word "gandoo" felt like a physical assault. He remembered his dad using it in the past, but he'd never known what it had meant until now. "Maybe I am being punished by God. Maybe I am cursed," Ali thought trying hard not to cry.

"Are you okay, Ali?" Haseena asked. Having read the letter, she now understood why Ali's face was so etched with pain.

"I'm fine. I'm shocked that they've found out about me," Ali said. "It means I can never go back."

"Were you considering going back?" Haseena asked in surprise.

"No, not really," Ali said lying.

"Well, you're lucky you left. What if they'd found out everything while you were there? What would you have done then? You'd better sign the Talak document. I'll post it back to them in a couple of days," Haseena said.

"Won't they find out that I'm still in touch with you when they receive it?" Ali asked.

"Don't worry, Ali. I can take care of myself. The sooner they get that divorce paper the sooner they'll stop hounding you and rebuild their own lives. That family must be hurting so much right now," Haseena said.

"I know, Haseena. I know," Ali said. "I should have listened to you and left before the wedding."

"I have a pen here," Haseena said, handing it to him.

Ali took the pen from her and opened up the talak document. A covering letter was attached to it from the Muslim Council in Small Heath, requesting that he divorce Sajda to free her from her marital responsibilities. The talak document itself was very simple. "I divorce thee," it stated on it three times with a space for a signature underneath for Ali and a witness to sign. Ali signed his name three times and dated the signature.

Haseena took the document from him and signed it quickly before returning it to her handbag. "That's the end of that chapter," she said looking at Ali's sad face. "Are you going to open another letter?"

"I don't think I can read any more," Ali said.

"Open them, Ali. Get it over and done with," Haseena said.

Ali took another envelope from the bundle and opened it. "It's from Yasmin," he exclaimed in surprise.

"Dear Brother Ali,

"I hope that you are well and in good health. Aneesa and I have tried in vain to get in touch with you, but there has been no response.

"We are all so worried about you.

"Why did you leave us so suddenly?

"Life is hard at the moment or should I say most times. It is quite unbearable without you. You at least can sleep at night knowing that we are only a phone call away, but we don't have the same peace of mind.

"What I think you fail to understand is the depth of our pain. If life could end when some one you love moves out of your life then we would have been no more.

"Unfortunately, God wants us to carry on living. The hungry heart has to feed, these restless eyes have to sleep, but this empty heart cannot be fulfilled.

"I love you so dearly. I'm sure you know that. What can I write to you about Mum? Even though you have been gone just days she misses you very much and spends most of her days crying. She hasn't been out of the house since you left.

"Grandmother has gone back to Pakistan. She was shocked and devastated by what you have done and has gone to pray with some of the Fakirs.

"It must be difficult for you to grasp, but you are our flesh and blood. You are important to us! Yet do we bear no significance in your life?

"I am sure in your heart of hearts you know what you are doing and maybe it is deliberate for whatever reasons. I pray that Allah will put some remorse into your heart, a little bit of tenderness for us and return you home to us safely.

"In the kingdom of God there is light. I pray that one day the darkness and gloom that falls upon us will be replaced by brightness and a happy future. Life is too short for neglect. Please come home to your responsibilities and your family.

"Khuda Hafiz and I pray I hear from you soon in whatever form.

"Yasmin"

"I can't believe it!" Ali said putting the letter down angrily. "I hate her! She's not mentioned once how they forced me into the marriage. She's asked me to come home."

"What did you expect from Yasmin. She can't see what's at the end of her nose at the best of times," Haseena commented.

Ali tore open another letter, hoping in vain that this would be better.

"Dear Ali,

"It's been a few days since you left me and every day since has been like hell for me. I feel that my life is a mess and I don't know how long I can cope.

"I feel sick from the moment I wake up in the morning to the moment I go to sleep at night. I used to love being me but

181

Amjeed Kabil

not any more. Now I'm just scared. My heart hurts so much, my head feels as if it's about to explode. I don't know how long it's going to be before I go insane.

"I have not been able to smile since my wedding day. You stole my happiness away from me.

"It's amazing how things can change in a few days. I want to be the way I used to be – happy and carefree – but I can't. I am crying as I write this.

"I am writing this from the bottom of my heart and what I write is the truth. I have a thousand things going through my head and it's driving me crazy.

"I've wasted my time on caring for someone who didn't give a toss about me. I suppose I must be a typical Pakistani girl, falling for someone she hardly knew, but having the feeling that she has to spend the rest of her life with that person.

"My father has found out that you say you're gay, but this typical Pakistani girl can't live without you, no matter what your problem is. I can help you overcome it. In my heart, I know that if you want to be normal, have a wife and children you will be able to. There is help available. I have looked into it, so there is no excuse. I am your responsibility now and only you can help me.

"Please come back. I would forget this unhappy time that I'm having at the moment. I do not have much of a future without you.

"I am visiting Mecca soon. My father is taking me. I have thought that I would be visiting God's house happy, but instead I'm burdened down with sadness. They say that God never forgives anyone who hurts others.

"Please prove to everyone that you are a decent person. Deep down I know you could be. You coming back would be a dream come true. Please make it come true for me. I'm desperate. Who knows what I might do.

"I will do anything to make you happy. I have money – we can settle down wherever and lead a quiet life. Please choose the life I want. We can get to know each other before anything.

"I can't live without you. I don't know how often I think of you. Let me do my duty and be a wife to you.

"Please be a husband to me. I beg you. I'm sorry but I am in love with you no matter what you say, and it's driving me insane. You might have your freedom but at my expense. I am

182

not good at expressing myself but gosh I hope I've convinced you about how I feel. I've shed so many tears for you in the last few days. I expect some happiness from you.

"Please I would really like to see you a.s.a.p. We have to talk face to face. I can come and see you or perhaps meet somewhere neutral. Please phone me or write to me at work.

"Please do this for me or I will write to you every week if you ignore my cries. If you're not up to phoning me send me a number where I can contact you.

"Sajda"

"It's Sajda. She wants to meet me," Ali said to Haseena. "She's so hurt." The ink had even run in places where her tears had fallen. "I have to call her and arrange a meeting. I need to explain to her why I left."

"You can't meet her, Ali. You've got to make a clean break," Haseena said. "You don't know what could happen if you met up with her."

"I owe it to her. I've hurt her so much, and it's the least I can do," Ali said guiltily, thinking of the pain that he'd inflicted on his wife.

"You can't meet her. You've signed the divorce papers, and that's the only thing that will help her to move on with her life," Haseena said.

"I have got to speak to her. I have to explain what happened," Ali said.

"Ali, for once please listen to me. Don't get in touch with the girl," Haseena said forcefully. "You're moving on with your life. Let her have the chance to do the same. Contacting her will be the worst thing you can do. Walk away from it."

"She's hurting so much, Haseena. I need to do something that will make her feel better. An explanation from me is all she might need," Ali said in anguish.

"Leave it, Ali, please," Haseena said. "You've got to let go."

Ali tried to stop himself from bursting into tears. He didn't want everyone in the coffee shop to watch him cry. He knew his friend was right. "Why didn't I listen to you in the first place?" Ali said miserably. "I can't bear to read any more letters. Will you take them with you?"

"Yes, of course," Haseena said taking the two remaining letters from him and slipping them back into her handbag. "I forgot to mention that your family has reported you missing to the police. They visited me this morning. You're going to have to report to a police station," Haseena said, knowing that giving Ali a practical problem to deal with might get his mind off the letters he'd read.

"They won't tell my family my whereabouts will they?" Ali asked.

"No. Apparently your family has told them that you've had a nervous breakdown, so they need to make sure that you're alive and well," Haseena told him.

"So, I just need to go and report to a police station?" Ali asked.

"Yes, simple as that, but take your passport with you," Haseena replied. "Anyway, Ali, I've got to start heading back. Will you be okay on your own? I really don't want to leave you, but it won't be safe for you in Birmingham."

"I'll be fine," Ali reassured her. "Don't worry about me. I've got Pete's address. I'll stay with him for a couple of nights until I've sorted a place out for myself."

"That's good to know. My train's leaving any minute, so I'd better go down to the platform. Oh, here's your car keys," she said handing them to him. "I've parked it on the street next to the station. I think it's called Conduit Street."

Ali took the keys and gave her a big hug. "Thank you for everything," he said gratefully.

"That's okay. I'm your friend, it's what friends do," she replied returning the hug. "Don't worry about coming to the platform with me. You've got lots to do. Derek wishes you all the best by the way. He couldn't come as he is on day shifts this week."

Haseena gave him another kiss before disappearing down the stairs to the platform leaving Ali alone. He hurried out of the train station to find his car. He located it quickly on the side street like Haseena had said and got into it. Starting the car, he noticed that Haseena had generously filled up the tank with petrol.

Following the directions that he'd copied from an A-Z map book in a newsagents at the airport, Ali drove quickly to Walton Street and parked outside Pete's house. He got out of the car and knocked on the door. The door was opened by a decrepit looking old woman. "What do you want?" she asked rudely.

"I'm looking for Pete. Does he still live here?" Ali asked her.

"Pete? Why are you looking for him?" she asked suspiciously.

"I'm a friend from university," Ali said.

"Well he doesn't live here anymore. He's moved to Wales," the woman said.

"He's moved out?" Ali asked, unable to believe the bad news.

"He moved out a few months ago. He used to lodge with me. I'm glad he moved out though, I was sick of him bringing strangers back home with him all the time," she grumbled. "I've stopped taking in lodgers now." With that the woman shut the door sharply in his face.

"What am I going to do?" Ali thought to himself. He'd pinned all of his hopes on Pete still living at this address. He hadn't prepared for the possibility of Pete not being there anymore. With only fifty-five pounds on him and nowhere to stay, Ali considered his options. A hotel would eat all of his money in one go. He could telephone Haseena and see if she could help, but she'd done enough for him already.

"I'll sleep in the car, tonight," he finally decided. It wasn't appealing, but it was the cheapest option as long as he could keep himself warm. There were some bargain discount stores that he'd driven past on Narborough Road on the way to Walton Street. They might sell cheap duvets.

Ali walked to the shops on Narborough Road, leaving his car behind. He found a store called Raj's Discount Store, which was run by a friendly Sikh man in a turban, and for eight pounds managed to buy himself a king size duvet.

It was still early when he got back to the car, and he had a few hours to kill before bedtime. Hiding his new purchase in the boot of the car, Ali went back to Narborough Road and found a pub to sit in. He ordered himself a small glass of lemonade and spent the next couple of hours sipping it slowly in a quiet corner, hoping that the landlord wouldn't throw him out.

Just before last orders, Ali went to the men's room, and used the toilet, before washing his hands and cleaning his teeth for the night and then left the pub.

Ali then went back to his car and drove to a quiet side street. However, it wasn't quiet enough, and he worried that someone might spot him sleeping in the car. What he needed was a secluded car park where he could sleep for the night.

It was only by chance while driving randomly through the streets of Leicester, Ali found a car park to a large DIY store that was tucked away behind a large canopy of trees.

Ali parked his car in a discrete corner of the car park and turned the engine and the headlights off. The car park was in total darkness and had an eerie feel about it. The store itself had the shutters down, and there was no one around.

Ali took his suitcase out of the car boot and emptied its contents in the leg space between the front and the back seats. He then folded the back seats down into the boot space so that the seats were flat, and took out his new duvet from its packaging and folded it in half before laying it flat over the back seat and the filled gap. Looking at the finished effect, he knew that he'd created himself a comfortable nest for the night.

He then got back in the car shutting and locking the door behind him, climbing into his nest, he settled down in between the folded layers of the duvet.

Ali found it very hard to sleep. The back of the car was cramped and uncomfortable. As the minutes passed by, Ali started to smell engine oil. The smell gradually became stronger, making him feel claustrophobic and sick.

Gasping for air and feeling a sense of panic, Ali wound one of the rear windows down. A cold gust of air blew in making him gasp. He quickly wound the window back up again leaving it open by an inch. He did the same to the windows on the other side, hoping that it would circulate the air around the car rather than giving him hypothermia.

He then settled back down in an attempt to sleep, trying to ignore the distant traffic noise coming through the open windows and not allowing his imagination to create terrifying visions of what might happen to him while alone in a dark car park at night. He wanted to cry at the unfairness of his predicament but managed to hold his emotions in check. Ali's eyes started to flicker and eventually they closed as he finally fell asleep.

Chapter Seventeen

"I'm homeless," Ali said to the small Indian woman sitting behind the reception desk. "Can I speak to someone who could help me to find somewhere to live?"

"Sorry, there's no one available to speak to you today," she replied dismissively without bothering to look up.

"But I'm homeless, and I thought I'd be able to get some advice here. The notice in the window says that you offer advice to homeless people," Ali said, taken aback by the woman's uncaring attitude.

"I told you that we have no one to talk to you right now," she said crossly. "If you really need to talk to someone, I can book you an appointment."

"Well, I'm free all day. So any time is convenient," Ali said.

"Three weeks," she said rifling through the pages of her desk diary.

"Sorry?" Ali asked, wondering if he'd heard right.

"I said it will be three weeks before anyone will be able to see you. The appointment diary is fully booked until then," she said continuing to flick through the pages of the diary again.

"I don't have anywhere to live now. I can't wait three weeks to talk to someone about it. I need some advice about it today. I can't sleep in the car for another night let alone for another three weeks!" Ali exclaimed despairingly.

"You can stay with your family. We have lots of people coming through the doors with the same problem, and we can't always help everyone straightaway," she said sighing dramatically in displeasure as if Ali was preventing her from doing something important.

"I don't have any family to stay with. If I did, I wouldn't be homeless now, would I?" Ali said feeling very frustrated.

"There's no need to talk to me like that. I've booked you an appointment in three weeks time, so you can come back then." The receptionist shoved an appointment card into Ali's hand and turned to the next person in the queue, ending the conversation.

Ali left the City Council's Housing Advice Center clutching the card in his hand. The notice on the window had clearly stated that the Housing Advice Center would be able to find homeless people temporary shelter and give advice on finding accommodation. It had said nothing about a three-week wait!

He'd stood waiting in the queue to be seen for over forty minutes in the hope that he'd solve his housing problem, but it seemed that it wasn't to be. He felt frustrated at his own predicament. All he wanted was somewhere warm to sleep and a temporary shelter would have been perfect.

It was going to be another cold night. Ali had spent the last two nights sleeping in his car. Today, he'd plucked up the courage to deal with his situation and actually do something about it, but it seemed that bureaucracy was holding him back.

Ali had left his car near a block of student flats on Putney Road, about half an hour's walk from the city center. It was convenient and the parking was free. It was also next to the car park he was using to park his car to sleep in overnight.

It was getting easier to sleep in the car. Ali had managed to get used to the traffic noise, and the raucous cries of students returning home after their late nights of partying. He feared the students the most but more out of embarrassment. The last thing he wanted was a group of drunken students discovering him asleep in his car and ridiculing him.

Ali was secretly pleased with the changes in himself. Less than a week ago, he would have feared the thought of being alone in a deserted car park after midnight. His imagination running riot with thoughts of vampires and ghosts, but he felt as if the experience had helped him mature.

It was early morning, and Granby Street, which ran through the heart of Leicester's city center, was deserted. Ali found this to be a blessing as he looked disheveled and unkempt. He headed towards the Shires, a shopping center which seemed to be the main place to shop in Leicester.

Ali entered the center and walked past a small bakery savoring the smell of freshly baked muffins. He considered buying a cookie, but the price of eight cookies for two pounds helped to change his mind. He had less than twenty-five pounds left, and with no certainty of any more money coming his way, he needed to make it last.

He decided instead to wait for lunchtime and buy himself a cheap bag of chips from the local chip shop he'd visited the previous evening.

Ali walked past the stores without bothering to look in the windows and took the escalator to the men's washrooms on the basement level.

Once in the washrooms, Ali stood at a washbasin, turned on the tap, took out his toothbrush and toothpaste from his jacket pocket and brushed his teeth. He looked around to see if anyone was watching, but the washrooms were empty. Using the soap from the dispenser Ali washed his face and then dried it on the paper towels provided.

He then pulled out a tube of hair gel from his pocket and used it to groom his hair. Despite his best attempts, he still looked unkempt. "I must have looked a right state, and she still didn't help me," he murmured to himself thinking back to his encounter with the receptionist.

His face looked like it had aged in the last few days. The creases on his face seemed to match the ones on his shirt and made him look haggard. Despite this, Ali felt satisfied for having made the effort. He then soaked a couple of paper towels with water and went into the toilet cubicle locking the door behind him.

He unbuttoned his shirt and used the wet paper towels to clean his armpits and chest, before promptly drying himself with some more tissue paper. He repeated the same procedure with his groin area, and then changed into a fresh pair of underpants that he'd brought with him.

Ali flushed the paper towels down the toilet, unlocked the cubicle door and walked out feeling a lot fresher. He glanced around and caught a man looking at him. The man held his gaze, making Ali squirm with embarrassment. Ali quickly turned away and hurried out of the toilets.

As he headed towards the exit of the shopping center, he had a sense of being followed. He looked back and saw the same man following him. It had to be a private detective. "He's found me," Ali thought in panic, his stomach clenching tightly in fear. He felt sick. All he wanted to do was to get out of the shopping center and hide.

"Hey, wait up! Why are you running away?" he heard the man's voice shout after him. Ali quickened his pace, fighting the urge to run, not wanting to attract the attention of the other shoppers.

Once outside, Ali sighed in relief, thinking he had managed to get away as he hurried down the street.

"Wait!" The man's voice was now even closer. Ali stopped. It was daylight, and he was in the middle of a main street in a town center. What could the detective possibly do to him?

"What do you want?" Ali asked turning around, trying to hide his fear as he faced the man. The man was dressed smartly in a navy blue pair of trousers and a white shirt and tie. He looked to be in his early forties and physically very trim. The lines on his face and the graying hair at his temples made him look distinguished and quite handsome.

"Nothing really. I just saw you in the Shires. I thought you looked really nice. I just wanted to tell you that," he said catching up with Ali.

"What?" Ali exclaimed incredulously.

"I think you're very sexy," the man said. "I'd like to buy you a drink."

"You're kidding right?" Ali asked feeling bewildered that someone would be attracted to him, especially in his current state. "I'm too busy. I've got things to do."

"Please, at least think about it. I need to drop off some paperwork at the office, but I can meet you in half an hour. What do you say?" the man asked.

"No, I'm sorry. I can't," Ali said starting to walk away.

"Please, I really like you. Just a quick drink. I can make it worth your while," the man said continuing to follow Ali.

"What do you mean you can make it worth my while?" Ali asked out of curiosity.

"I can tell you're running away from something. I can help you. Let's meet for a drink, we can chat and get to know each other. If you wanted to get to know me better then you could earn yourself a little bit of money. If you wanted you could even stay a couple of nights at my place," the man said.

"Go away," Ali stormed angrily. "I'm not a fucking rent boy," he cursed, horrified by the indecent proposal.

"Don't be like that. I just want to treat you right and help you out a bit. Give you somewhere to stay for a couple of nights. What do you say? I promise I won't force you into anything you don't agree to," he said sincerely.

"Go away," Ali said. "If you carry on pestering me, I'll report you to the Police."

"Listen, I don't mean to pester you. If you're interested in my offer then meet me at the pub on Dover Street in half an hour. Please?" he asked.

Ali did not respond. He knew he needed money and somewhere warm to sleep, but this was not the way to do it.

"I really like you and want to help you out," the man said gently. "I'll jot down the directions to the pub. If I don't see you there in half an hour then I'll take it you're not interested." He took out a pen from his jacket and wrote the directions onto a piece of paper.

"Here," he said shoving the piece of paper into Ali's hands. "I hope you'll be there. It's not far. It's just on the other side of town. My name's Andy by the way. What's yours?" he asked.

Ali didn't reply, not wanting to give away too much about himself. "Well I hope you turn up," he said looking at Ali longingly before heading off.

"What is it about me?" Ali muttered to himself. This was the second time since running away that he'd been approached by another gay man. "I can't be that camp. Maybe it's because they can sense that I'm vulnerable and needy," he finally concluded.

Ali spent the next few minutes agonizing over what to do. In some of the clubs that he had been to there had been a seedy element with young men offering themselves for cash to older men. He had never thought that he'd be in a position where he'd be considering doing the same.

"What have I got to lose," he finally thought, having made his decision. "I'll go and meet him, then I can decide how far I'm prepared to go for somewhere to stay and a bit of cash."

Ali followed Andy's written instructions and found the pub. It was next to some dilapidated old buildings that were in

193

the process of being torn down to make way for a car park. Ali entered the pub nervously through the front door that was hidden behind some scaffolding. Inside, the pub was poorly lit, the curtains were drawn and the lights dimmed low, which gave it a nice atmosphere, but it was clear that it was also to conceal the faded décor and the drinks spilled on the carpeted floor.

In the corner by the bar, were several stacks of newspapers and magazines. Ali walked over and picked up something from each pile, *The Pink Paper*, *QX Magazine*, and *Bent*. They were all free publications for the gay community. Ali went up to the bar, walking past a table of middle-aged men in tight white t-shirts. They stared at him and whispered to each other, making Ali feel self-conscious. He blushed knowing that he didn't fit in, especially not with his crumpled clothes.

"What am I doing here? I should be trying to find somewhere to live," Ali thought. He turned around having decided to leave the bar.

"Hi, what would you like to drink?" he heard the barman ask.

"Can I have a small lemonade and ice with a slice of lemon," asked Ali, changing his mind and turning around to face the barman.

"Yes of course, sweetheart," the barman said and poured the lemonade into a large pint glass. He added ice and lemon and finished it off by putting a cocktail umbrella in the glass with a camp flourish. "I've poured you a large glass, sweetheart, but I'll only charge you for a small."

"Thank you very much," Ali said gratefully.

"That's okay, honey. That'll be ninety pence," he said sweetly with a pretty smile.

Ali carefully counted out the coins. He didn't have much money left. In fact after buying the drink he knew that he had exactly twenty-three pounds and fifteen pence in his pocket.

He found a table that faced the door so that he could see Andy when he walked in and sipped the lemonade while flicking through the gay publications.

Turning though the pages of *QX*, Ali came across listings for escort services at the back of the magazine. There were pages and pages of adverts of men with photographs of themselves in swim shorts showing their torsos or completely naked, their faces blurred out. "Lots of people do it. It can't be that bad," Ali thought.

Ali heard the door open and glanced up as Andy walked in through the door. "So you came," he said grinning cheerfully. He kissed Ali on the cheek and plonked himself down in the chair opposite.

"I had nothing to lose, I suppose," Ali said, trying not to sound glum.

"Well, I'm glad you did. I've not been able to stop thinking about you. Let me get you a drink," he said looking at Ali's nearly empty glass.

"I'll just have another lemonade with ice," Ali said.

"Have something stronger," Andy suggested. "Maybe a glass of white wine?"

"No, I'll stick to the lemonade, but could you get me a bag of peanuts and a packet of cheese and onion crisps please?" asked Ali hungrily.

"They serve food here. Are you sure you don't want a proper meal?" Andy asked.

"No, I only want a snack," Ali said. He would have loved to enjoy a proper meal, but didn't want to feel indebted to anyone.

"I'll just be a few moments," Andy said getting up. He gave Ali a slobbery kiss on the lips as if buying a small snack for Ali gave him permission to push the boundaries.

Ali watched him as he ordered at the bar. He tried his best not to feel nervous, but the butterflies in his stomach didn't help. "What am I going to do?" he thought. He felt so nervous and sick with worry.

At the table next to the bar, Ali caught the eye of the group of middle-aged men staring at him. He blushed again and looked away hoping that they weren't judging him.

"Here you are," Andy said returning to the table and handing Ali the drink and snacks.

"Thank you," said Ali, tearing into the packet of crisps and stuffing them into his mouth enthusiastically. It was the first bit of food to pass his lips since the previous night.

"So who are you running away from?" Andy asked as he watched Ali eat.

"I'm not running away from anyone," Ali replied, between a mouthful of crisps.

"Oh..." Andy murmured skeptically.

"I'm just visiting Leicester," Ali said, not wanting to reveal too much. "It's a nice place to visit," he added.

"You don't have to tell me if you don't want to, but you shouldn't lie," Andy said, not wishing to pry. "I do know you're homeless; otherwise, why would you be freshening up in public toilets?"

Ali didn't reply, not knowing how to deny the truth.

"Listen. You don't have to worry. All I want to do is help you," Andy said earnestly.

"That's really kind of you," Ali said.

"Do you want to come back to mine?" Andy asked suddenly.

"I'm not sure," Ali said. He'd finished all the snacks and had stopped eating. He felt his stomach making worrying noises, and he stared nervously down at the glass of lemonade in front of him shamefully.

"I'll pay you a hundred pounds for the night. You won't have to do anything you don't want to," said Andy, cajoling him. "I want to have sex with you, and you need some money right now and a place to stay. This way we can help each other out."

"I don't know..." Ali said unconvincingly, tempted by the offer.

"It will cost you an hour of your time, and you'll have earned yourself a bit of money for yourself," Andy said persuasively. "If you don't want to stay the night, you could leave straight away."

"I suppose it should be okay," Ali said.

"So are we going spend all day sitting in the pub or shall we go to mine," Andy said getting up. "I live round the corner from here, above a nightclub I manage."

Ali followed him silently out of the pub. He felt confused by his own actions. It was all happening so fast, but he let himself go along with it. A few weeks ago, he would have viewed anyone accepting money for sex from a moral high ground. "I still have some money. I don't need to do this," he thought just as Andy turned a corner. He considered making a run for it in the opposite direction, but his legs failed to follow through with the thought.

"We're here," Andy announced as he unlocked a side door to the nightclub, and led Ali up a flight of stairs.

"Welcome to my home," Andy said opening the door to his apartment and inviting Ali inside. He shut the door behind and locked it shut.

Ali's heart started racing. He felt trapped. His mouth felt dry, and he couldn't stop shaking. He suddenly felt frightened.

"So ... here we are," Andy said turning round to face Ali. He moved towards him and kissed Ali on his lips. Pushing Ali roughly against the door, he grabbed hold of Ali and kissed him again, attempting to thrust his tongue into Ali's mouth this time. Ali kept his mouth tightly shut.

"What's wrong?" Andy asked crossly.

"I'm really sorry. I can't do this. I thought I could, but I can't," Ali said shakily trying to push Andy away. "I don't feel right doing this. I'm really sorry."

"What? You can't do this you fucking prick," Andy shouted. "We made a deal, so stick to it." He pushed Ali violently against the door and attempted to pull his jeans down.

"Leave me alone," Ali cried, pulling himself out of Andy's tight grip.

"Look, you stupid bastard, it's a bit too late to back out now. All you have to do is pretend to enjoy yourself, and afterwards I'll pay you," Andy screeched.

"I'm really sorry I can't do this. I'm really sorry. I want to leave, please," Ali said trying to choke back his tears.

"Just get your fucking clothes off," Andy screamed at him.

"I'm not doing this. I have to go. I didn't mean to mess you about," Ali said trying find an escape route. Andy stood in front of the door blocking his only exit.

"You're going to have to finish what you've started," he said menacingly as he started to unzip himself.

"Leave me alone. Let me leave," Ali pleaded. "I don't want to hurt you, but I will if I have to."

"That will just make it more fun. I'll pay you extra for that," he said, coming at Ali with both hands stretched out. "This is so much more fun," he gasped breathlessly.

"Leave me alone," Ali cried, but Andy tried to grip him in a headlock. Without a second thought Ali punched him hard in the stomach, making Andy double over with a loud howl of pain. Ali followed this with a kick in the general direction of Andy's crotch.

"You fucker," Andy screamed in pain. "I'm going to hurt you so bad ..." Ali didn't wait for him to carry out his threat. He pushed past him, unlocked the door and raced down the flight of stairs. He opened the door to the outside and started running. He didn't stop until he reached the safety of Granby Street.

He stood in a shop doorway gasping breathlessly. He shook from the adrenalin rush. He felt ashamed by what he had done and knowing that he'd been so foolish. "What is wrong with me?" he muttered angrily.

"I have to go back home. I can't live like this anymore. I've had enough. I'll tell them that I had a breakdown and beg their forgiveness," Ali muttered miserably as he wandered down the street in despair, heading back to where he had parked his car.

As he turned the corner to a side street, a large poster in a shop window caught his eye:

"OPENDOOR LEICESTER – SUPPORT & ADVICE FOR YOUNG 16-25 YEAR OLDS. FREE ADVICE ON HOUSING, PREGNANCY, AND BENEFITS. CALL INSIDE."

"This is it!" Ali thought excitedly staring at the poster. He tried the door to the building, but it was locked. The lights in the window were off, and it seemed the place was shut. Ali spotted a doorbell hidden to the side of the building and started to press it desperately. Just as he was about to give up, he saw someone appear at the door. It was a young black woman. She frowned at Ali from behind the glass panel in the door, and unlocked it reluctantly.

"What do you want?" she asked sternly, opening the door.

"I saw the sign," Ali said pointing at the sign in the window. "I need someone to give me some advice."

"We're closed for lunch," the woman said. "We'll be open at two."

"I'm homeless. I need some help to find somewhere to stay," Ali cried, tears coming to his eyes. "I've been to the Council, and they won't see me for another three weeks. I just don't know what to do anymore."

"Come back at two," the woman said to Ali, her demeanor mellowing and becoming friendly. "I'm not allowed to let you in before then. We should be able to help you find somewhere."

"Thank you," Ali cried gratefully. "Thank you very much."

"I'll see you at two. My name's Sheila. Ask for me when you come back," she said smiling. She then shut the door, locked it behind her and disappeared back into the building.

Ali left the doorway filled with renewed hope, putting his decision to return home on hold for the time being.

Chapter Eighteen

Ali tried the handle to the door and was pleased when it pushed open. He followed the arrows printed on sheets of A4 paper stuck on the walls that directed to the Opendoor office. The arrows led him down a flight of stairs and into the basement of the building. The stairs came to an end in front of a big door.

Ali knocked on the door and waited. When no one answered he pushed the door open and entered. The office was quite small with no visible windows and space for only two desks. It looked like any regular office with computers at both desks. A fax machine and a photocopier were situated in one corner.

A small wicker basket overflowing with loose condoms sat in the center of one of the desks with a hand written notice reading, "Play it safe – help yourself to free condoms."

"I'm here to see Sheila," Ali said timidly to the woman sitting with her head down behind one of the computer screens.

The woman glanced up looking disturbed. "She's popped out to the loo. Take a seat," she said pointing to one of the chairs, and went back to the work she was doing on the computer.

Ali sat down and waited impatiently, feeling apprehensive about meeting Sheila. What if she couldn't help him after all? Ali looked up each time he thought he heard someone enter the room.

"You came back, then," he heard a woman's voice say, and looked up to see Sheila.

Ali nodded a shy yes, feeling stuck for words

"Would you like a mug of tea?" she asked him pleasantly, trying to put him at ease.

"Yes please," Ali said gratefully.

"Sugar? Milk?" she asked.

"Milk, no sugar please," Ali replied.

Sheila disappeared behind a small screen at the back of the office and reappeared soon after with two steaming mugs of tea. "We'll go into one of the interview rooms," she said walking past him to another door.

Ali got up, followed her into the small room and closed the door behind. It was a stuffy little room with two tatty office chairs in it and nothing else. "Sit down," Sheila said gently. Once Ali was seated, she handed him the mug she was holding.

"Thank you," Ali said, and sipped the tea before putting it down on the floor to the side of the chair.

"What's your name?" asked Sheila.

"Ali Mirza," Ali said.

"So how can Opendoor help you?" she asked.

"I'm homeless," Ali said. "I don't have anywhere to live. I was hoping that you might be able to help me find somewhere to live. I don't have much money to find somewhere myself."

"So where have you been sleeping?" asked Sheila.

"In my car," Ali replied, his voice sounding mournful. "I spend the day walking and keeping myself warm. At night, I go to my car to sleep."

"That must be terrible for you. What happened to make you homeless?" asked Sheila giving him a reassuring smile in encouragement, knowing that he was finding it hard to talk.

"I had a disagreement with my family. It meant I had to leave home," Ali said.

"What was the disagreement about?" Sheila asked.

"I can't talk about it," Ali said cautiously, finding it painful to talk and open up his memories of the last few days.

"I'm sorry, Ali, but I'll need to know more about your situation in order to help you," said Sheila. When there was no reply forthcoming from Ali. "I'm sorry I can't help you unless I know the facts," she continued. "It's painful talking about things that have hurt us, but you've already done the hardest thing by coming here. Was it drugs?"

"No it wasn't drugs," Ali replied.

"In your own time, Ali," Sheila murmured gently.

"I was forced into an arranged marriage," said Ali unhappily. "I ran away after the wedding night because ... well because I'm gay."

"Did your parents know you were gay?" asked Sheila without signs of surprise at Ali's words. She had heard this tale before from many young Asian men who came to the office.

"Yes. I told them in my last semester at University. They wouldn't accept it and put it down to stress from my studies. When I finished my degree, they badgered me to move back home, and I did," Ali told her.

"Well, you're very brave for leaving. Not many people would have had the strength to leave," Sheila said with empathy.

"It was very hard," Ali said, trying to hold back the flood of tears that threatened to burst from his eyes. "I can't go back to Birmingham as my family is still looking for me. I've got to start a new life here in Leicester, but I can't do that without somewhere to live."

"We'll be able to help you find a place to stay," Sheila assured him. "If you don't find somewhere straight away, we can refer you to Nightshelter. It's an overnight hostel for homeless people. They'll allow you to stay there from nine in the evening to eleven in the morning. They've got washing facilities there, so you'll be able to freshen up."

"It would be nice having a bed to sleep in and a shower. I'm not sure if I could cope sleeping another night in my car," Ali said.

"How old are you?" Sheila asked him suddenly.

"Twenty-four," Ali told her.

"That's a shame. If you'd been seventeen, we could have got Social Services to find you somewhere to stay. Let's go back to the main office, so you can start making some phone calls," Sheila said getting up.

She opened the door and led Ali back into the main office. "Here's a list of all the long stay hostels in Leicester," she said picking up a booklet from her desk and handing it to Ali. "Take a seat and start phoning them."

Ali sat down on the chair that Sheila pointed to. He picked up the telephone handset and opened the first page of the booklet. "What shall I say?" he asked turning to Sheila, unsure of the approach to take.

"Say that you are being supported by Opendoor. Tell them that you're homeless and ask if they have any vacancies," Sheila suggested.

"Okay," Ali said gratefully.

"Telephone HITS Homes Trust first," said Sheila encouragingly. "I think they've got some vacancies coming up."

"Okay," Ali said.

"Well, go on then," said Sheila smiling, bemused by Ali's lack of confidence.

Ali turned the pages in the booklet, found the number for HITS Homes Trust, and dialed it. The phone was answered immediately. "Is this HITS Trust?" Ali asked.

"Yes, how can I help you?" asked a female voice.

"I'm at Opendoor. They've advised me to give you a call. I'm currently homeless and wondering if you have any vacancies," Ali said hesitantly.

"We're actually interviewing for two vacancies today. Did you want to be considered?" the female voice asked.

"Yes, please," Ali cried eagerly unable to believe his luck.

"We'll need a referral from Opendoor before we can interview you," the woman said.

"Oh my God!" Ali screamed in excitement to Sheila. "They have vacancies, and they're interviewing today. They need a referral from you. Would you refer me?"

"Yes, of course," said Sheila.

"They'll refer me," said Ali turning back to speak to the woman on the phone.

"Excellent, can you get here for three o'clock?" she asked him.

"Yes, I think so. Where are you?"

"We're on Evington Road," she said giving him a house number. "What's your name?"

"Ali Mirza," Ali said.

"Okay, we'll need a referral faxed to us straight away," the woman said urgently. "If we don't have a copy of that referral when you get here, we won't be able to consider you. They should have our fax number."

"I'll let Sheila know," Ali said happily.

"I'll expect to see you at three. Try not to be late," the woman said sternly before putting the phone down and ending the call.

"They're interviewing me at three. Do you think you'll be able to fax a referral to them before then? They won't interview me without one," Ali said.

"I've partially filled a referral form out while you were on the phone," Sheila said waving the form at him. "You just need to fill in your personal details." She handed him the form and a pen to complete the missing information.

"This is only an interview, so don't build your hopes up too much," Sheila cautioned when Ali handed the completed form back to her.

"I know, but it feels like I am finally doing something constructive," Ali said excitedly. "I've got to get to Evington Road for three. Do you know how I can get there?"

"It's too far to walk, and you don't really have that long to get there. If I were you, I'd get a bus from the Haymarket," she advised him.

Ali gave her a confused look. "Is that in the center?" he asked.

"It's not far. When you come out of this building, walk back to Granby Street and then onto Gallowtree Gate. You'll eventually come to a junction where you'll see the Haymarket shopping center on your right. Walk through it, and the bus terminal is on the other side," Sheila instructed. "Get the number twenty-two, and it'll take you to Evington Road. It shouldn't be more than a ten minute ride."

"I think I should be able to find it," Ali said positively.

"Good luck," said Sheila getting up. She came over to him and gave him an unexpected hug fondly. "If they don't take you on, we'll find something for you, so don't worry. Just be honest with them."

"Thank you so much Sheila," said Ali shyly removing himself from her embrace.

Ali followed Sheila's directions, found the bus terminal and jumped on the bus as soon as it arrived. He looked out of the window worriedly, trying to spot the street sign for Evington Road as the bus drove slowly out of the town center, stopping to pick up new passengers along the route.

Feeling increasingly worried that he may miss his stop, Ali got up and asked the driver to let him know when the bus arrived at his destination. He then sat back down impatiently looking out of the window.

"It's your stop coming up now, me duck," the bus driver suddenly called out in a Leicestershire accent just as the bus came to a halt outside a busy row of shops.

Ali got up hurriedly and thanked the driver as he stepped off. He walked along the road checking the number of each building that he passed. He finally reached an old three-storey Victorian building with a large metal sign by the side of the door for HITS Homes Trust.

Ali rang the bell and waited.

"Who is it, please?" a woman's voice asked from the intercom.

"Ali Mirza, I have an interview for three o'clock," Ali replied.

"Come in. You're already five minutes late," the voice said sharply. "We're in the main office. Take the door to your left as you come in."

"Thank you," Ali said politely and walked into the building when the door clicked open. There was a large brightly painted blue door to his left with glass in it. Ali could make out some figures behind it. Taking a deep breath, Ali knocked on the door and stepped inside without waiting for a reply.

"Hello, Ali, I'm Naureen," a short Pakistani woman said getting up from behind a large office desk and shook Ali's hand "I'm the Manager for HITS Homes Trust. These are the two support workers who work on the scheme, Trevor and Sarah," she said introducing him to the two people seated on the chairs next to her desk.

"Nice to meet you," Ali said nervously.

"Sit down," Naureen said, pointing to an empty chair in front of her desk before returning to her own chair.

Ali sat down on the chair facing the panel of three. His confidence had completely evaporated since stepping into the room, and he felt worse realizing that this was going to be a proper interview. Naureen's expression seemed quite warm, but the two support workers looked very serious. They both held small notepads resting on their laps ready to start making notes. It felt like the start of a job interview.

"I'll give you a brief introduction about the work that we do here at HITS Homes Trust, and then we'll ask you a few questions. We will be making some notes to help us remember what you've said," Naureen informed him.

"Okay," Ali said his voice wavering.

"HITS Homes Trust was set up to support young vulnerable people between the ages of eighteen and twenty five," she said as if reading from a memorized script. "We offer furnished accommodation and day-to-day support for all our residents. The staff are trained counselors and will provide emotional support and a counseling service. We work closely with local colleges and employers to help find work or places on training courses for our residents. Would any of what we do be of any use to you?"

"Yes. All of it," Ali said.

"We manage two supported housing schemes including this one. The other one is based on Maidstone Road. They are all one bed flats and come fully furnished," Naureen continued.

"Can you tell us a little about yourself?" Trevor asked after Naureen's dialogue.

"I already mentioned in my telephone call that I'm homeless. My family forced me into an arranged marriage, but I ran away the day after getting married," Ali said with downcast eyes, not wanting to see their reaction to his words. He felt especially apprehensive about Naureen's reaction knowing she was Pakistani and Muslim, so he didn't mention his sexuality. What if she responded in the same way as his family?

"What made you run away?" Trevor asked.

"It wasn't right for me," Ali said.

"Why?" Naureen asked.

"Because I'm gay," Ali replied murmuring his response not looking at Naureen in case he saw an adverse reaction.

"That must have been difficult for you. Do you think you'll go back home?" Trevor asked.

Ali considered the question. "No," he finally replied after a long pause. "When things are not going well I sometimes think about going back. Then I remember how unhappy I was."

"How do you think you would benefit from living in supported accommodation?" asked Sarah looking up from her notepad.

"It would give me a home. I've been sleeping in my car for the last few days. I also need help finding a job. It would be nice to talk to someone and sort my head out," Ali said.

"What are your goals?" asked Sarah once she had finished jotting down his answer on her notepad.

"I don't have any long-term goals right now. All I want is to find a place to stay and then I can start looking for a job," Ali said.

"How long do you think you would need to live in a supported environment?" Trevor asked.

"I don't know," Ali said. "Maybe a year I guess."

"If you're not successful in getting a place here what will you do?" Naureen asked.

"I don't know. I really don't know," Ali said. All his hopes rested on getting one of the vacancies. He had not considered what he'd do if he didn't.

"Well, that's all the questions we have. We are trying to keep the interviews as short as possible," Naureen said. "Do you have any questions for us?"

"How many people have you interviewed," Ali asked, curious about the level of competition.

"You're the fifth and the last person we're interviewing," Naureen told him.

"When will you be able to let me know if I've been successful or not?" Ali asked.

"We're giving everyone a call back in half an hour. As you don't have a fixed address we can either telephone Opendoor and let them know the outcome or you can wait in the lounge area," Naureen said.

"I'll wait in the lounge, if that's okay," Ali said.

"You can go back out through that door," Naureen said pointing at the door Ali had entered. "The lounge is through the door opposite. We'll let you know when we're ready."

"Thank you," Ali said getting up. He smiled at everyone before leaving the office and going to the lounge, hoping that he had given them a good first impression.

The lounge was typical of a family room. There was a blue sofa and chair in the center of the room, with a mahogany coffee table. A large crowded bookshelf stood in one corner, while in the other corner, a television set flickered.

Ali sat down on the side of the sofa closest to the television. He hadn't watched television for days and tried to pay attention to the flickering images, but his attention was on more important things. "I want a place to stay," he thought. He felt sick with trepidation. "What if they turn me down? What am I going to do then?" The only reason he surmised he would be turned down would be because of Naureen, especially if she was anything like Yasmin.

Ali turned his attention to the television screen, trying to distract himself from the nervous wait, but the door opened startling Ali and making him jump. It was Naureen and Trevor.

"We've made a decision," Naureen said with a stern and serious look on her face. Ali's face dropped at seeing her expression. She looked as if she was about to deliver some bad news. He didn't want to hear the words, knowing he wasn't prepared for them.

"We've decided to offer you one of the vacancies," Naureen said her face bursting into a smile.

"Really?" Ali asked in disbelief unable to believe what he'd heard.

"Yes, really," she said. "Trevor will sign you up for the property right away. I'll leave you in his capable hands and let him go through the details with you. I've got to make some calls to the other people we interviewed."

"Thank you, Naureen," Ali said feeling overwhelmed. He couldn't believe his luck. He had been so wrong about Naureen.

"You're welcome, Ali. I know that we'll be able to help you sort yourself out," Naureen said. She came over and shook Ali's hand before leaving the room.

"So, you must be pretty chuffed?" Trevor asked.

"Yes, I can't believe it. I can now finally sort myself out," Ali said.

"Good. We're all pleased for you. We all felt you would benefit the most from our help," Trevor said. "Your flat is going to be in the Maidstone Road complex. I'll go through the paperwork with you, and then you can have the keys to your new place."

Trevor spent the next half hour explaining the conditions of tenancy to Ali before getting him to sign the tenancy agreement. "You'll be entitled to full housing benefit which will pay your rent until you find a job," Trevor told him after helping Ali to complete a housing benefit claim form. Ali tried to pay attention to the rest of the information Trevor gave him, but there was too much to take in when all he wanted was the keys.

"Here are the keys to your new home," said Trevor finally handing Ali a set of keys. "You need to come back to the office tomorrow, so I can take you to the job center and get you signed up for Job Seekers Allowance. It's another benefit you're entitled to."

"Okay," Ali said taking the keys. "Thank you very much for all your help. You don't know how grateful I am."

"I'm just glad we could help," Trevor said modestly. "Are you moving in tonight?"

"Yes, if that's okay?" Ali asked.

"Yeah, that's fine. You'd better go and make a start then. Here's a map showing you how to get to Maidstone Road," he said handing Ali a photocopy of a page from an A-Z. "Don't forget I'm seeing you tomorrow," he reminded Ali.

"I won't," Ali said getting up. He gave Trevor a wave on his way out.

It was dark and raining outside, but that did not dampen Ali's spirit. He had the keys to his new home safely tucked away in his pocket and he was happy. It was wonderful to know that he wasn't going to spend another night in the car. He smiled contentedly at the thought.

Ali walked back to the student halls with a new spring in his step. The rain was getting his hair and jacket wet, but he didn't care. He got into his car and using the map that Trevor had given him, managed to drive to Maidstone Road in record time.

The building housing his new flat was set away from the main road and on the edge of a newly developed housing estate at the bottom of two tower blocks. Ali parked his car and eagerly raced to the building. He opened the main door, let himself in and went up the brightly lit staircase to his flat, which was on the first floor.

Ali struggled with the set of keys, trying to open the door to the flat. Eventually, he found the correct key and went inside. It was dark inside. He found a light switch, but after pressing it several times, he realized that the electricity was switched off. The light from a street lamp outside a window allowed Ali to see his new home as his eyes adjusted to the dim light.

The room that he'd stepped into was a large lounge. Ali could make out a sofa and a coffee table. He walked through an adjoining door, which led into the kitchen. It had everything, a cooker, a washing machine and a microwave. Ali could even make out pots and pans set out on the work surfaces in the dim light.

Another door opened into a bedroom with a double bed. Ali sat down on the bare mattress and surveyed his surroundings. It was perfect. He didn't even need to buy anything. Everything he needed was here. He couldn't believe his luck.

Tomorrow, he would have to sort out the electricity supply and then telephone Haseena to let her know that he was okay. For now, all Ali wanted to do was to get on the bed and sleep.

He considered going to his car and bringing all his belongings in, but he didn't want to leave the comfort of his new home, not even to get the duvet from the car. In the end, Ali took his shoes off and curled himself into a ball on the bed, fully dressed and wearing his thick jacket, which was still slightly damp.

Feeling secure and safe for the first time in ages, Ali let go of all the pain he'd been suppressing and let the tears flow. His pitiful crying echoed loudly in the bare room. It felt as if his heart was going to burst when he let himself think about Steve and life without him. He hugged himself in comfort as his body shook, wracked by grief at the loss. Eventually, his mind turned to thoughts of Sajda, and his tears turned to those of guilt.

In the morning, things would be better, but for now he let the tears of pain flow freely.

Glossary

Chapter 1

Goree – English Girl

Salwar and kameez suit – Salwar are loose trousers and the kameez is a long shirt

Ammi – Means mother in the Urdu language

Sharara – A traditional suit for women

Dupatta – A long scarf essential to Indian and Pakistani suits. It is long seen as a symbol of modesty in South Asian women.

Hajj – Is the Pilgrimage to Mecca in Islam

Kafir – It is a term used to describe a non-Muslim

Hijab – Clothing or demeanor that protects modesty by creating a barrier in this case it is a head scarf, covering the hair and ears

Eastenders – Popular English Soap

Mecca Medina – An Islamic pilgrimage site

Chapter 2

Aloo paratha – Indian butter bread layered with potato

Samosas – Savory Pakistani snack made from fried triangular pastry filled with peas, potato and fried onion.

Chapter 4

Abbu jee – Dear father/ Father dearest

Ammi – Mother/mom

Shah Jee – Meaning Sir when speaking to someone in authority

Chapter 5

Urdu – National language of Pakistan

Jang – Daily Pakistani newspaper

Halal – Meaning permissible in this case meat slaughtered to Islamic specifications

Chapter 6

Kuthie – Bitch

Mir-pouri – A Pakistani dialect based on Urdu

Jungalee – Wild/ primitive

Saag – Spinach

Lamb pilau rice – A rice dish first cooked in oil and then in a sauce containing either vegetables or meat

Roti – Pakistani bread

Chapter 7

Mehndi – Henna ceremony at a Pakistani wedding

Bollywood – The name given to the popular Indian film industry

Mosque – Place of worship for followers of the Islamic faith

Aishwarya Rai – Highest paid Bollywood Actress and model

Shahrukh Khan – Highest paid Bollywood male actor

Aap Jaisa Koi (Someone like you) – Popular Bollywood song from the film Qurbani

Qurbani – Seventies Bollywood hit movie

Kali – A Hindu goddess

Bindi – A forehead decoration available in a self adhesive form

Saris – The sari is long strip of unstitched cloth worn by Indian and Pakistani women, ranging from five to nine yards in length, which can be draped in various styles

Rani – Means Queen in Hindi

Chapter 8

Kurtha – A long shirt worn my Pakistani men

Chapter 9

Dost – Friend

Henna – Natural dye used to create temporary body art

Sehra – A headdress worn by the groom during the marriage that has garlands hanging that covers the face of the groom.

Ma- sha-allah – A term of greeting

Imam – Religious leader

Nikah – Wedding contract between bride and bridegroom

Lehnga suit – A Pakistani suit worn usually for weddings

Chapter 10

Parathas – Indian bread made using butter

Chapter 16

Gandoo – Meaning gay used derogatively

Talak – Divorce

Fakirs – Spiritual recluse

Khuda Hafiz – A term of farewell

About the Author

Amjeed Kabil was born in the West Midlands, England in 1972 and currently lives in Birmingham, England. He has worked for several years in the Social Housing field, which has included working with young, vulnerable homeless people. This has given him ideas for several books. Amjeed Kabil is currently working on his second novel. For further information about Amjeed Kabil, visit: www.amjeedkabil.co.uk.